WHAT PEOPLE ARE

Mike Dellosso has a winner here.
acters. Compelling plot. Soul-stirring implications and
some of the best writing I've seen.

—ALTON GANSKY
CHRISTY AWARD FINALIST, ANGEL AWARD WINNER,
AND AUTHOR OF *ANGEL* AND *ENOCH*

With *Darkness Follows*, once again Mike Dellosso
proves himself a master of twisty, creepy, edge-of-your
seat suspense. As if that weren't enough, he infuses this
story with characters who matter, and even more so
with head-rattling truths that echo long after you turn
the last page. That the story itself—which links two
lives across a century and a half—is both intriguing
and entertaining is sweet icing on an already delicious
cake.

—ROBERT LIPARULO
AUTHOR OF *COMES A HORSEMAN*, *GERM*, AND THE
DREAMHOUSE KINGS SERIES

If you're ready to be grabbed by the proverbial throat
from the moment you start and want that rush to continue to the end, then *Darkness Follows* is your book.
Twists, turns, and a compelling finish make this novel
a fine addition to the Mike Dellosso library.

—JAMES L. RUBART
BEST-SELLING AUTHOR OF *ROOMS* AND *BOOK OF DAYS*

Hold on for a fast-paced journey that satisfies on a
number of levels.

—ERIC WILSON
AUTHOR OF *NEW YORK TIMES* BEST SELLER *FIREPROOF*

Taut, tense, and frightening. A high-speed ride that
will keep you guessing until the end.

—TOSCA LEE
AUTHOR OF *DEMON: A MEMOIR*

Mike Dellosso's brilliant light shines into the dark places of the human heart and illuminates our most terrible fears.

—ERIN HEALY
AUTHOR OF *NEVER LET YOU GO* AND
COAUTHOR WITH TED DEKKER OF *KISS AND BURN*

Mike Dellosso could very well be the next Frank Peretti.

—C. J. DARLINGTON
AUTHOR OF *THICKER THAN BLOOD* AND
COFOUNDER OF TITLETRAKK.COM

Mike Dellosso, an astonishing new voice in supernatural thrillers, cements his right to be grouped with the likes of King and Peretti.

—SUSAN SLEEMAN
THESUSPENSEZONE.COM

Mike Dellosso has once again brought us an engaging thriller full of gut-wrenching suspense and strong spiritual truth.

—JAKE CHISM
THECHRISTIANMANIFESTO.COM

FRANTIC

MIKE DELLOSSO

REALMS

Most CHARISMA HOUSE BOOK GROUP products are available at special quantity discounts for bulk purchase for sales promotions, premiums, fund-raising, and educational needs. For details, write Charisma House Book Group, 600 Rinehart Road, Lake Mary, Florida 32746, or telephone (407) 333-0600.

FRANTIC by Mike Dellosso
Published by Realms
Charisma Media/Charisma House Book Group
600 Rinehart Road
Lake Mary, Florida 32746
www.charismahouse.com

Cover design by Justin Evans
Design Director: Bill Johnson

Visit the author's website at www.MikeDellosso.com.

Library of Congress Cataloging-in-Publication Data

Dellosso, Mike.
  Frantic / Mike Dellosso. -- 1st ed.
      p. cm.
  ISBN 978-1-61638-480-7 (trade paper)— ISBN 978-1-61638-639-9 (ebook)
1. Kidnapping--Fiction. I. Title.
  PS3604.E446F73 2012
  813'.6--dc23
                                      2011039349

First edition

12 13 14 15 16 — 987654321
Printed in the United States of America

Dedication

For Jen, your dedication to our family inspires me!

For Laura, I love seeing you grow in your creativity and passion.

For Abby, never lose your attention to detail and your determination to do your best.

For Caroline, your smile is infectious and brightens every room you enter.

For Elizabeth, so innocent. Those baby blues could inspire a thousand stories.

Acknowledgments

EVERY TIME I write one of these acknowledgment pages I'm reminded of how many people go into the making of a book, how many people have left their fingerprints on it. Really, if we want to get philosophical about it, the number is countless. Everyone who has ever known me has left a fingerprint on my life, and since each story is a product of who I am and what I've experienced, they've all had a role in the making of this book. But since we're shooting for a certain page length here and not looking to top the charts on the boring scale, I can only name a few of the many.

First, I need to recognize my wife, Jen. She puts up with a lot from me, more than she should have to. Living with someone who spends time in another world, especially one of his own making, can't be an easy task. We have our moments of friction, but mostly we handle it with grace, in large part due to her belief in me as a writer.

I also need to say a few words about my four little ladies. I love writing and would continue to do it even if I remained anonymous and didn't make a penny, but since I do make pennies and we depend on those pennies, I need some motivation to keep at it. My daughters—Laura, Abby, Caroline, and Elizabeth—provide much of my intrinsic motivation. Every time I look at them I'm reminded why I drag myself out of bed before sunrise every day and do this writing thing. And I'm reminded why I strive to make each book better than the one before it.

Now, I want to thank:

My parents…more than anyone else, they played a role in forming me into the person I am today. They've contributed so much to my storytelling simply by contributing so much to my life.

Les Stobbe…an agent full of wisdom and patience. I can be impulsive and impatient at times, and he's become very good at reining me in and putting things into perspective.

L. B. Norton…an editor who is both insightful and careful, she walks a fine line and does it with apparent ease and grace. She helped fine-tune this story and bring out the best in it. Editors deserve more credit than they get, and LB is at the top of that list.

Debbie Marrie and Deb Moss…my editors at Realms. Debbie was the first to believe in me, and her support has never wavered. She's stuck with me this far, which amazes and humbles me. I hope she never regrets it. Deb is my literary mom who makes sure my manuscript's shirt is tucked in and hair is combed before it goes out in public. More than once she's had to do that lick the thumb and get the food off my face mom-thing.

The marketing, publicity, and sales teams at Realms…for all they do to make my books and me visible. The design team…for the eye-catching covers.

My readers…you give me the extrinsic motivation to keep writing. I love your feedback. A lot of you have been with me from the very beginning, and the rest have jumped on board since then. I hope you're enjoying the ride as much as I am.

My God and Savior…without Him in my life, all this would be an act of futility. He gives me purpose. Whatever glory there is goes to Him.

Chapter 1

THE NIGHT MARNY Toogood was born it rained axheads and hammer handles.

His grandfather made a prediction, said it was an omen of some sort, that it meant Marny's life would be stormy, full of rain clouds and lightning strikes. Wanting to prove her father wrong, Janie Toogood named her son Marnin, which means "one who brings joy," instead of the Mitchell she and her husband had agreed on.

But in spite of Janie's good intentions, and regardless of what his birth certificate said, Marny's grandfather was right.

At the exact time Marny was delivered into this world and his grandfather was portending a dark future, Marny's father was en route to the hospital from his job at Winden's Furniture Factory where he was stuck working the graveyard shift. He'd gotten the phone call that Janie was in labor, dropped his hammer, and run out of the plant. Fifteen minutes from the hospital his pickup hit standing water, hydroplaned, and tumbled down a steep embankment, landing in a stand of eastern white pines. The coroner said he experienced a quick death; he did not suffer.

One week after Marny's birth his grandfather died of a heart attack. He didn't suffer either.

Twenty-six years and a couple of lifetimes of hurt later, Marny found himself working at Condon's Gas 'n Go and living above the garage in a small studio apartment George Condon rented to him for two hundred bucks a month. It was nothing special, but it was a place to lay his head at night and dream about the dark cloud that stalked him.

But his mother had told him every day until the moment she died that behind every rain cloud is the sun, just waiting to shine its light and dry the earth's tears.

Marny held on to that promise and thought about it every night before he succumbed to sleep and entered a world that was as unfriendly and frightening as any fairy tale forest, the place of his dreams, the only place more dark and foreboding than his life.

On the day reality collided with the world of Marny's nightmares, it was hotter than blazes, strange for a June day in Maine. The sun sat high in the sky, and waves of heat rolled over the asphalt lot at the Gas 'n Go. The weather kept everyone indoors, which meant business was slow for a Saturday. Marny sat in the garage bay waiting for Mr. Condon to take his turn in checkers and wiped the sweat from his brow.

"Man, it's hot."

Mr. Condon didn't look up from the checkerboard. "Ayuh. Wicked hot. Newsman said it could hit ninety."

"So it'll probably get up to ninety-five."

Mr. Condon rubbed at his white stubble. "Ayuh."

He was sixty-two and looked it. His leather-tough skin was creased with deep wrinkles. Lots of smile lines. Marny had worked for him for two years but had known the old mechanic his whole life.

Mr. Condon made his move then squinted at Marny. Behind him Ed Ricker's Dodge truck rested on the lift. The transmission had blown, and Mr. Condon should have been working on it instead of playing checkers. But old Condon kept his own schedule. His customers never complained. George Condon was the best, and cheapest, mechanic around. He'd been getting cars and trucks through one more Maine winter for forty years.

Marny studied the checkerboard, feeling the weight of Mr. Condon's dark eyes on him, and was about to make his move when the bell chimed, signaling someone had pulled up to the pump island. Condon's was the only full-service station left in the Down East, maybe in the whole state of Maine.

Despite the heat, Mr. Condon didn't have one droplet of sweat on his face. "Cah's waitin', son."

Marny glanced outside at the tendrils of heat wriggling above the lot, then at the checkerboard. "No cheating."

His opponent winked. "No promises."

Pushing back his chair, Marny stood and wiped more sweat from his brow, then headed outside.

The car at the pump was a 1990s model Ford Taurus, faded blue with a few rust spots around the wheel wells. The windows were rolled down, which probably meant the air-conditioning had quit working. This was normally not a big deal in Maine, but on a rare day like this, the driver had to be longing for cool air.

Marny had never seen the vehicle before. The driver was a large man, thick and broad. He had close-cropped hair and a smooth, round face. Marny had never seen him before either.

He approached the car and did his best to be friendly. "Mornin'. Hot one, isn't it?"

The driver neither smiled nor looked at him. "Fill it up. Regular."

Marny headed to the rear of the car and noticed a girl in the backseat. A woman, really, looked to be in her early twenties. She sat with her hands in her lap, head slightly bowed. As he passed the rear window she glanced at him, and there was something in her eyes that spoke of sorrow and doom. Marny recognized the look because he saw it in his own eyes every night in the mirror. He smiled, but she quickly diverted her gaze.

As he pumped the gas, Marny watched the girl, studied the back of her head. She was attractive in a plain way, a natural prettiness that didn't need any help from cosmetics. Her hair was rich brown and hung loosely around her shoulders. But it was her eyes that had captivated him. They were as blue as the summer sky, but so sad and empty. Marny wondered what the story was between the man and girl. He was certainly old enough to be her father. He looked stern and callous, maybe even cruel. Marny felt for her, for her unhappiness, her life.

He caught the man watching him in the side mirror and looked at the pump's gauge. A second later the nozzle clicked off, and he returned it to the pump. He walked back to the driver's window. "That'll be forty-two."

While the man fished around in his back pocket for his wallet, Marny glanced at the girl again, but she kept her eyes down on her hands.

"You folks local?" Marny said, trying to get the man to open up a little.

The driver handed Marny three twenties but said nothing.

Marny counted off eighteen dollars in change. "You new in the area? I don't think I've seen you around here before. Lately, seems more people have been moving out than in."

Still nothing. The man took the money and started the car. Before pulling out he nodded at Marny. There was something in the way he moved his head, the way his eyes sat in their sockets, the way his forehead wrinkled ever so slightly, that made Marny shiver despite the heat.

The car rolled away from the pump, asphalt sticking to the tires, and exited the lot. Marny watched until it was nearly out of sight, then turned to head back to the garage and Mr. Condon and the game of checkers. But a crumpled piece of paper on the ground where the Taurus had been parked caught his attention. He picked it up and unfurled it. Written in all capital letters was a message:

HE'S GOING TO KILL ME

Chapter 2

E VERY CLOCK IN the world came to a sudden stop.

Marny stood there like an idiot as the seconds ticked by, staring at that piece of paper with its spiderweb of folds and strange handwriting. The words were scribbled hastily, not like his idea of a girl's careful script at all. Her face was in his head again. That mahogany hair, the sloping lines of her jaw, her eyes, those thoughtful, sad eyes. Sweat ran down his temples and the back of his neck like he was made of ice and melting in the late morning sun.

Finally he snapped out of his daze, looked down the road—the car was gone by now—and headed back to the garage. Proactive was not a word commonly used to describe Marny Toogood. But that day, at that moment, he felt he had to *do* something. What, he had no idea. No plan, no marching orders. But there was something about the girl, something about the way she postured herself in the backseat of that car, something about her hands and her shoulders and the dip of her mouth, and something about those eyes that drew him to her, connected them on some metaphysical level that he couldn't understand. What he did understand and what pried him out of his comfort zone and pushed him to action was the fact that the driver of the car, that strange man with no personality, was going to kill her—at least she *believed* he was going to kill her—and as far as Marny was concerned, he was the only one who knew about it.

By the time he made it back to the garage he wasn't even thinking; he was just doing, acting on pure instinct. Mr. Condon dropped his checker piece and stood so fast his metal chair toppled over and clanged loudly on the concrete floor.

"Holy jumpin', boy, what's the matter?"

Marny tried to talk, but his tongue wouldn't work. "The–the–the…" He waved the paper like it was trying to fly away and he had it by one wing.

Mr. Condon held up both hands. "Now just settle yaself, Mahny. Ya look like ya ready to pass out." He glanced outside. "Did they drive off without payin'?"

Marny shook his head and waved the paper again.

Mr. Condon took it from him. His dark gray eyes moved over the words several times. He glanced at Marny, then back at the paper, then at Marny again. "Do ya believe this?"

Sweat began to soak through Marny's shirt, sticking it to his chest and back. He barely noticed. "I have to do something. The car."

The tone of Marny's voice and the sweat leaking from his pores must have been enough to convince Mr. Condon. "What kind was it? Make and model? I'll call Petey."

Petey—Pete Morsey—was a local cop. Mr. Condon always kept track of who was working what shift in case he needed to call in a gas thief or some other criminal who happened upon Condon's Gas 'n Go with malicious intent. In the two years Marny had worked there, no cop had ever been called.

Marny's mind went blank. He tried to picture the car in his head, but all he could see was the girl's face—her sad mouth, those penetrating eyes—and the hurried writing on the crumpled piece of paper—HE'S GOING TO KILL ME.

Mr. Condon put a hand on Marny's shoulder. "Mahny, come on, son. Think."

Finally it came to him. "It was, uh, a Taurus, light blue, nineties." Like the temperature outside.

"Did ya recognize the driver?"

Marny shook his head. "I don't think he's local. I have to go after them."

Time was running out. If he didn't leave now, he'd have no chance of catching up to the car. The garage sat on a stretch of State Road 137 where, heading north, there were no turnoffs for a good five miles. If he left now, he still had time to at least see where the car was headed.

"I'm callin' Petey," Mr. Condon said. "You stay put, ya hear? Let Petey handle this." He headed for the office and the phone.

In the rear of the garage Mr. Condon kept a fully restored 1976 Chevy Nova. He'd bought it ten years earlier at an auction for next to nothing and put more than it was worth into it to get it back to mint condition. The keys were hanging on a nail above the tool table. Marny opted for the horsepower of the Nova over the fuel efficiency of his own 1990s model Subaru.

He got in, shoved the key into the ignition, and turned it. The engine growled to life and snorted like a hopped-up thoroughbred. A clear path led to the bay door and out of the garage, and with his foot on the gas Marny put down some rubber finding it. Behind him Mr. Condon shouted something, but Marny was already too far away and couldn't hear him over the engine.

State Road 137 was a long stretch of asphalt that shot fairly straight through a forest of white pine, hemlock, and spruce. Leaving Mr. Condon and the garage behind, Marny pushed the Nova down the road with one thing now on his mind: the curse. There was a pretty good chance that if he got involved in the girl's plight, things would not turn out well. Nothing positive came from anything he did. The thought made his palms sweat and the steering wheel slick.

But then the girl's face was there again, hovering in his mind like a ghost, beckoning to him, and despite his history of twenty-six years of hurt and frustration and despair, despite his own self-esteem issues, despite the curse, he felt urged, pushed... *chosen*. This was a call to action, something he'd never felt before.

Rounding a slight curve to the right, going much faster than the posted speed limit, he noticed the light blue Taurus up ahead a good half mile. Marny took his foot off the accelerator and let the Nova slow. His heart rate went the opposite direction. There was no turning back now, and suddenly his mind went blank. Now what? He was no match for the hulk of muscle and fat behind the wheel of that Taurus. And the driver didn't look like a man who could be reasoned with.

After another mile the Taurus's brake lights illuminated, and the car turned right. Marny didn't remember any road there. As he drew nearer, he found it was not a paved road at all but an unmarked gravel lane. In his twenty years of living in Thomason, Maine, he'd never before noticed it. It was only wide enough for one vehicle, and at first Marny thought it must be a driveway. Maybe someone recently purchased some land back in the forest and laid this path as a throughway. But the lane didn't look new; it had two worn ruts where the gravel had been kicked away by years of tires traveling it. On either side the forest encroached with creepy curiosity and formed an almost complete canopy above. Slowly he drove the Nova down the lane, around a couple bends until it came to a fork.

Marny stopped the Nova and got out, walked up to the Y and listened. Over the gruff hum of the Nova's engine he could hear nothing but the steady chirp of crickets and the loud, irregular buzz of cicadas. His watch said it was nearing noon, but in the forest it was more like dusk, as if time had slipped away and seven hours had somehow been lost in the matrix of the universe. It was decision time. His instinct told him that based on his past record, it didn't matter which path he took, it would be the wrong one. He thought of Robert Frost's poem and the road less traveled, but both of these options appeared less traveled. He thought about doing eeny meeny miny mo, but it seemed too juvenile. Flipping a coin would be appropriate, but he didn't have a coin on him.

And that's when he noticed the tire track in the gravel that split to the left. It was subtle and shallow and he'd almost overlooked it, but now that he saw it, it flashed at him like a neon sign in the middle of a Maine forest. So left it was.

The lane wove through the forest for another half mile before ending at a clearing. Marny stopped the Nova short of getting a full view of the area, shut off the engine, and walked the rest of the way. Staying to the far left of the lane, hiding among the undergrowth and pine trunks, he got his first view of the clearing. In the center stood a large house.

Chapter 3

THE HOUSE WAS no monument to architectural genius.

A two-story box with a wide front porch, clapboard siding, and rusted metal roof, its paint was peeling in places. One of the first-story windows along the side of the house had been broken and was now covered with a sheet of plywood. The porch sagged on one end because the brick foundation beneath it had crumbled under the weight. The grass in the clearing was patchy and knee-high.

At the far side of the house sat the Taurus, engine still ticking.

The heat wasn't as intense here in the forest as it had been at the Gas 'n Go, but it was still hotter than Mainers are used to. But despite the heat the windows of the house were all shut. Marny stood statue-still for a minute, listening, but all he heard were the natural sounds of the forest and the unnatural tick of cooling metal.

Carefully, making as little noise as possible, he picked his way along, circling the house, staying a good ten feet behind the tree line and concealed in the shadows of the heavy pine branches. Once he thought he saw movement in a window, but it was either the reflection of a cloud moving overhead or a bird passing by. When he came full circle, he thought about pulling out his phone and calling the police, letting Pete handle the whole thing like Mr. Condon said, but there was no reception. Wireless service was spotty in this part of Maine, nothing out of the ordinary for a state that was 90 percent forest and had only forty-one residents per square mile.

After a minute or so of arguing with himself—one side making the point that since he now knew where the house was he could just drive to a landline and call Pete, let someone with a gun and more courage than he had handle matters; the other side contending that if he left, that gorilla might kill the girl while he was gone—Marny made up his mind.

For reasons he didn't understand, he decided to stay. He supposed it had something to do with the girl's eyes and that scribbled note HE'S GOING TO KILL ME. It brought something out in him that he'd never felt before.

The best thing to do, he decided, was to get a closer look at the house, peer into a few windows, and get a feel for the layout. And maybe he'd see the girl again. Maybe the gorilla would be grooming himself or preoccupied with eating metal, and Marny could slip in undetected and rescue the girl.

Heart in his throat and blood thumping in his arteries, he stepped from the tree line into the clearing and bolted for the house. Once there, he squatted next to the concrete foundation and wiped sweat from his eyes. Knees bent, staying low to the ground, he positioned himself under a side window and slowly stood so just his eyes cleared the sill. There was a large living room, sparsely furnished with a blanket-covered sofa and two wooden ladder-back chairs. No carpet, no window treatments, no pictures, no personality whatsoever. And no girl or gorilla.

Moving to the next window, he found more emptiness. This one looked into what should have been a dining room but had no furniture at all. Nothing to say anyone lived there, nothing that called the place a home.

Around the back of the house were two windows looking into the kitchen and a pair of metal cellar doors, the kind that swung up and out. The kitchen was empty, but at least there were signs of life. The sink was full of dirty dishes, and a trash can overflowed. So the first floor was unoccupied; they must be on the second floor.

Marny knelt by the cellar doors. This was the best way to gain entry to the house unnoticed. Carefully and slowly, so as not to make a sound, he raised one door. Surprisingly, it opened with only a low moan. The other one did as well. Eight concrete steps descended to a wooden door. Down the steps he went, and he rested his hand on the door latch. The metal was cool, a stark contrast to his sweaty palm. He could feel his heart beating through his hand and into the steel handle. He was about to try depressing the latch when a memory made him pause.

There was one other time he'd tried to play the hero, one other person he'd tried to rescue, and it hadn't ended well at all. An image of his mom's face materialized in his mind. Marny had her mouth and nose, and the few times he'd heard her laugh he realized they shared that too.

When Marny was five, Janie Toogood had remarried. Marny was sure that at the time she thought she was doing the right thing. He needed a father, and she needed a husband. They both needed the extra income. Janie's job as a clerk at Cudworth's Hardware just didn't bring in enough to support the two of them.

Janie didn't introduce Marny to Karl Gunnison until they were engaged and a week from being married. The first time Marny met him, Karl called Marny "Buster" (but in his Maine accent it came out "Bustah"), punched him in the arm hard enough that it hurt, and told him he was going to be his new dad; what did he think of that? Marny didn't think anything of it. He'd never had an old dad, didn't even know what a dad did.

That first year he found out quickly what a dad did: went to work during the day and spent the evening sitting in his chair in front of the TV throwing down Pabst after Pabst.

The introduction of Karl Gunnison into their lives was the beginning of a whole new world of trouble for Marny and Janie, trouble that ended in tragedy sixteen years later.

Marny pushed the memory from his mind. Everyone deserved a second chance to be a hero.

Again he almost abandoned the plan and ran for the Nova. He

didn't have to get involved. He could pretend he never found the note, never even saw the girl or the gorilla or the Taurus. Never went to work that day. He could go on with life as it was and pretend none of this ever happened.

But it *was* happening. He *had* gone to work and seen the gorilla and the girl and found the note—HE'S GOING TO KILL ME. He *did* follow the Taurus and find the house.

The house where the girl was.

The girl with the eyes that kept haunting him, pleading for him to intervene and do something, anything.

Maybe this was his chance for redemption.

Then again, maybe this would go the same way the rest of his life had gone, and both she and he would wish he'd never gotten out of bed that morning.

Swallowing past the lump in his throat, he was just about to squeeze the latch when he heard the crunch of dry grass behind him. Before he could swing around, something hit him in the back of the head. He momentarily blacked out, came to, and found he was leaning against the wooden door and sliding down. His legs buckled. He faded in and out, and the concrete stairs melted before him.

Then everything went black.

Chapter 4

THE LAND BETWEEN sleep and wakefulness is a plot of unsteady ground.

But somewhere between those two worlds Marny gained some form of awareness, enough to realize he had been dreaming of Karl Gunnison. He tried to open his eyes, to break the surface of consciousness, but found the throbbing in his head pulling him back into sleep. He was back in the living room of his old home. He touched the sofa, the coarse fabric, drew in a breath. It was as if time had folded and he had somehow passed from this decade to that one unscathed. Everything was exactly as he remembered it, even the floor lamp with the shade that was slightly off-balance and leaned to one side.

Footsteps behind him broke the silence of the room and his memories. They were coming from the kitchen. He spun around and found Karl standing in the doorway, Pabst in one hand, bag of chips in the other. Big boned and thick chested, he appeared larger than he was. With his bushy beard and bald head, beady eyes and thick accent, he was every bit the forklift driver at Waldron's Seafood. For some reason the sight of him after five years and after what happened between them didn't surprise Marny as it should have.

Karl was wearing his Carhart bibs and yellow-stained white T-shirt. "What ya doin' here, Bustah?"

Marny said nothing.

"Ya deaf?" Karl held the can to his mouth and took a long swig. "Where's ya mother? Ya dirty lobstah. How dare ya come 'round here again."

Though he'd been born and raised in Maine, and though he'd worked at a seafood supplier for most of his adult life, Karl Gunnison hated lobsters. Said they were dirty scavengers who lived on the bottom of the ocean cleaning up nature's waste. Of course, the language he used to describe his hatred for Maine's number-one crustacean was a bit more colorful.

To Karl, Marny was a scavenger too. The big man cursed and walked toward him. He was headed for his favorite chair, where he'd spend the rest of the evening being served beer after beer by Janie, his wife, his servant.

Marny stood his ground, fully expecting Karl to pass right through him like an apparition. After all, he wasn't real, right? He was a figment of Marny's imagination, a trick of the neural connectors in his brain.

Karl came and stood before Marny, inches away, so close Marny could smell the beer on the breath from his nostrils. He was an inch or two shorter than Marny, but much wider and thicker. Draining the rest of the beer from the can, Karl shook it and, keeping his eyes on Marny, turned his head slightly and said, "Janie! Bring me another beer, will ya?"

Marny said nothing, did nothing. He knew how this all ended. It was impossible for Karl to be real, but still every muscle in Marny's body grew so taut it quivered.

Karl narrowed his eyes and belched loudly. The breath that wafted over Marny's face almost made him gag. "Outa my way, Bustah."

Marny wasn't moving. But when Karl shoved him hard enough that he lost his balance and almost went down, he had to rethink this reality. If Karl was real enough to walk through time and bully Marny once again, what else was he capable of?

Karl laughed and shook his head, sat in his chair. "Janie! My beer, I'm waitin'."

From the second floor Marny heard a voice he'd not heard in five years but longed to hear every day. "Just a minute."

"I ain't got a minute. The game's about ta start."

Every cell in Marny wanted to walk up to Karl Gunnison and knock him in the back of the head. Maybe grab a lamp and bust it over his skull. But every molecule in him wanted to climb the stairs to the second floor and see his mom. Dream or no dream, reality or fantasy, she was there, and he had a chance to see her again. He hadn't dreamed of her since her death, and her image, the sound of her voice, the feel of her motherly touch had begun to fade.

He crossed the living room and stood at the bottom of the staircase. It ascended in front of him like a ladder into another dimension. From his chair across the room Karl glared at Marny.

"Ya better stay put, Bustah. She needs ta learn ta obey." He shook his head and looked away. "Sheesh, it's like trainin' dogs, livin' with the two a' ya."

Anger flared inside Marny like an oxygen-fed fire. He'd only stood up to Karl once; it was time to do so again. Besides, this was nothing more than a dream; what could happen?

"Shut up," he said through clenched teeth. "Don't you talk about my mother that way."

Karl grabbed his empty beer can and stood. "Or what? Ya gonna do somethin' 'bout it? Ya little good-fah-nothin'."

"You're a piece of garbage," Marny said and meant every word. He hated Karl Gunnison. Hated the fact that his mother had married him. Had substituted him, a beer-drinking chauvinist pig, for the father Marny had never known, but who sounded like he'd been a gem of a man. He hated that Karl was here in his life again, climbing out of his mind and still bullying him from the grave.

Karl grunted, cursed loudly, and threw the can at Marny. Marny flinched, but the can hit its mark and got him on the shoulder. It too was real.

Mom called from the second floor. "Marny, is that you? You home already?"

Marny put one foot on the bottom stair and was stopped by Karl's voice, low and thick.

"Ya go up those stairs and I'll kill ya, hear?"

"Marny?" Mom again. "We need to talk."

Her voice bewitched him, like a prize bass tricked by a well-crafted lure. He knew she wasn't there. She'd been dead some five years. But if her mirage was as real as the one of Karl, he'd play along just to see her one more time. He went to the second step.

Karl mimicked his move and took one step closer to him. "Bustah, I'm warnin' ya. Not one more step." He raised his voice. "Janie, my beer."

At once Marny moved and, skipping the bottom step altogether, took the staircase two steps at a time. Karl roared and was at the base of the steps in no time, but Marny was already more than halfway up. At the top the stairs suddenly disappeared from beneath his feet. They slanted downward as one, as if on hinges, and became a sliding board. Marny's feet went out from under him, and he slid back down toward the raging Karl. Karl's eyes were like fire and his mouth hung open like a steel trap ready to spring. Marny groped at the banister, tried to find purchase. A little over halfway down he caught one of the rungs and stopped his descent.

Karl cursed again and lunged. Marny clawed at the banister and got his feet under him enough to pull himself up the staircase-turned-sliding board to the second floor. At the bottom of the stairs Karl was acting the part of a raving lunatic—cursing, waving his arms; his face turned shades of red darker and darker. Finally he turned and punched the wall, then dropped to his knees.

Mom's voice came from around the corner. "Marny, come here. I need to talk to you."

The hallway extended both to the right and left, just like their old home. He moved cautiously down the hallway to the left, past the bathroom, past a closet, and into her room, not knowing what to expect. She was sitting on the bed folding laundry. She smiled at him as she had done a million times when she was alive.

Marny's mouth formed the word Mom, but no sound came out. Tears blurred his vision until he dashed them away.

Janie patted the bed beside her. "Sit, Marny."

He didn't, though. He couldn't. He knew she wasn't real. She looked like his mom, sounded like her, and if he went to her and held her, she'd feel and smell like his mom too, but it wasn't really her. It was his mind, this dream, deceiving him. He stayed where he was.

Janie's eyes turned sad, and she put down the shirt she was folding. It was one of Karl's work shirts. "Why couldn't you just leave well enough alone, Marny?"

Marny knew she was talking about that day five years ago. The day he'd had enough and decided to do what he should have done sooner, the day he'd stood up to Karl Gunnison.

"You had to interfere, and look where it got us."

He wanted to tell her to stop, please stop, but the signal wasn't making it from his brain to his mouth.

"Sometimes"—she looked at her hands and twisted them nervously—"sometimes I wish I'd never had you."

Please, he couldn't take anymore. He'd wondered if she ever felt that way, ever wished he'd never been born that stormy night. Her life would not have taken so many wrong turns. Hearing her say it, though, was almost too much for him to bear. His legs went weak and nearly buckled.

"Your father would still be here. Your grandfather. Little Billy Tillman. Sarah Williamson. Adam Bitfield." She put a fist to her mouth as if fighting back tears. "I never would have wound up with Karl." Then she looked Marny dead in the eyes, and what he found there was not love or sympathy or forgiveness—any of which he would have gladly welcomed—but accusation and blame. "And I'd still be here."

He started to cry then, couldn't hold back the tears. They

streamed from his eyes and down his cheeks. He tried to say something, to apologize, to beg her to love him still, but his mouth
was not cooperating. All that came forth was a weak moan. He
couldn't take any more and turned to leave the room. Her voice
followed him.

"It's your fault, Marny. All your fault."

Chapter 5

THE DEEPEST DARKNESS has a substance all its own.

For Esther, there was nothing about the darkness that was comforting or inviting, yet it was familiar—the overwhelming emptiness of the room, the smell of mildew and soil, the dampness in the air. She'd spent some time in this cellar, this dungeon.

She felt her way through the blackness, arms extended in front. Her foot bumped against something hard, and the tinny sound of metal echoed off the stone walls. She bent and felt along the ground. There, a paint can. The one she'd used for a makeshift chair the last time she was here. It had kept her from sitting on the damp floor. That time she'd only been locked in the cellar for half a day.

Moving along the wall, one hand following the rough foundation, the other extended in front of her, Esther crept with shortened strides until she came to the workbench. There were no tools on it, of course; they'd all been removed years ago.

Her hand felt along the top surface. The wood was coarse, but not enough to produce splinters. It had been worn to a glossy, creviced landscape by some long-dead carpenter who had once owned the home. She found a square wooden leg and ran her hand down it until she nudged something human, alive.

A head. *His* head. So it *was* him. A quick exhale escaped her lungs, and she almost laughed.

Esther dropped to her knees and caressed the man's face with both hands. Yes, it was him; there was no mistaking it. She knew he would come. He had a face that said he would.

The man turned his head slowly and moaned.

Esther combed her fingers through his hair. "Shh. It's okay. It's okay to wake up."

This was the man who would prove himself to be a hero. She'd seen it in his eyes back at the station. She had a knack for reading people, and as soon as she saw him, she knew he was the one.

His heart was bigger than he realized, and he had courage he knew nothing of.

Marny came to in fits and starts, clawing his way to consciousness like a drowning swimmer trying to make it to the surface only to be pulled under again by the riptide. He opened his eyes in a flutter but saw nothing, only darkness, felt a hand on his shoulder, his head, then blacked out again, tugged back to the depths of nothingness, the tentacles of unnatural sleep wrapped firmly around his ankles.

Again his eyelids stuttered open, and this time he heard a voice, a woman. Not his mother. He couldn't make out what she was saying; her words garbled together like someone speaking under water. He tried to move but felt like he'd gained at least a hundred pounds. Then the tentacles were there again and under he went, back into the noiseless depths of the black sea of nescience.

Immediately the voice came again, accompanied by the hand on his head, then his face. It was soft and warm and reminded him of his mother's hand. Could it be? The voice didn't match. He tried to talk, to say her name—*Mom*—but his throat felt like sandpaper and wouldn't work.

The woman's voice again. This time her words were clear and lovely. Her voice was like that of an angel.

"Hey, wake up. You have to wake up."

Marny opened his eyes fully, a task that proved much more difficult than it should have been, but still saw nothing. Was he blind? He remembered the blow to the back of his head and panicked at the thought of it having knocked out his eyesight.

The woman must have sensed his fear. Her hands found his face. "Shh. It's okay. We're in the cellar. It's dark."

It was her, the girl from the car. It had to be.

Pulling himself to a sitting position, Marny felt his ankles and found they were shackled.

"I have the key." She groped in the dark, then the clink of metal and the sound of a lock dropping open.

Marny swallowed hard, lubricating his dry mouth and throat. "What time is it?" He was disoriented, lost in a vacuum. He had no idea how much time had elapsed since he was knocked on the head. It could be minutes, hours, even days.

"Eleven."

"In the morning?" Had he slept almost an entire day?

"At night."

He rubbed his ankles. "I thought I was supposed to rescue you."

"Everyone needs a savior." He could hear the smile in her voice.

"Thanks." He had never been anyone's savior, not even a hero.

Her next words caught him by surprise.

"We need to get my brother."

Brother? There was someone else in this house with her and the gorilla? But the note said HE'S GOING TO KILL ME. *Me.* Not us.

"Your brother."

"He's upstairs, on the second floor. I can't leave without him. He's eleven."

She sounded very confident. Like this whole botched rescue attempt was all part of some grand plan that was already worked out and it was a certainty that they'd all make it out alive and safe. All three of them.

Marny stood and stretched the tightness from his back and hips. She took his hand in hers, and it almost made him shiver. He'd never held a girl's hand before, never wanted to get that close to someone he would eventually in some way disappoint, hurt, or worse.

"This way." She tugged on his hand.

They took a couple strides before she stopped suddenly. "Wait."

"What?"

She tightened her grip just a little. "I'm Esther."

"Okay."

There was a pause, long enough that he thought something was wrong.

"Do you have a name?"

"Oh, yeah. Marnin. Everyone calls me Marny."

"Good enough." She pulled on his hand again and led him through the darkness.

He wondered how she knew her way around in the dark so well, but then figured she must have spent time in this cellar too, enough to be able to get around blind. The thought angered him.

"Here are the steps to the first floor."

Another pause. They didn't move, didn't advance up the stairs.

"What's wrong?" Marny said.

"The house..." There was a slight quiver to her voice, enough that it made him swallow, and this time he firmed his hand around hers. "It's not like other houses. He–he has it rigged."

"Rigged?"

"Rigged to keep us in."

Marny didn't like the sound of that. "What do you mean?"

Esther hesitated, and he could hear her struggling to find her breath. "It's not like other houses. You'll see. Just stay with me, and we'll find our way out."

Slowly they began to take the stairs, one step at a time, their shoes making muffled scrapes against the boards. Sweat beaded on Marny's forehead and chin again, and he could feel his palms growing wetter by the second. His heart thumped so loudly in his chest he swore Esther could hear it, but she said nothing.

At the top of the stairs he felt the door against his shoulder.

"This is it," Esther said, her voice just above a whisper. "Remember, stay with me. I know the way. I know where William is."

"William?"

"My brother. The house was built to keep him in and others out."

"I probably don't want to know why."

"You'll find out soon enough."

"Wait."

"What?"

"There's something you need to know."

"Okay."

"Look, I'm not a hero, not a savior, not anything. I'm just a guy who followed a note from a girl who needed help. I don't know what I'm doing here."

"Then why did you come?"

Good question. Great question, in fact. "I don't know. Maybe I shouldn't have."

Her free hand found his face and rested on his cheek. "Marny, you are a hero. You don't know it yet, but you are."

Marny wasn't comfortable with her high expectations. He'd disappoint her, he knew. The stage was all set. "Just don't expect too much. I'll do what I can."

"I believe in you," Esther whispered.

Marny couldn't tell if she was speaking to him or trying to convince herself.

With that she turned the doorknob, the mechanism clicked, and the cellar door opened on quiet hinges.

Chapter 6

MYSTERIES AND PORTALS to other worlds often lurk behind closed doors.

The door opened all the way, and they found the first story illuminated by the soft light of a floor lamp. Esther looked exactly as Marny remembered her from the Gas 'n Go. Her eyes still penetrated him, as if looking through the orbs in his head and peering directly into his soul. He felt naked and vulnerable in front of her and let go of her hand.

"Stay with me, Marny," she said. He loved the way her lips moved when she said his name.

They rounded a corner and found themselves in the living room. Esther had said the place was rigged, but other than being sparsely furnished and in desperate need of a good dusting and vacuuming, nothing here looked out of the ordinary. Marny took quick note of the walls and flooring, expecting to find tiny holes out of which darts tipped with exotic poison would fly, but found nothing. The floor had no hinges signifying a trap door. He scanned the ceiling. No battle-axes dangled from pendulums.

Esther took his hand again and tugged on it. "William is this way. We have to hurry."

Marny followed her through the living room and to the staircase leading to the second floor. She started up, but he hesitated.

"What's the matter?"

He had an image of the stairs collapsing into a sliding board like the ones in his dream and of the floor at the bottom opening up and swallowing them whole. "The stairs. Are they rigged?"

"No."

"Then what is?"

Esther relaxed her grip on his hand. "The doors. The windows. The house is secure."

The front door. He hadn't even noticed it. He glanced quickly at the windows but noticed nothing odd about them. They weren't barred, and they appeared to have standard locks on them. Nothing that couldn't be unlocked.

"We have to hurry," she said. "Before he wakes up."

"William?"

"Gary."

The gorilla. If he was unpleasant fully awake, Marny didn't want to find out what he was like upon being wakened from a deep sleep.

Halfway up the stairs Marny had the urge to break free of her grip, dash to the first floor, and throw himself out a window. But he resisted and climbed the rest of the way to the second floor. At the top of the stairs was a hallway. A bathroom was directly ahead, and to both the right and left were closed doors.

Esther let go of his hand. "Stay here. I'll be right back."

She went left and was back in a minute with a young boy dressed in jeans and a T-shirt. He had short brown hair, the largest coffee-colored eyes Marny had ever seen, and a left arm that was withered and deformed, bent at the elbow with a small, twisted hand on the end. It was smaller than the other hand and had only four fingers. The boy smiled at Marny, and in his eyes Marny found the sympathy and love he had longed to see in his mother's.

"You must be William."

The boy said nothing.

"I'm Marnin. People call me Marny."

Esther took William by his withered hand and pulled him. "C'mon, we have to move quickly." She turned to Marny. "Focus on me, Marny, nothing else. I can get us out, but we have to move quickly before he wakes up. Hold William's hand."

William smiled at Marny again and offered him his good hand.

At the bottom of the stairs they were back in the living room of the gorilla's house. It was dark outside, and that put a lump of dread in Marny's stomach.

They crossed the living room with large, quick strides, Esther first, then William, then Marny. Halfway across, a loud bang came from the second floor. Esther stopped, her eyes wide.

The gorilla was awake.

Esther gave William's hand a quick tug, and they dashed to the front door.

That's when Marny noticed the locks. Ten of them, dead bolts, from the top of the door to the knob.

"They're set up so you don't know which is locked and which is unlocked," Esther said. "You think you're unlocking one, and you're really locking it."

"Can you open it?"

"I think so."

Upstairs, floorboards creaked and a door slammed open.

Esther went to work on the locks, flipping some to the right, some to the left.

Marny noticed how badly her hands shook and touched her shoulder. "Steady," he whispered, "but hurry."

Heavy footsteps pounded across the floor above them, and another door clunked against the wall. Gary must be in William's room, discovering that his ward was not there.

Esther let out a tight whimper, brushed hair from her face, and tried the doorknob. Nothing.

The gorilla pounded the wall and grunted. He hollered something unintelligible that sounded like "don't dance with the chocolate car," though Marny doubted he was the dancing type, and he hadn't seen any chocolate car parked outside.

Esther and Marny locked eyes, and there was no mistaking the fear in hers. William still gripped Marny's hand. He looked to be the calmest of the trio.

Gary was at the top of the stairs now, breathing hard and grunting like a silverback ready to charge.

Esther grabbed the doorknob again with both hands, shook it violently, turned it, but nothing happened.

Marny let go of William's hand and lifted the table lamp. Bringing it to shoulder level and holding it like a battering stick, he lunged at the window. The cord pulled away from the socket, instantly bathing the room in darkness, but the lamp merely bounced off the glass. By the filtered light of the moon he tried again, but again the base of the lamp rebounded off the glass and nearly knocked him off-balance. Safety glass, probably bulletproof too. He eyed one of the ladder-back chairs; it was worth a try.

They were out of time. Gary stomped down the stairs, shouting "Nooo!" all the way.

Esther shrieked and moved to the side. William was there, his small form in front of the door. What a contrast it was; in the midst of such chaos, such confusion and nonsensical horror, the child remained so calm, so poised. His good hand was busily switching the dead bolts.

The gorilla came into view, roaring and clenching his fists. He wore baggy jeans and a white V-neck T-shirt that was too small for his thick frame. Coarse black hair covered what was exposed of his chest.

Two things happened simultaneously then. Marny picked up the lamp and threw it at his attacker, catching him along the side of his head and shoulder, and the front door swung open with only a slight creak.

The lamp succeeded in slowing Gary, but only momentarily. It was enough time, though, for Marny to shout "Get outside!" and all three of them to exit the strange fortress designed to keep an eleven-year-old boy captive.

Outside, the moon's light was brighter and cast the clearing and forest in a silvery lunar glow.

"To the car, there." Marny pointed to the gravel lane where the Nova was parked just out of sight.

Esther and Marny grabbed William's hands again and ran to the car, William hobbling but never stumbling. Midway there Marny heard Gary exit the house and cast a long line of expletives their way as if they were a hook intended to snag and reel them back in.

"Hurry." Now Marny led the way, pulling his two companions along. They made it to the Nova, threw open the doors, and jumped in, Marny in the driver's seat, Esther and William in the back. The key was right where he'd left it in the ignition. He turned it, and the engine roared to life. Mr. Condon took good care of his prized possession.

Gary had just hit the gravel lane when Marny flipped on the headlamps and stepped on the gas. He didn't have time to pull the car around, so he just floored it, intending to circle the house and head back down the lane the way he'd come.

But Gary had a different idea. He dived for the car and landed on the hood with a solid thud, groping for anything to hold on to. His hands found the windshield wipers. Marny yanked the wheel hard left, causing Gary to lose his hold and slide off the hood, taking one of the wipers with him. His nails scratched along the paint like an obnoxious student dragging his fingers across a freshly wiped chalkboard.

The Nova handled the turn decently enough, slipping only once in the loose soil, but as they came back around the house, Gary was waiting. He crouched at the waist like a football linebacker ready for a bone-crushing hit. Marny pressed the accelerator closer to the floorboard.

But right before they made contact, Gary launched himself into the air, the devil in his eyes, his mouth a malicious snarl, and landed solidly on the windshield. A circle the size of a watermelon appeared in a million jagged lines, but the glass didn't break. Gary rolled up and over the roof of the car, thudding and bumping along until he slid off the back.

Marny didn't go back to see if he was okay. He was sure no jury in the country would find him guilty of vehicular manslaughter after what they'd been through. Instead, he pointed the Nova in the right direction and made haste back to the main road.

Throughout both assaults, neither Esther nor William had said a word. Now, back on the paved road, the Nova's tires humming quietly on the asphalt, William spoke for the first time.

"Where are you taking us, Marnin? Somewhere safe, I hope."

Marny hadn't even given that a thought. He couldn't take them to his apartment above the garage; he was certain that would be the first place Gary would look. He glanced at William in the rearview mirror. "We're going to see a friend of mine. Mr. Condon."

Chapter 7

GARY WANTED TO hit something. He *needed* to hit something. So in spite of the pain in his shoulder he thumped the only thing close enough to hit, the ground. The earth did not shake, nor did it open beneath his hand. He was, after all, just a man and prone to failure like any other man. In fact, he was quite accustomed to failure. At one time he'd had hopes of being a minister, even attended seminary in Massachusetts and afterward served in a few churches. But his past eventually caught up with him there too and drove him out of each ministry until he was no longer of use.

But this failure was colossal. Not acceptable.

He'd lost the boy.

Immediately the voice was there in his head, disappointed, saddened, the voice of despair and condemnation.

He is your responsibility, your charge to protect, even with your life if needed. This is your holy calling. You have been chosen by the Almighty to watch over His anointed one, to shepherd him.

And with the voice, as always, came images, just momentary glimpses, like the flashes of a camera. A boy. Not *the* boy, but another. Same twisted arm, though, and deformed leg as well. And the face of an angel. He's in a wheelchair. That's it. That's all it ever was. Brief images, tiny explosions of a distant memory. He knew this boy, of course, and every day was haunted by him.

Though he was gone in the flesh, his spirit lived on, roaming to and fro, clinging to Gary.

And there was another reminder, the scars. Gary looked at his hands, his arms. The smooth, glossy skin would never let him forget, never let him escape the failure that had altered the course of his life, defined it in every way.

He grabbed his head with both hands and rolled to his back. The impact with the car had jammed his shoulder, but that pain was nothing compared to the damage his spirit now suffered. He'd underestimated the boy and his gift. Underestimated the girl. The curious visitor—the gas station attendant—was no surprise, though. From the moment Gary caught him looking at Esther, he'd known he'd have to deal with the stranger sooner or later. He should have killed him when he caught him snooping around the house, but instead he'd locked him in the cellar, intending to deal with him in the morning.

At times the killing didn't bother Gary, but at other times he wondered if there'd been enough of it already. He had so much blood on his hands, and the faces...they haunted him when he closed his eyes. The look they gave him right before he took their life, before he drained it from them like water from a spigot, was one of frantic terror. But none of them were innocent, not really. None were righteous.

Except the boy. The anointed one.

Again the voice was there. *Only the anointed matters. Those who reject him or stand in the way of his protection must be punished. No mercy shall be shown for sinners.*

"Stop!" Gary climbed to his feet and paced the clearing. He spoke aloud so his voice could rise as an offering, a sweet-smelling incense, from the forest floor to the heavens. "Forgive me. Please, I didn't mean that. I didn't mean to lose him. I didn't mean to fail. And those words..." It bothered him when he used vulgarities, when his mouth turned foul. "Forgive me."

The boy needs you. You must be willing to die for him. A good shepherd lays down his life for the sheep. Are you willing to do that?

"Yes. I'm willing." He'd thrown himself in front of the car, hadn't he?

Gary lumbered to the house and grabbed his car keys. His shoulder still throbbed, but he ignored the pain. He had to get the boy back. He had to please the voice. He had to fulfill his duty. And his duty was to protect the boy. He was the guardian, the defender. The boy was special, the anointed.

Walking back to the car, keys in hand, Gary clenched his hands into fists.

The boy needs you. He can't defend himself. Look at him, vulnerable, scared. Prey for the wolves. He needs you.

"I'll find him. I promise."

Gary could not resist the urge to obey the voice. He chalked that up to it being his holy calling. Before the foundations of the earth he was elected to be the boy's protector. From the first time he laid eyes on the boy and his twisted arm and leg, he knew how he would spend the remainder of his life. He had a purpose for existing. Nothing else mattered. No other life was as precious.

The Taurus started on the first try, and Gary didn't waste any time getting out of the woods and onto the main road. He pointed the car in the right direction and hit the gas. He had time to make up. He had a sheep to rescue.

Chapter 8

NEAR-DEATH EXPERIENCES ARE rarely pleasant and almost always disturbing.

Marny still shook from his confrontations at the house: his dream of Karl and his mom, then the encounter with the gorilla. He massaged the steering wheel with both hands, checked the rearview mirror.

Once the Nova settled into a comfortable speed, Esther climbed up front and fastened the seat belt. "William's sleeping."

For a few long seconds Marny said nothing, just watched the dark figures of hovering pines, the sentinels of the night, whiz by in so many blurs.

After checking the mirrors again he said, "What was that back there?"

"The house or the monster who lives in it?"

"Both."

"It's a long story. How much time do we have?"

"Twenty-five, thirty minutes."

Esther sighed, looked out the side window. "The pines are so peaceful, aren't they? Their strength is immeasurable, yet they cause no harm."

"Except when they fall on you."

She looked at Marny, and even in the darkness of the car he could feel the heaviness of her eyes. "Thank you for coming for us."

He shrugged. "It was—"

"Don't say it was nothing, Marny. It was anything but nothing. The moment I saw you I knew you were a hero. I knew you were the one."

"The one?"

"The one with a heart big enough to help us."

Her words hit him in the chest and nearly took the wind from his lungs. His mother used to accuse him of having a heart big enough to fit the world in, but he never believed her. "You don't know the whole story," he said. "You probably don't want to spend too much time around me. I'll get you to Mr. Condon's and let him take it from there. You two will be in good hands."

She turned toward the window again and studied those peaceful giants she so admired. After a minute she cleared her throat. "He's our uncle, our mother's brother."

It took Marny a second to get whom she was talking about. "The gorilla."

"Gary. Our father left us after William was born. He couldn't bear the sight of his own son. Mom tried to make it on her own for a few years, but just wasn't able to, so she took us to live with her brother."

"The gorilla."

"Yes. Gary. He was single and had this great big house in the woods he'd just moved into. Plenty of room for all of us. She died when I was seventeen and William was seven. Four years ago. He's kept us with him these last four years because of William."

"What about William?"

"He's special."

"Is that what you call it?"

"No. We call it cerebral palsy, but that's not what I'm talking about."

She had him intrigued now. "Go on."

"There's nothing to go on about."

"You said he's special."

She glanced at the backseat where her brother was sleeping soundly. "He has abilities...gifts."

"Is that why he was able to get the door open back there?"

"Yes."

"So what, he knows how to pick locks, that kind of stuff?"

Esther laughed a little, and even in the dark her smile was bright. "No, nothing like that."

"So is he some kind of genius, boy wonder kind of deal?"

"No, not like that either. It's hard to explain. You have to just believe it."

"Okay." Her enigmatic answers were keeping him at an arm's length. Maybe that was for the best. He planned to dump them both in the lap of law enforcement when they got to Mr. Condon's and then step out of their lives forever...before the dark storm clouds that followed him would catch up to them and he would have one more regret to add to his long list.

Up ahead he saw the porch light of Mr. Condon's place, a beacon of safety and rest. "There it is."

Esther shifted in her seat and looked back at William. "He'll keep coming after us, you know. This isn't over." She drilled him with those haunting eyes. "No one can keep us safe, Marny."

Those were not the words he wanted to hear.

Chapter 9

I T WOULDN'T BE hard to find them.

The voice was persistent in Gary's head now. He'd agitated it, gotten it concerned. It doubted him. But he was, in fact, very resourceful when he needed to be. He remembered seeing the gas station attendant and the older man playing a game in the garage bay when he pulled up to the pump. Playing a game instead of doing their job meant they were more than coworkers; they were friends. He'd also noticed the curtains in the windows above the garage. Living quarters. And by the way the punk dressed and acted, Gary didn't think it was much of a stretch to presume he was the one who occupied those quarters. Low-rent accommodations.

He pulled into the gas station lot and cut the engine. The Nova was nowhere in sight. He grabbed a rag from the passenger seat and got out of the car. The garage was on a stretch of road that was mostly uninhabited; there were no other buildings in sight, no homes, no one to hear the sound of glass breaking.

Above, the starlit sky appeared to shimmer and undulate. Gary liked nighttime in Maine. The pines absorbed any residual light, causing the darkness to be blacker than what was experienced in other parts of the country. Sometimes, when the boy and his sister were asleep, he'd creep out of the house, lie on the ground, and gaze at the starry sky, get lost in it. As a boy he did the same thing, except he'd climb out his bedroom window and lie on the roof of the porch. Midnight was always his favorite time.

Along the side of the garage a wooden staircase led to the second-story apartment. Gary climbed the steps, wrapped the rag around his right hand, and punched a hole in the door's window. He didn't even flinch when the glass shattered. Reaching through the mouth of jagged teeth, he flipped the lock on the knob and opened the door.

The interior was dark and the furniture a collage of black humps. It smelled of cleaning fluid and pine. At least the punk wasn't a slob.

Gary clicked on his penlight and moved it around the apartment in wide arcs. Nothing seemed out of the ordinary. Kitchen table with two chairs, sofa, recliner, TV in the corner. Nothing matched, but it wasn't worn either. In fact, the place looked barely lived in. The punk surely did little entertaining in this bachelor pad of his.

Moving from room to room, running the light's beam along the floors, over the furniture, and up and down the walls, Gary surveyed the entire two-room living area and found nothing worth noting. He even fingered through a stack of bills on the kitchen counter but came up empty. In the living room he sat on the sofa and propped his feet on the coffee table. He needed a few minutes to rest and think.

A thought came to him then, an inclination. The punk would probably go to Condon's house looking for help, maybe to call the police. Gary leaned forward and picked up a framed picture on the table. It was of a woman and a boy, the punk at a younger age, maybe seven or eight. The woman was smiling, but it wasn't genuine. There was something sad about her, wounded, and for an instant Gary felt sorry for her. There was pain in her eyes, the same pain he dealt with. He had an urge to throw the picture across the room, but instead he set it back on the table. It toppled and fell over.

After relieving himself in the punk's bathroom, Gary exited

the apartment and followed the wooden stairs back down to the ground level. At the door that opened to the station's office and waiting area, Gary again wrapped the rag around his right hand and put his fist through the window.

Once inside, he found the office and pulled out his light. It didn't take long to find Condon's home address. In the top drawer of the desk was a small stack of personal bills.

Gary tapped the envelope against his chin. He had to get the boy back. It was literally a matter of life and death—for him; for the boy, the anointed one. He'd failed to uphold his one solemn duty, and now he had to redeem himself. He'd go to Condon's house, and if the threesome wasn't there, well, maybe Condon would know where they were.

Gary could be very persuasive. And resourceful.

Chapter 10

M R. CONDON TOOK great pride in two things, his garage and his home.

When Marny wheeled the Nova into the driveway and parked behind Mr. Condon's Chevy pickup, Esther said, "Wow, seaside paradise. Nice place."

Mr. Condon lived fifteen miles from the garage in the quaint coastal town of Pine Harbor. His house was a small bungalow with a wide porch that overlooked the broad waters of the Penobscot Bay. He'd lived there alone since his love, his wife, Sarah, died of uterine cancer some eight years earlier, and when he wasn't tinkering with cars at the garage or digging in the dirt, he could be found sitting in his favorite rocker, sipping hot tea and watching the lobster boats go by with their catch. To the right of the house was a one-car garage where Darla, Mr. Condon's other love, resided: a partially restored 1972 Buick Riviera Boattail. The interior was pristine, while the exterior had been stripped and primed but still awaited its first coat of paint.

Having done all the remodeling and landscaping around his shoreline house himself, Mr. Condon spent most of his free time maintaining it and working on Darla.

The bungalow was a nice place, the kind of house Marny saw himself owning someday. From the driveway, a winding flagstone path curved through the front lawn and up to a wide porch populated by natural wood wicker furniture. The porch was surrounded by clumps of witch hazel and sweet fern, and at the corner of the house stood a midsized black willow. Another stone path led around the side of the home, under a breezeway that connected the house to the garage, to an expansive deck that overlooked the bay where one could sit with a blanket and watch a spattering of colorful buoys bob in the dark seawater.

Marny looked at his watch. It was nearly midnight. Mr. Condon was not a night owl; he preferred the early morning hours and watching the sun rise.

Esther got William from the car, and they walked to the front porch, but before Marny could knock on the door, Mr. Condon threw it open. "Holy jumpin', Mahny. What'd ya do?"

He was in an old pair of khakis and a faded T-shirt, and his hair showed no sign of being awakened from sleep.

He looked from Marny to Esther to William, and understanding dawned in his eyes. "Well, come on in. Can't have ya standin' out there in the dark."

Once inside, introductions were made, and the threesome followed Mr. Condon back to the kitchen, where he told them to sit at the table. "I'll get the tea," he said. "You do the talkin'."

While Marny told him the entire story from start to finish, Mr. Condon busied himself with heating the water and steeping the tea bags. When he finished, he set the mugs on the table, leaned against the counter, and folded his arms.

Marny didn't know if Mr. Condon believed his story or not. His employer had no reason to doubt Marny; he'd never lied before and certainly had never concocted any tale about a fortressed house and a crazed maniac who enjoyed throwing himself at moving vehicles.

"That all of it?" Mr. Condon said.

Marny hesitated. There was one thing he'd left out. "Almost."

"Well, let's have it."

"The Nova. The, uh, windshield might need some attention."

Mr. Condon didn't say anything. He stood there for a few

seconds, slowly nodding his head. Then his eyes shifted from Marny to Esther and finally landed on William. "What's so special about ya, son?"

William looked at Esther, then at Mr. Condon. Marny wasn't sure William understood the question.

Then William shrugged. "I don't know."

"He doesn't realize there's anything special about him," Esther said. "He doesn't do it intentionally. It's his gift."

Marny wanted more than that. "Doesn't do what intentionally? What's this gift thing?"

Her eyes dropped to the table and the mug, then found Marny again. "Faith."

It felt as if the air had been sucked out of the room by a giant straw. *Faith?* That was it? Marny thought it'd be invisibility or superhuman strength or the world's greatest mime routine...but *faith?* He almost laughed.

William looked at Marny and cocked his head to one side. His good hand reached across the table and rested on Marny's. "Why are you disappointed, Marnin?"

He spoke in an almost rhythmic manner that was oddly peaceful. His brown eyes studied Marny for a moment, then went to something more interesting on the wall.

Marny's chagrin must have shown on his face. "I guess I expected something else."

"Like?" Esther said.

He shrugged. "Like the ability to manipulate the laws of physics or read minds, or telekinesis. Something powerful."

Mr. Condon smiled. "Son, there's nothin' in the world more powerful than faith." He looked at William and winked, then pushed away from the counter. "I'll call Petey, let him know you three are safe. He'll come right over. That all right?"

"Fine by me," Marny said.

Esther turned to Marny, eyebrows raised. "Who's Petey?"

"Local cop on patrol. Mr. Condon called him back at the garage."

"And he's coming here?"

"Sounds like it."

Mr. Condon took the phone and walked to the front room in the house, the living room. Marny was about to apologize to Esther and William for his disappointment when a bright light appeared and moved along the back wall of the kitchen. A car's headlights. Marny's heart skipped a few precious beats. It could be Pete, or it could be...

Mr. Condon appeared in the archway between the kitchen and living room, his eyes wide, mouth tight. "Get in the cellar. All three a' ya."

Chapter 11

Marny wasted no time with questions.

The door to the cellar was in the kitchen. It opened quietly, and he sent Esther and William down first.

Mr. Condon grabbed his arm and leaned close. "Listen, Mahny, if things go bad, ya take them to the lighthouse. My boat is docked there. The keys are under the seat. Go to Booker Island and wait for daybreak, then find help." He looked Marny right in the eyes, and for the first time Marny saw fear in the lines of his friend's face.

Marny nodded. "I'm not the boatman you are, but I think I can manage. Let's hope it doesn't come to that."

"Hope and pray, Mahny. Hope and pray." Mr. Condon patted him on the shoulder and gave him a nudge down the steps. "Now go on. And take care a' them."

He shut the door, and Marny descended the steps. The cellar was nothing special, just four concrete walls, a concrete floor, and a low ceiling. A furnace sat to one side, the washer and dryer opposite it. Along the walls were stacked cardboard boxes in no particular order or pattern. The rest of the floor space was taken up by boat and auto supplies and a push mower and garden tools. The room smelled like oil and cut grass. Opposite the wooden staircase, along the far wall, was a walkout door to a patio overlooking the Penobscot. The house was built into a hill with the cellar level exposed in the back.

No sooner did Marny's foot hit the concrete floor than a loud knocking resonated through the wood framing of the house. Marny looked at Esther and William. They were huddled together under the staircase watching him, waiting to see what he would do.

He put a finger to his mouth.

The knock came again, and this time was followed by Mr. Condon's footsteps along the hardwood flooring. He moved toward the front door.

The lock on the door jiggled and voices could be heard, Mr. Condon's and Gary's. Marny couldn't make out what they were saying, but the conversation grew in intensity and finally resulted in a loud wet knock, breaking glass, and a grunt.

Heavy footsteps crossed the floor, accompanied by a muffled scraping sound. A chair slid and rattled, and the floor shook from a sudden thud. The men were in the kitchen.

"Where are they?" Gary's voice was low and serious. Silence for a few moments, then louder, "Esther, I know you're here. Bring the boy out or the old man dies. Do you want that on your conscience?"

Marny shook his head slowly. Esther pressed a hand to her mouth. There were tears in her eyes. William buried his face in his sister's shirt.

A volley of loud smacks and groans came from above.

"Where are they?" Gary again. He waited a second or two, then followed with another smack. Mr. Condon's moan was pitiful.

Marny's stomach twisted around itself like a sailor's knot, and nausea burned in his abdomen. He rounded the staircase and quietly ascended the first four steps so he could peer under the door and into the kitchen. He could see two legs of the table, the chair legs, and Mr. Condon's sneakers. One foot was flat on the floor, the other was tipped and resting on the outside edge. Gary's footsteps moved across the kitchen, something clunked, then they moved back until his boots came into view.

"There's always ways of making people talk," Gary said. His voice was calm now, conversational, as if he were discussing the day's weather with dear Mr. Condon. "Do you know what this is? Of course you do; you're an educated man."

He raised his voice so Marny, Esther, and William could know what it was as well.

"It's a garrote, ligature, used for strangulation. I loop this cord around your neck and progressively tighten it. The pressure collapses your carotid artery, cutting off oxygen to the brain. At first you'll feel woozy, light-headed, then the pressure will grow so great it will compress your trachea and you'll experience a choking sensation. I can assure you it isn't pleasant, not one bit, but it has a way of getting someone to talk."

There was another slap, another moan, then, "Now, where are they?"

A pause.

"Fine then. Because of your hardened heart you will be punished. You will share in the suffering of our Lord in hopes that your soul may be cleansed and the darkness in it banished."

This declaration was followed by a struggle and the sound of someone being strangled. Mr. Condon gagged, wheezed, gurgled. His feet twisted and stamped on the floor. An awful image dangled before Marny's mind's eye: Mr. Condon's eyes bulging, face red, lips turning purple as the cord dug into his neck.

Marny clenched his fists and ground his molars. Sweat broke out all over his face. He wanted to rush up the stairs, throw open the door, and wrap his own hands around Gary's neck. He'd been mistaken. Gary was no gorilla. He was a monster, as Esther had said.

But instead he tumble-slid down the steps, grabbed Esther by the arm, and pulled her and William across the cellar. Things had sufficiently gone bad, and he was getting them out of there.

The cellar door to the patio opened easily, and all three of them stumbled outside. Despite the cooler temperature of the night, sweat drenched Marny. To their right, a quarter mile down the coast, was a lighthouse privately owned by Mr. Condon's neighbor, who allowed him to dock his lobster boat there. It sat at the end of a rock pier that jutted another quarter mile into the bay.

"C'mon," Marny said. "The lighthouse."

But before he finished the word, a sharp *woop-woop* pierced the night air. The siren of Petey's patrol car.

"The police," Esther said and pulled up.

"Petey." Marny hesitated and briefly entertained the thought of going back into the house and seeing what the outcome of all this would be. But he quickly shook off the notion and took Esther by the arm. "C'mon. Let him handle things. We need to move."

Esther didn't question him.

They headed down a sloping bank to a pebbly beach dotted with clumps of boulders. Moonlight shimmered on the water like a white oil slick, but beyond, a few hundred yards out, the horizon was nothing but blackness, an empty gulf, as if the world really were flat and just dropped out of sight. Out there somewhere, a good mile off the coast, was Booker Island. The air coming off the water, blowing out of that dark abyss, was moist with the smell of salt and seaweed.

Behind them, the house was quiet. To any passers-by it would seem to be just another seaside bungalow whose occupants had turned in for the night and were snug in their beds, listening to the rolling ocean through screened windows.

Marny wanted to look back, but he couldn't yet. He had to put distance between the three of them and Gary; he had to press on toward the lighthouse. It was their place of refuge now, their way out of this nightmare.

When they were a little over halfway to the pier, a shot rang out and cut through the air so sharply Marny almost felt its impact. He stopped and spun around. The lighted windows of the house on the shore made for a serene picture that contrasted violently with what had occurred within those four walls.

Had Petey taken care of Gary? Had he shot him and rescued Mr. Condon?

Hope swelled in Marny.

Until he saw the figure standing on the patio, silhouetted by the lighted door of Mr. Condon's home.

Gary lumbered down the bank and took off after them in a full sprint.

Chapter 12

MARNY HAD KNOWN that sooner or later Mr. Condon's affiliation with him would catch up to his friend.

It did everyone. Sooner or later.

And this time it had caught up to Pete Morsey. Which was why, in spite of the fond feelings he already had for them, Marny was determined to part company with Esther and William. But not before getting them to safety and out of the reach of their crazed Uncle Gary. He wasn't about to abandon them prematurely. He might be self-deprecating and overly cautious, but he wasn't a jerk.

Marny was surprised by how fast William could move with that gimpy gait of his. Years of accommodation and substitution must have trained his muscles to overcompensate with what they had to work with. William and Esther held hands as they hit the pier.

Looking back, Marny was relieved to see that Gary had gained no ground on them. He was malicious and hateful, but he was also big and lumbering, a lummox, not in the least swift of foot. But navigating the pier would slow them all down. It consisted of Prius-sized boulders aligned in three rows and ran the length of a quarter mile, sticking out into the Penobscot Bay like an aging finger. Most of the boulders abutted each other tightly, leaving no room between them, but occasionally there was a gap the size of a tire. They had to be careful to stay on top of the boulders and not find one of those crevices. If one of them caught a foot and went down, Gary would be on them like a Rottweiler on a rabbit.

The moonlight cast odd shadows across the pier, masking the places where the gaps were. At one point William slipped and would have gone down if Marny hadn't grabbed him by the shirt and steadied him.

Navigating the boulders slowed William even more than Marny had anticipated. Gary was gaining on them. They were a little less than halfway along when their pursuer stepped onto his first boulder.

"We need to move faster." Marny's voice quaked and cracked with fear.

"He can't," Esther said.

Marny had a thought. It wasn't often he came up with a good idea, and even less often one that would save lives.

He stopped Esther and William, crouched low, and told William to get on his back.

Esther looked at him like he'd just crossed the border to Crazyland.

Gary was gaining quickly now. He might be a lummox, but his footing on the boulders was proving to be surprisingly nimble.

"Quick. Get on."

William glanced at Esther, then climbed onto Marny's back. He was small for his age and couldn't have weighed more than eighty pounds. A load to carry, yes, but not unbearable. Marny found himself able to run the boulders quite well with William perched on his back. But he still had a good quarter of the way to go, and his lungs were already burning.

Out of breath and struggling to find words, Marny said to Esther, "Go ahead and get the boat started. The key is under the seat cushion. You start it like a car."

She touched William's arm, nodded at Marny, then took off ahead. Marny realized then how slowly he was moving and pushed himself to go faster. Adrenaline surged through his veins even as the buildup of lactic acid in the muscles of his legs threatened to end this whole ordeal. But he couldn't stop, not now. He was almost there. A hundred yards more to go. He wanted to look back and see where Gary was, but he didn't dare for fear he'd lose his footing and go down.

Up ahead, Esther climbed aboard Mr. Condon's boat and fished around the seat for the key.

Seventy-five more yards. Marny's legs felt like lumps of clay moving through mud. Each step on each boulder was a chore that took every ounce of his strength and focus.

Esther stood, and a second later the engine roared to life.

Fifty yards. He could hear Gary's footsteps behind them now. The monster was gaining.

"The rope," Marny hollered, but his voice was so weak and strained he didn't know if Esther could hear him or not. "Get the cleat."

Apparently she did hear, because she jumped out of the boat and unwound the rope from the cleat on the small dock.

Twenty-five yards. Marny's foot hit a divot in one of the boulders and buckled his knee. He had no idea how he hung on and didn't go down. He could hear Gary's labored breathing behind him now. The gorilla couldn't be more than thirty or forty feet away. Esther climbed back into the boat and got behind the wheel. Hopefully she'd be ready to throw the throttle as soon as Marny and William hit the boat's deck.

Ten yards now. He bore down and pushed his body to the limits of what it would give him. His legs were numb. He had to will them to move, to take one more step, one more step, one more step. Finally they were there, at the dock. It sat maybe five feet lower than the boulders, and a ladder descended to the planks below. Marny skipped the ladder and made the jump. His legs hit the dock and collapsed beneath him, throwing William from his back.

"Go!" He shoved William in the direction of the boat. The boy scrambled to his feet and hobbled ahead.

On his back, legs throbbing, Marny looked up. Gary stood on the pier above him. His face glistened with sweat in the moonlight, and his deep-set eyes were hidden by shadows. His chest heaved, lungs wheezed.

Marny managed to climb to his feet, to his numb and useless legs, and get himself to the boat. Right before he reached the end of the dock the whole thing shook from the impact of Gary landing on it. Marny tried to leap from the dock to the deck of the boat, but his legs gave out from under him. He tumbled off the edge of the dock, hit the back of the boat, and rolled in. Immediately the engine growled and the vessel lurched forward, leaving Gary standing on the end of the dock.

With legs spread wide and the dock rocking in the boat's wake, Gary pounded his chest and beat at the air. "You can't get away from me! I own you."

His voice carried across the hard water until it sounded like it was in the boat with Marny, like Gary was standing next to him, screaming into his ear.

"There's nowhere you can go to hide from me. I'll find you!"

Marny had no doubt he would keep his promise.

Chapter 13

THE BOY WAS there again, in his wheelchair with his withered limbs.

Gary had landed awkwardly, straight-legged, and the impact of his feet with the dock had sent a jolt up his legs, through his spine, and into his head. And the shock had produced the image of the boy, just a child.

The voice was there again too.

How could you let this happen? You're supposed to protect him. You're his guardian.

Gary tugged at his hair with both hands and thought about throwing himself into the bay. "Please, don't. I'll get him back, I promise. I will."

You are the guardian of the anointed; you must take this seriously. It is a high calling and not one to be taken lightly.

He ground his molars and leaned against the pier. "I take it seriously. It's my life. *He's* my life. There's nothing else. I'll find him."

Then, before the voice could scold him anymore, he turned, climbed the ladder to the pier, and took off back toward the mainland singing a song he'd learned many years ago: "Loving shepherd of Thy sheep, keep Thy lamb, in safety keep; nothing can Thy power withstand, none can pluck me from Thy hand."

The song kept the voice quiet. Or at least drowned out its droning.

When he got back to Condon's house, he went inside and surveyed the scene. Condon was dead at the table, the cop on the floor. The place was a mess. Broken glass, spilled tea, broken furniture. But surprisingly, not much blood. It hadn't taken Gary long to overpower the cop and take his weapon, but the altercation was violent. The shot to the cop's head had shut down the brain, which canceled the heart. Little blood oozed from the hole just above the right eyebrow. He'd straighten and clean the place up, not leave a trace of ever being there, but first he had to attend to the bodies.

Gary saw the killing as necessary. It was never something he enjoyed or even desired, but the protection of the boy had to come first, even at the expense of other lives. Some must die so one could live. And besides, anyone who stood in the way of his calling, who interfered with his duty, brought potential harm to the anointed one, and that must be dealt with. That was a sin punishable by death.

He crossed the kitchen, careful not to step on any broken glass and track it through the house, and stopped at the table. He lifted Condon's body by the head and sat it upright in the chair. The head lolled to one side and the jaw dropped down. Blank eyes stared at the counter.

Gary touched the forehead lightly. "May the God of grace show mercy on you. May He forgive your sins and heal your broken spirit. May your soul not be tormented in hellfire forever and ever."

Even sinners deserved to be prayed for.

He then released his hold on the old man's head. The body slumped in the chair and toppled to the floor. Gary let it lie there while he went to the cop's body near the sink. He rolled the body over and again touched the forehead lightly. "May God have mercy on your soul and not collect the debt you owe Him. May He forgive your trespasses and grant you access to heaven."

Gary then got up and exited the house. He'd come back later and clean the place. First he had something else he needed to deal with. He hated the idea of it but it was necessary, for the boy's sake, for the mission, his duty. For the anointed one.

The nearest houses to Condon's were half a mile down shore, in the town of Pine Harbor—except for one, a single-story home set not fifty yards away. The occupant had to be dealt with. It was all too possible he'd seen or heard something—the Taurus, Condon's odd late-night visitors, the gunshot, the trio's run along the shore-line—that would raise suspicion and later identify Gary and put the cops on his trail. There could be no witnesses, no interference of any kind. And besides, if the boy and his sister returned with the intruding stranger to find Condon gone, the first place they'd go would be the neighbor's home seeking aid. This would be a fine opportunity to instill upon them the gravity of the situation, the weight of Gary's dedication to retrieving and protecting William.

The neighboring home had weathered-shingle siding, a high-pitched roof, and a wide, sprawling patio. Leading from the patio to the house was a pair of sliding glass doors, and on the other side of the glass was a tiny white dog barking at him. Its yelps were not audible at this distance, but by the way it hopped about and ran back and forth the length of the doors, it was obvious that it was barking up a storm.

Gary hated dogs.

Chapter 14

OVER THE COURSE of the mile-long trip from the Pine Harbor pier to Booker Island, Marny had the boat at every bit of thirty knots.

And he knew that despite Mr. Condon's objection to using his lobster boat for anything but relaxing, his friend would have been proud.

Every summer in Maine the lobster boat races took center stage. Towns like Boothbay Harbor, Rockland, and Pine Harbor all participated, and lobstermen from up and down the coast showed up to put their vessels on display. The top speeds the boats obtained was right around thirty knots—about thirty-five miles per hour, to landlubbers.

And though George Condon often said his vessel was the fastest in the water, he never entered a race. He used his boat solely for relaxation, for getting away from the stresses of the world that took place on land, for letting the rhythm of the ocean lull away all anxiety and worry, and for catching the occasional lobster— not for creating more stress by engaging in competition. He said it with every bit of sincerity he could muster, but the twinkle in his eye said otherwise. Marny had always gotten the impression that once Mr. Condon was finished with the garage, there would be some races in his retirement.

As the boat bounced over the crests and troughs of the Penobscot

Bay, sprays of salt water shot out from either side, creating a dramatic wake. Regardless of what the temperature had been like during the day, the air was cool and damp on the water. Esther and William sat in the rear, huddled close together. Occasionally Marny glanced back at them, but his focus was on the black horizon ahead, watching for the first glimpse of the island. He'd kept the lights off on the boat, opting to hide in the darkness so Gary would have no idea which way they headed. Now, though, being in the middle of the bay with only the moonlight to guide them and the thought of the depths below teeming with sea creatures of all kinds, he was having second thoughts and almost flipped on the floodlights. He drew in a long breath, wiped his palms on his pants, and calmed himself. Hitting the lights would be a fatal mistake. For now, the darkness was their ally.

Booker Island was named after William F. Booker, the first owner. He was a newspaperman who owned the *Portland Press Herald* and was a philanthropist extraordinaire. He purchased the island in 1967 to ensure it would never be inhabited but remain in its natural state. But Booker had no immediate family, and when he died, the island was put up for auction. The bidding came down to Mr. Condon's neighbor, Edward Tuttle, and a New York City entrepreneur who wanted to put a bed-and-breakfast and tennis courts on it. Mr. Tuttle won the bid by paying nearly five million for the hundred-acre island, more than a million more than what it was worth. He then bought the lighthouse and pier from the town of Pine Harbor for another million.

No one ever knew where he got that kind of money. Some supposed he inherited it from wealthy distant family in Augusta, others speculated he accumulated it over years of gambling or horse racing or some other unseemly method. Mr. Tuttle never defended himself and never told.

As the island came into view, Marny slowed the boat to ten knots and steered it to the right. He'd been there once before with Mr. Condon and remembered where the dock was. The island humped out of the water like a silver-embossed, spiny turtle shell. Around the edges the pebbled beach quickly gave way to exposed granite, and from there clumps of wild strawberries, lupine, buttercup, and hawkweed. The center of the island was forested by a large army of spruce, protecting the land from intruders intent on disturbing the natural habitat and upsetting the balance of the wild.

Marny and his new friends wanted to do neither; they only wanted to find solace for the night.

As the boat rounded the right side of the island, Marny throttled back even more and aligned it with the dock. A hand gently touched his arm. William stood there, looking up at him.

"What is this place, Marnin?"

Marny pulled back on the throttle so it was almost at an idle. "Booker Island. We'll be safe here for the night."

William placed his hand over Marny's on the throttle stick. "Thank you for helping us."

"You're welcome, William. I couldn't just let Gary take you back, could I?" The boat pulled up alongside the dock, and Marny cut the engine.

William paused. "Yes, you could have. But you didn't."

He was right. Marny could have just walked away from the note; he could have escaped that evil house on his own; he could have left them with Mr. Condon and split. He could have, but as William said, he didn't. From the moment Marny first saw Esther in the backseat of that car, something about her drew him in, an irresistible force. There was nothing sensual about it. She was attractive, yes, in a wholesome kind of way, but that's not what seized him. It was her eyes.

The boat nudged the dock and knocked William off-balance. He stumbled and caught himself on the wall of the cabin.

Marny reached out and steadied him. "You okay?"

"Yes, Marnin. I'm fine. Thank you."

Marny went to the rear of the boat and stepped up onto the dock. There he fastened the rope to the cleat.

"We'll stay here for the night?" Esther stood with feet wide, trying to maintain her balance on the undulating vessel.

"Yeah." Marny offered his hand and helped her onto the dock. "We'll go around to the east side and make a fire. That way we can watch the coast. Mr. Condon has blankets somewhere on the boat." William took his hand, and Marny helped him onto the dock as well. "Let me get some stuff and we'll head over."

"It's so dark," Esther said.

"Yeah, out here on the water you don't get the light pollution from the coast. The darkness is real."

"Can he get us?"

"No way. He doesn't even know we're here. Probably doesn't even know this island is here. Unless he's psychic or has some wicked night vision, we're safe. He's not psychic, is he?"

"No. Not that I know of." She was quiet for a moment, head tilted back, watching the stars play their games in the night sky. "But what if he does figure out where we are?"

"Then he'd have to swim a mile in fifty-degree water...or fly. Any other way and we'll hear him coming long before he reaches the island. But he can't know we're here."

William looked at Marny, and there was sadness in the boy's eyes. "He'll come," William said. "He won't stop until gets what he wants."

"And what's that?"

"Me, Marnin."

Chapter 15

MARNY WAS TEN the first time he saw Karl Gunnison hit his mother.

He was sure the jerk struck her before then, plenty of times probably, but Marny was never around and she'd done a good job of hiding the bruises, both physically and emotionally. She was in the kitchen washing the dinner dishes and Karl was in his Barcalounger in the living room watching Monday night football. Marny remembered the game too. Broncos and Redskins. Karl hated John Elway, and Elway was tearing up the 'Skins. The jerk was in a bad mood. Marny sat on the sofa, half interested in the game, while Karl called Elway every name in the book and then some Marny was sure he'd made up. Then he got started on the Redskins. Regardless of what Janie said about swearing in the house, Karl gave Marny a lesson in the finer uses of English vulgarities on a daily basis.

Halftime arrived, and Karl got up to go to the bathroom. When he returned, he dropped back into his chair, belched loudly, and hollered for Janie to get him another beer. Only she didn't hear him over the water running.

He hollered again, but still the water ran and Janie hummed, oblivious to the storm brewing in the living room. Marny tried to defend his mother, but Karl told him to shut his mouth and mind his own business.

Finally the jerk let loose with a conglomeration of expletives Marny had never heard used in the same sentence, got up with much drama, and stomped into the kitchen. His face was red and the veins in his neck stood out like vines crawling up a tree trunk.

Marny followed, his heart beating so hard he could feel it in his earlobes. Something bad was going to happen.

Karl walked right up to Janie, who was so focused on the dishes and so lost in the tune in her head that she never even saw him coming. He grabbed her by the back of the neck and pushed her face into the soapy dishwater. Marny was sure she'd drown right there in front of him in the kitchen sink. But Karl didn't hold her under long, just long enough that when he let her up she was spitting and sputtering and gasping for air.

Then he smacked her right on the cheek. She spun around and dropped to her knees, never making a sound. Soapy water puddled around her on the linoleum.

Marny hollered, "Leave my mom alone!" He made a move to help her, but Karl's look drove him back. The jerk didn't even look human. Didn't look animal either. It was something else Marny saw, something evil. Marny backed out of the kitchen and stood in the doorway while his mom tried to compose herself.

Karl stood over her, hands on his hips, and shook his head. "Look at ya," he said.

Marny could hear the smile in his voice.

"On your knees like a dog. Next time I tell ya t'fetch somethin' ya better do it."

Marny hated Karl Gunnison. He was the only person Marny ever wanted his curse to catch up to. And finally it did. In the worst possible way.

The Maine sky at night has to be one of the most beautiful spectacles nature has to offer. In the absence of any kind of light pollution, stars a million deep dot the sky like crushed diamonds on black velvet. The constellations are all there, doing their cosmic waltz, as are galaxies and planets. The universe seems both near and flat, like one could extend a hand and dot the stars with a fingertip, and boundless, a vast endless expanse of lights and bodies suspended in an infinite sea of blackness.

The threesome stood at the edge of the forest, looking out at where the sky met the sea, and Marny couldn't tell where one ended and the other started. William drew near and stood close enough so his shoulder rested against Marny's side. Esther stood on his other side.

"It's beautiful, isn't it?" Her voice was low, almost a whisper, as if to speak any louder would somehow disturb the pattern of stars and throw the universe out of sync.

"I'm sorry I got you into all this," Marny said. For some reason he thought if he'd just let well enough alone, Esther and William would have somehow worked things out with Gary on their own. His involvement had only brought them trouble...

She turned her face toward him and put a hand on his arm. "We were already in it. You saved us. Our hero. Thank you."

"I need to get you two to safety and then bow out, be on my way." He had no idea what he was going to do. With Mr. Condon gone he no longer had a job or a friend.

Head tilted back, still looking at the stars, William said, "You can do more than you think you can, Marnin."

"What's that supposed to mean?" Marny said.

William was quiet, still, watching the stars twinkle and glisten.

"Ever hear of the Midas touch?" Marny said. "Everything turns to gold? I have the opposite. I've been trouble for anyone who's ever known me. What I touch turns to mold."

Esther tilted her face toward the sky. "Did you ever read the Bible?"

The Bible? "Sure. As a kid." From as early as Marny could remember his mom had taken him to church every Sunday—until she married Karl. Her new husband forbade her to go to church, so she sneaked into Marny's room at night and read him the Bible. He wondered where Esther was going with this.

"Do you remember the parts with all the names? So and so begat him and he begat this guy and so forth."

"Yeah. The boring stuff."

"Right. Pages and pages of names and genealogies and ancestries. Pages of people."

"Pages of boring."

She paused, but he could tell she wasn't finished.

"Look at them." She still watched the stars. "Look how many, how majestic. Do you know what the Bible says about the stars?"

"God made them?"

"It says, 'He made the stars also.' That's it. Pages and pages of people's names and families. Pages most skip right over. And one sentence about the stars. Like it was an afterthought. Kinda tells you what's more important to God, doesn't it?"

She turned to Marny again. He kept his eyes on the night sky and the endless field of stars. He knew where she was going with all this now, and it made him uncomfortable.

"He loves you, you know. More than all those stars. He loves you. And you're important to Him. You just need to believe in Him…and in yourself. He does."

"He does what?"

"Believe in you. He knows the size of your heart. He knows there's a hero in you, someone willing to give his own life for others."

"Until now others have lost their lives because of me."

Esther's hand found Marny's, and she held it tight. At that moment he wished the mainland would sink into the ocean, and Gary along with it. He wished the sun would never rise again and the stars would never burn out. He wanted to spend the rest of his life here on this island with Esther, just like this.

"God's love can reach you wherever you are," Esther said. "He loves you more than all those stars."

A lump formed in Marny's throat. That was the same thing his mother told him every night, that God loved him more than the stars. That he was God's star. Marny released Esther's hand and stepped back from the two of them. It couldn't last forever. The mainland was still there, and the sun would rise in the morning. And Gary would be waiting for them, along with Marny's curse.

"I'm gonna build us a fire." Marny turned toward the forest. "Getting chilly out here."

Chapter 16

DEEPER INTO THE forest the darkness thickened and loomed like a black fog, discouraging anyone from entering.

While Esther spread the blankets on the ground and built a fire pit with stones, William and Marny gathered sticks along the tree line. The forest was where the things of the night lurked, and Marny was just fine staying on the rocks along the island's edge.

William came to him, arms full of yard-long sticks. "Ready to build the fire, Marnin."

Marny was surprised at how much the boy could carry despite his withered arm. "Okay, let me just grab a few more larger sticks and we'll be ready."

He grabbed a ten-foot, partially rotted branch and dragged it behind him to where Esther was preparing the site.

When they arrived, she stood and smiled. With the moonlight at her back and gleaming off the edges of her hair she looked like a messenger sent from heaven, halo and all. Mr. Condon kept three wool blankets on the boat, and she had all three spread on the grass surrounding a small ring of stones. "Will this do?"

"It's perfect."

"Are we going to camp out here, Marnin?" William asked.

"Looks like it. You okay sleeping under the stars?"

"Mm-hm."

"Great. How about you stack the sticks in the ring there, and we'll get this fire going." It struck Marny then that they had no matches.

Esther interpreted the look on his face correctly. "Are there any in the boat?"

"I don't know. I'll go check." Marny ran over the grass and granite to where the boat was docked and rooted through the storage compartments. There were flares, but he didn't want to waste them on starting a campfire. They might need them for their intended purpose before the night was over. In a first-aid kit he found one pack of water-resistant paper matches.

Returning with his find, he held the matchbook over his head, victorious. "Cavemen would have killed for just one of these, and we have twenty."

He crouched low with his back to the breeze, tore a match from the cardboard book, and struck the head across the phosphorous strip. The match ignited, then promptly fizzled. Marny tried again. Then several more times. The moist, steady breeze that blew off the water and combed over the island proved too much for the tiny flame on the end of the match. He tried cupping his hands around the lit match, shielding it from the air, but as soon as the fire neared the pile of dry sticks, it was extinguished.

Marny looked up at Esther and William, huddled close together. He found hope in their faces, and trust. And it made his cheeks burn. Their belief in him was unearned and soon to be dashed like a glass bottle against the rocky shore of the island.

No one spoke.

He tore another match from the book, slid it along the strip, and quickly cupped the flame in his hands. Carefully, with one hand shielding the flame from the ocean air, he put the match to a clump of dry grass and pine needles he'd gathered and stuffed under the larger twigs and sticks. The tinder ignited immediately and burned quickly. The fire spread, hungrily devouring the dry fuel until it was gone. But the flames proved too weak to take to the sticks and too fickle to withstand the steady breeze. Within seconds, what promised to be a sustaining fire had withered and faded to nothing.

Marny stared at the open matchbook. With one match left he looked at William, then Esther. "This is it. Wish me luck." He struck the match, cupped his hand around it, and held it close to a branch of pine needles. The flame ignited one needle, then two, then a twig and more needles. Marny blew on it, giving it the oxygen it craved...and promptly blew it out.

He dropped back on his butt and put his head in his hands. Without fire they'd freeze; overnight temperatures were forecast to dip into the upper forties. Their only other option was to head back to the mainland, where a very unhappy Gary no doubt waited.

Marny heard movement and looked up. William had crouched low and hunched over near the pile of sticks. His brow tightened and lips drew into a thin line. He worked his good hand under the sticks, held it there, then shut his eyes. Marny was about to ask him what he was doing when a faint glow appeared where his hand was. At first Marny thought the boy had found an unused match and succeeded where he'd failed nineteen times. But William didn't pull out his hand. The glow grew brighter and larger. Now light radiated up through the sticks and illuminated the curves and angles of William's face, giving him a ghostly appearance. With his eyes still closed and the glow brightening even more, William held his hand there, showing no sign of being in pain or awe. His face went calm, relaxed. His lips moved almost imperceptibly. Suddenly a tongue of fire appeared and licked at the sticks. William opened his eyes and jerked his hand away from the flame. Within seconds the fire had spread to the rest of the sticks and engulfed most of the small pit.

William scooted next to Esther and put his head on her lap. She wrapped them both in a blanket and met Marny's eyes.

"What was that all about?" he said.

William shrugged and closed his eyes. Esther stroked his hair with her hand and began to sing a song Marny had never heard before. It was beautiful, melodic, haunting. Sounded like an old hymn, maybe Scottish. Slowly, like the melting of butter on a hot griddle, William's body relaxed, and he slipped into sleep.

The fire was going full tilt now and quickly engulfed the dry branches. Marny placed more wood on the flames and inched himself around so he was closer to Esther.

"What did William just do? With the fire?" He couldn't help his curiosity.

Esther continued to stroke William's hair. "He believed."

"Is that why Gary is after him?"

"Why?"

"Because of these... magic tricks he does."

"It's not magic, Marny. Magic is for stories and dreams and those who play on the dark side of things."

"Like Gary and his house."

She looked out at the bay, which emptied into the ocean, so vast, so deep, so black, undulating and moving in a rhythm not of this world, stirring with mystery. "Yes."

Marny poked at the fire with a branch, then tossed it in. "You said he was going to kill you. Your note."

"He will when he gets what he wants."

"What's that?"

She was about to answer when their fireside conversation was interrupted by the muffled sound of something moving in the forest.

Chapter 17

MARNY GRABBED A branch from the fire and stood.

A flame hung onto the end of the stick for a second, then died. Esther stared at him with wide eyes. He knew what she was thinking because it was no doubt the same thing he was thinking. Apparently Gary didn't mind swimming a mile in fifty-degree water, and now he was tramping through the woods in sopping wet clothes. It didn't make sense, but the sounds they heard didn't lie.

Again they heard the soft uneven crunch of pine needles and the rustle of branches. Definitely footsteps. Marny took a stone from the fire ring in his other hand. Sticks and stones wouldn't be much of a defense against Gary's bulk, but he felt he needed something to defend himself—to defend *them*—with.

William remained asleep, and Esther stayed where she was. Marny moved forward, stepping lightly on the island grass so as to remain as noiseless as possible. Chances were that Gary had followed the light of the fire and seen them already, but in case he hadn't Marny wanted to remain as concealed as he could for as long as possible.

He gripped the stick in his hand way too hard and could feel it pulsating from the thrum of his heart.

The sounds grew closer, right up to the forest's edge, and Marny froze. If there was ever a disadvantage, he had it. Standing there in the open with no cover at all, he was a target begging to be hit.

His primitive weapons would do no good against the darkly veiled shots from a handgun.

The thing in the woods ran left, moving quickly, brushing through boughs of pine and rustling the forest floor. It stopped, then returned to its original position. Whatever it was, it was big, the size of a man. But it moved quickly and with the agility of an animal. Marny couldn't picture Gary, with his mass and weight, moving like that.

Two glowing orbs appeared and hovered maybe five feet from the ground. Human eyes didn't glow in firelight. Marny balanced the rock in his hand, then tossed it at the spot where the eyes seemed to float in space. The stone landed with a thud, and the animal took off with a crunch of pine needles and deadened *whoosh* of branches until the sound diminished to nothing and they were left with the noises of the island once again, the crackle of the fire and rhythmic ebb and flow of the water.

Returning to the fire ring, Marny threw the stick back on the flames and sat next to Esther. She looked at him, her eyes wide and expectant.

"Just a deer or something checking us out." His hands shook, and to his ears it sounded like his voice did also. This time it was only a deer; next time it could be Gary. Marny was confident Gary wouldn't be able to approach the island without their knowing it, but if there was one thing this day had already proved, it was that stranger things could happen.

He could tell Esther knew what he was thinking. She always seemed to know what he was thinking. Either she had a special gift like her brother did, or Marny was just that transparent. He suspected the latter but certainly didn't rule out the former. Again, stranger things had already happened.

Esther looked around, studying the darkness, then said, "Do you have a plan for if he comes?"

A plan. Marny wasn't one for plans. His life was lived from the seat of his pants, not from formulating plans to reach goals and operating on a schedule of planned events. His only plan was to stay alive, get Esther and William to safety, and then get as far from them as possible. In the short time he'd known her he'd already grown very fond of Esther, and he wasn't about to put her safety—and possibly her life—in jeopardy by sticking around.

He picked up a stick and poked at the fire while trying to think of an answer that would sound as though he'd been pondering the subject of what-ifs. Nothing came to him. "Um, run?"

"Not much of a plan."

"I suppose I'm not much of the planning type. I usually just, you know, take life as it comes."

There was silence between them then, and Marny was certain she was wishing she'd never dropped her note at that gas station for that attendant to find. Someone else would have been much more help, better prepared to protect them, and would maybe even stand up against Gary.

"I'm sure you'll do the right thing when the time comes."

Her confidence in him was humbling. He didn't deserve it, but somehow it made him feel better to know someone thought he was more than just an affliction waiting to upset people's lives and take their loved ones.

"Why did you pick me?" He hoped she'd say something eloquent and encouraging, something that gave new life to his mission, infused him with resolve...so when she said, "I didn't have any other choice," his already suffering ego dropped a few notches.

"Gary doesn't go out but to the general store and gas station," she said. "He'd never gone to your station before because it's too close to home. He usually goes to the Agway in Ellsworth. It's self-service, so he doesn't have to talk to anyone. He takes me along to keep me separated from William. He's afraid I'll steal away with my little brother while we're alone in the house. I don't run in to too many people."

Okay, so she hadn't chosen him. He just happened to be the only warm body she came in contact with.

"It was God's will. You're the right one, Marny." She said it like she was putting the final thoughts on an argument she was determined not to lose.

Marny wasn't sure about the God's will part, but he couldn't deny that fate had had a hand in all this. He could only hope fate would also have a hand in getting them off this island safely and getting Esther and William away from Gary for good.

"Do you believe that?" she said.

"Believe what?"

"That you finding and reading my note was part of God's plan?"

"I told you I'm not the planning type."

"But God is. Nothing happens by chance. Every aspect of our lives, the good, the bad, the losses and victories, they're all planned. Nothing catches God by surprise."

And that's what Marny had a problem with. He knew what the Bible said, the major parts anyway. His mother's nightly readings were still in his head somewhere. The all-knowing, all-loving God thing had him stumped, though. There was so much suffering, so much hurt. The three of them—Esther, William, and himself—were perfect examples of the hurt this world could produce. And that was part of God's plan?

Marny placed another stick on the fire. "I never did understand that."

"You don't have to understand it, just believe it. It's called faith."

"The gift William has."

"Yes. But we can all have faith."

Marny was getting uncomfortable with the conversation. His mother had faith, and look where it got her. "You better get some sleep."

"You can't hide from it, you know."

"I'm not trying to hide from it, just understand it."

Esther glanced around. "Are there snakes around here?"

He shrugged. "I'm sure there are, but they won't come close to the fire."

"What if it goes out?"

"It won't."

"How do you know?"

He looked at her and smiled. "Have faith."

She adjusted William and lay down next to him so his head was on her arm. "Good night, Marny. My accidental hero."

Chapter 18

DOING THE LORD's work wasn't always easy or clean.

Gary stood on the patio behind the large seaside house. He'd waited an hour for the dog inside to quiet down and disappear into a back room.

A whispered prayer left Gary's lips and wafted away on an ocean breeze. He was God's servant. At times he questioned what the Lord required of him, but he'd immediately scold himself or sometimes even inflict pain upon himself, cleansing through suffering.

The voice was always there, his unseen schoolmaster.

Corralling your mind and bringing it into submission is a constant struggle. But what the Lord demands should be your priority. The servant is never greater than his master.

Entrance to the house was gained easily, almost too easily, verifying that this appointment was arranged by God Himself. The home's occupant was also a chosen one. He had been chosen before creation to partake in this most important mission. The aura of providence was in this place; Gary could feel it, smell it, even taste it in the air.

Moments after stepping into the house, he was met by the dog, apparently awakened by the whisper of the door opening. It was a small dog and easily silenced. Its neck was no thicker than Gary's wrist.

With the dog in one hand, he moved through the house quickly, room to room, searching for the sleeping inhabitant, the chosen participant in the work of the Lord. They all had their roles to play. Gary's was that of protector and guardian, this man's was that of a sacrifice. But hadn't they all been sacrifices? Unlike the others, though, this man's would only be temporary—momentary, in fact—for a far greater place awaited him on the other side.

Gary found the bedroom on the first floor and the owner of the house asleep in his bed. A CPAP machine sat firmly in place over his nose, making the sleeper look like a space traveler en route to another galaxy, sleeping away light-years of travel. The pump hummed quietly on the nightstand. Gary placed the dog on the bed beside its master and whispered another prayer.

The man slept peacefully on his back, hands crossed over his chest, eyes moving rhythmically beneath his closed lids. Gary wondered what images his reverie held, if they were pleasant or nightmarish. He supposed a man of this stature and standard of living, a man of this age and maturity, would entertain only enjoyable dreams. But one could never be sure.

In the darkness of the room, with only the dusty light of the moon filtering through the windows to light his path, Gary embarked on a journey few in this world have been asked to take. He knelt beside the bed and placed a hand lightly on the sleeper's leg.

"You have been chosen to partake in the work of the Lord. His anointed is among us and must be protected. I am his protector and must fulfill the instructions given me by Almighty God." His words came out as serpentlike whispers, barely piercing the stillness of the room, not disturbing the sleeping sacrifice.

"Your gift to the Lord will be rewarded in paradise, your suffering will be smiled upon. Through suffering we are cleansed, through death we are glorified."

He then stood and breathed another prayer asking for strength and courage. The duty given him was not an easy one, but something was asked of everyone, and what had been asked of him was small compared to what others had given.

Gary pulled in a deep breath and blew it out. His hands were trembling, not out of fear or apprehension, but out of awe for what had been asked of him, for it was the stuff of angels and God Himself. He had been given the power over life and death, the right to take life or give it freely. He felt with all humility that he was not worthy of such a duty. Some died because they opposed the work of the Lord—like Condon and the cop—but others because they were *part of* the work of the Lord. Some might call them collateral damage, but Gary didn't see it that way, not at all. They were partners, brothers in the mission, warriors worthy of the highest honor. They were sacrifices, giving everything, and would gain eternity.

"Your time has come," he whispered to the sleeper. "May your perfecting be swift and glorious."

Gary stepped outside and breathed in the cool, salty air coming off the bay. One day he'd like to own a home near the sea, maybe one just like this one. Maybe this one…if the Lord so blessed.

He turned and came face-to-face with himself in the glass of the sliding patio door. His reflection always annoyed him. He'd always been on the heavy side. In school his gym teacher once called him "thick," but Gary knew what that meant—fat. In recent years he'd put on more weight and lost some hair. And then there were the scars covering most of his hands and arms. Freakish things. The Lord's chastisement.

Turning away from the man in the glass, he crossed the lawn in silence, taking in the moment, basking in the satisfaction that came with serving the Lord and accomplishing His task. No matter how difficult the journey or high the price, the warmth of the light on the other side, *His* light, was always worth it.

But Gary's reprieve was cut short; there was still work to do. There was the matter of retrieving the boy and disposing of those who sought to harm him. They were not sacrifices, not brothers on the journey; they were the enemy, violators, perverters of God's calling. He would feel no remorse when administering the justice they deserved.

Gary looked out across the vast sea rolling in the moonlight. It seemed to have a life of its own, breathing in time to the rhythm of God's creation, sharing his heartbeat. Out there somewhere was the boy, the anointed one, and he would soon be under Gary's protective shelter again.

They would come back to the house to see if dear Mr. Condon had survived. They would go to the neighbor for help and find the seriousness of their transgressions, how far the tentacles of their sins had reached. They would hope to retrieve the car.

He would do what had to be done tonight, then come back in the morning and wait for their return.

Chapter 19

S LEEP IS AN overcoming force, a need that will not be spurned. Marny stayed awake as long as he could watching the flames dance in the darkness, occasionally throwing on another dry stick and gazing as the fire slowly consumed it. But around two in the morning the arrhythmic snapping and crackling of the flames accompanied by the perfect timing of the ocean's roll tugged at his eyelids. More than once he dozed, only to be jerked awake by the reflex in his neck. He'd adjust himself, breathe in a couple lungfuls of cool ocean air, stretch, then try again.

Esther and William slept surprisingly well. Marny would have thought two people in their predicament would find sleep difficult to come by, a prize just out of reach. But they'd slipped so suddenly and peacefully into that world of dreams that it almost seemed unnatural.

He thought of what Esther had said about God and His will. She truly believed God had brought them together for a reason. That it was no accident that he was the attendant at the gas station Gary never stopped at who picked up her note and read it. That it was God who prompted him to follow Gary and rescue her from the house of horror.

Marny thought about it, but he wasn't convinced. Life was too random, too chaotic, too cursed to say that God had His way and it was all working out accordingly.

Then he thought about what she'd called him: her accidental hero. She was being facetious, of course. She didn't believe in accidents, and he was no hero. If anything, he was an antihero. And if she knew the truth about him, she'd take William and both of them would swim the mile in fifty-degree water back to the mainland. It was that bad.

But no matter how much he tried to coerce both his muscles and mind into staying awake, the fatigue and stress of the day eventually caught up with him, and he drifted into sleep, where his mind conjured awful visions.

He was in a darkened room, no light at all, sitting on his haunches in the corner. Karl's voice was there, deep and gravelly, strained, half grunt, half speech. He said something about showing him respect, but Marny didn't catch the whole thing. He wasn't sure if Karl was talking to him or to someone else.

Karl's voice drew nearer in the darkness, a bodiless phantom closing in. Then Marny picked up another sound: a wet thumping sound, like he was swinging around a piece of raw steak. Was the jerk going to bludgeon him with a slab of meat? Marny tried to push back farther into the corner, but the wall would not give even an inch. He pulled his knees up closer to his chest and buried his face in them. If Karl was going to kill him, he at least wanted his eyes closed when it happened.

Karl's footsteps stopped just inches from Marny, and the click of the light switch echoed in the room. Light surrounded him now, but he kept his face buried and eyes closed.

Karl nudged him with his foot. "Look at me, ya little piece a' garbage. Look what I done."

Marny kept his face buried. He knew the moment he opened his eyes and lifted his head, a thirty-two-ounce steak would rattle his brain and the beating begin.

Karl nudged him again, this time harder. "Hey, garbage boy. Look what I done. Look at ya now. Not such a tough guy, ayuh?"

Marny opened his eyes and lifted his head. Bile surged up his throat and stung the back of his tongue. Karl did have a piece of meat in his hands, only the meat was no cut of steak; it was Marny. He held the other Marny up with one hand gripping the back of his head and the other arm around his waist. He was limp and appeared dead. His face was so bloody and disfigured Marny wouldn't even have recognized himself if it weren't for the University of Maine sweatshirt he'd worn so often in those days.

The bile was there again, but Marny swallowed it down. He was too scared and mad to vomit. In a fit of rage like he'd never experienced in real life, he jumped up and launched himself at Karl. The jerk dropped his punching dummy and stopped Marny's attack with a stiff forearm to the chest. Marny went down hard and lay there next to his pulverized twin. Karl stood over him, sweat dripping from the tip of his nose, a string of saliva connecting his parted lips. He breathed heavily, too heavily for the little work he'd done to knock down someone half his weight. With one of his meat-hook hands he grabbed Marny around the ankle and dragged him out of the room and down the hallway. Marny tried to fight back, but his arms were paralyzed. Had Karl hit him that hard? He felt no pain, just paralysis.

At the end of the hall was the staircase that led to the first floor. Without hesitation Karl swung Marny around and shoved him at the steps. Marny bounced violently down the flight, hitting each stair with either his back or arms until he came to rest on the floor at the bottom. Still he felt no pain, but fear had seeped into every cell of his body—intense fear, like he'd never felt before. He was sure Karl was going to follow him down those steps and beat him into a slab of meat as he had his twin. But when he looked up the stairs, Karl was gone and his mother was there. She wore her favorite flowered dress and had her hair all fixed up like she did on Sunday mornings. Tears came to Marny's eyes, and he whispered her name.

"Marnin." Her voice was calm, casual. "You didn't kill me...but you might as well have. It was your fault. You provoked him, and you know he always took it out on me."

The tears flowed now; Marny couldn't control them. "No."

"Don't deny it. I swear, you're such a victim. If you would have only minded your own business, none of it would have happened."

Karl appeared behind her, but she didn't seem to notice. He too looked calm now. Gone were the rage, the bulging veins, the reddened and sweaty face.

Mom continued, oblivious to the monster right behind her. "How many times did I tell you to mind your own business? Huh? But you just couldn't."

Fear suddenly seized Marny, clamped down on him like a vise and tightened his throat. He tried to warn his mother about Karl, but no words would come. It was as if someone had stuffed a rag in his throat.

At the top of the stairs Karl smiled at Marny, a wolfish grin that dripped malice, then gave his mother a hard push right in the middle of the back. Her head snapped back, and she lurched forward and for an instant was in a free fall down the steps. Her body hit the first step a quarter of the way down and tumbled end over end until right before she landed on him...

Marny jerked awake so hard his neck spasmed. Pain shot up the side of his head. It took him a second to orient himself. The sun peeked over the watery horizon an eternity away, but dawn had arrived and the sky was deep shades of orange and red. It had to be a little before five o'clock. The fire pit was now nothing more than a pile of charred sticks. Esther was still asleep...but William was gone.

Panic jumped into his chest. William was *gone*. Had Gary crept up on them in the still of the early morning hours and taken him? Marny was supposed to stay awake, guard Esther and William, make sure this very thing didn't happen, but he'd slept so soundly.

Looking around, he saw nothing but granite, grass, shrubs, and pines. No William.

He stood and scanned the island again, making a complete turn and finding nothing that clued him to William's whereabouts. How was he going to tell Esther he'd lost her brother? He assured her he'd stay up and keep the fire going, told her to have faith in him. His hands began to shake and a cool sweat broke out on his face.

But before he could stutter something, Esther stirred and opened her eyes. She rubbed at them, then pushed herself to sitting.

"Where's William?" Her sleep-stained eyes darted around the small encampment.

Marny just looked back at her dumbly. His silence said it all.

She said with some urgency, "Marny, where's William?" She was giving him every opportunity to come up with a perfectly rational explanation for why her brother, the one with the special gift, the one wanted by crazy Gary, was missing.

"I…I don't know."

Chapter 20

ESTHER STOOD AND swiveled around, anger and panic burning her cheeks.

She came full circle and drilled Marny with narrowed eyes. Her breathing was shallow, labored. "You don't know? You were supposed to be watching."

His eyes dropped to the grass and stones. "I know. I fell asleep."

"But you said you'd stay awake; you said you would." She started to walk away from the fire, then stopped and turned around. "Well, come on. Let's see if he's on the island. He may have wandered off."

She wasn't ready to accept the reality that Gary may have been there as they slept, stepping silently around them, watching, planning, taking her brother. That would be the end of her world.

She took off ahead of Marny, heading farther east, following the rocky shoreline around the island. To her left, across an expanse of choppy water, lay the coast of Maine, a dark gray smudge on the horizon. To her right, towering pines formed a wall behind which lay acres of wooded land hiding secrets she had no desire to unveil. She only wanted to find her brother.

Picking her way over rocks and around boulders, Esther fought off the guilt that nudged at her heart. She shouldn't have snapped at Marny like that. Did she really expect him to lie awake the entire night and keep watch?

But he'd said he would; he'd told her to have faith. She

MIKE DELLOSSO

wondered briefly if she'd made a mistake in choosing him, if he wasn't the one she thought he was. But he had to be, not because she'd chosen him, but because, in reality, she hadn't chosen him. Because he'd chosen her. It was his decision to follow her note and rescue her and William from Gary's clutches. Where had that compulsion come from?

She knew where. It was all part of providence, something she didn't fully understand, couldn't fully understand, but simply accepted.

She stopped and called William's name, waited a few seconds, then glanced back at Marny. He was keeping his distance, allowing her the space she needed to cool down. With his head hung low, hair in his eyes, and hands in his pockets, he looked the picture of remorse and defeat. Again guilt pricked at her.

But the guilt was quickly pushed to the side by a growing sense of panic. What if Gary *had* been on the island last night? What if he had taken William? Why hadn't she heard anything? She wasn't that deep of a sleeper. Over the years, with Gary as unpredictable as he was, she'd trained herself to sleep light and be ready to move at the slightest noise or disturbance. Had she been that exhausted from their escape from Gary that she'd slipped into a coma-like sleep?

Halfway around the island's edge she climbed a grouping of boulders and peered over the top. Her heart leaped into her throat. There, in a small cove, William stood almost knee-high in a tide pool, holding a starfish in each hand. He looked at her, held his hands high, then went back to studying the creatures he'd found.

Esther's legs suddenly felt weak, and she sank to the ground.

Marny knelt beside her. "He's fine."

Esther sighed. "Yeah. He's fine."

"I'm sorry I fell asleep."

"Don't be. You only gave your body what it needed. I'm sorry for snapping at you."

"You call that snapping? That was a pat on the back compared to the verbal beatings Karl used to give me."

"Karl?"

"My stepfather. He had a way with words. Real classy guy."

They were both quiet for moment, watching William fish in the tide pool for creatures washed in from the bay's depths and captured in the shallow trap. He set the starfish down and retrieved a small lobster, no bigger than the palm of his hand.

Finally Esther said. "I don't know what I'd do without him. He's so strong, so sure of everything."

"It seems the feeling is mutual. He needs you too."

She shook her head. "He doesn't need me. He just pretends he does."

"Have you ever seen your father since he left?"

"No. I was ten when he left. I loved him so much. He was my hero. He used to call me Squirt and take me to McDonald's in Freeport every Saturday morning for breakfast. I looked forward to Saturday all week. It's when I had him all to myself, just the two of us."

"And just like that he left?"

She hesitated, refusing to let the memory of that day crawl back from wherever she had cast it. "Just like that. He couldn't handle the thought of having a son who was both physically and mentally challenged. When Mom died, the courts found him and gave him the option of taking us back, but he refused."

"And you've never looked for him?"

"How could I? Gary keeps close tabs on us. I've thought about it. I have this dream that someday he'll just show up on Gary's porch and demand to take us back. That he'll be my hero again and rescue us."

William turned his head to look at Esther. His lips were tight, jaw set, brow furrowed. He said, "We need to get off this island."

Chapter 21

WILLIAM'S WORDS PUCKERED Marny's skin in a wave of goose bumps.

Marny looked out across the bay and saw nothing but a single organism with a million different moving parts oscillating to a cadence all its own, moving ever closer to them but never gaining ground. Colorful buoys dotted the water, bobbing quietly in time with each other.

William held several starfish like they were jewels. He looked at the mainland as if he could see across the mile of open water and had found something there that scared him, something headed their way. He turned and met Marny's eyes for a moment, then glanced away. "We have to get off this island, Marnin," he repeated.

"Why? Is he coming?"

His eyes fixed on the dark streak on the horizon, William nodded and carefully set the starfish back in the tide pool. He wiped his hands on his pants. "Is the boat ready to leave, Marnin?"

Esther stood, walked to William, and offered him her hand.

"We should get going," she said. "He's never wrong about this stuff."

The view across the water was still empty. No boats approached. No sea monsters with numerous tentacles loomed just below the surface.

Marny nodded. "Okay, let's go."

They headed back to the campsite, gathered the blankets, threw some dirt on the fire pit, and climbed aboard the lobster boat. Right before Marny turned the key to fire up the engine he heard a low thrum in the distance. Looking up, he saw another lobster boat a good three quarters of a mile away, headed in their direction. His throat tightened and his palms began to sweat. It could be nothing, just a lobsterman getting an early jump on his traps. Not unusual at all. But it could be something far more sinister too, more venomous than a multitentacled sea monster with an appetite for human flesh. It could be Gary.

William and Esther had climbed into the boat and taken seats in the back. Marny turned around, caught William's eye, and nodded toward the approaching vessel. "Is that him, William? Is that Gary?"

William didn't even look at the boat. Marny could tell that somehow he just instinctively knew. "No." He was a child of few words, but when he spoke, what he said carried the weight and significance of a thousand grandiloquent words.

Esther seemed surprised by her brother's answer. "No? That's not Gary coming for us?"

William shook his head. "Not yet."

"Then who's that?" She pointed at the lobster boat now a half mile away. It was traveling at cruising speed, no more than fifteen knots, and did not appear to be in any hurry to get to their little sanctuary in the middle of the bay.

William shrugged. "I don't know."

Marny wasn't going to wait around and see. "Hold on." He pushed the throttle forward slowly, and the boat backed away from the dock. He turned it and shifted, then inched the throttle forward again. Slowly it gained speed. Marny didn't want to full-throttle it back to the mainland as he'd done last night getting to the island. There was no need to alarm the approaching lobsterman.

At a quarter mile from the island they passed the other boat with a good forty yards between them. The lobsterman was an elderly man with a deeply creviced face and wiry gray hair and beard. He wore yellow bib overalls over a long-sleeved gray shirt. They made eye contact, and Marny nodded and gave a little wave. The lobsterman drilled him with a squint-eyed glare and returned neither sign of cordiality.

It didn't take long to make it back to the lighthouse and dock the boat. Walking the pier back toward the rocky shoreline, Marny had a stone in the pit of his stomach. He kept expecting Gary to jump out from behind a boulder and show them the meaning of brutality.

When they stepped off the pier and onto the pebbly beach, he said to Esther, "I think we should go to Mr. Tuttle first. We can call the police from his house." He glanced at Mr. Condon's place down shore a little bit. "I don't want to go back in there unless we have to."

"I think we should just get the car and go," Esther said.

"Go where?"

"Into Pine Harbor, away from here, anywhere else but here."

Marny glanced at the two houses again. One held the remnants of violence and murder and the thought of seeing Mr. Condon's pale, lifeless face; the other held the hope of aid, shelter, a place to call for help. "Mr. Condon has another car, and the keys are in his house. But I'm not going in there unless it's the last resort. Let's see if Mr. Tuttle can help us first."

Esther said nothing.

"You okay with that?"

"I just don't want to be around here any longer than we have to."

The fear was evident on her face, in the tone of her voice.

"I don't either, but I think the safest place right now is inside Mr. Tuttle's house."

"Okay. I trust you."

Those were not the words Marny wanted to hear. If he failed, it could be the end of all three of them.

They climbed a flight of rough-hewn logs set into the embankment that served as stairs from the beach to Mr. Tuttle's property.

The yard was a wide expanse of some of the thickest, greenest grass Marny had ever seen, perfectly manicured. The house, thirty yards off the shore, was magnificent and stately. The entire back facade was lined with windows so one could see the beauty of the bay from anywhere in the house. A sprawling two-tiered patio made the transition from yard to house a welcome one. Marny walked up to the back sliding door and knocked. Mr. Tuttle didn't answer, nor did Molly, his middle-aged Maltese, bark.

Marny knocked again, louder, but there was still no answer. And no Molly.

The interior of the house was carefully furnished and decorated in a coastal decor where driftwood and ships' artifacts were abundant. It appeared to be empty.

"Maybe he's not home," Esther said.

Marny looked at William as if he were a fortune-teller and could disclose the whereabouts of Mr. Tuttle and his little white toy dog. William stared back at him with wide eyes but said nothing.

After knocking one more time with no response, Marny tried the door and found it open. Not surprising. Mr. Condon told him once that Mr. Tuttle never locked his doors. He was a gentle and trusting man who harmed no one and expected the same grace shown back to him. He had made no enemies on his way to making a ton of money—a colossal feat in itself.

"Mr. Tuttle?" Marny's voice echoed in the massive vaulted-ceiling great room. A small loft was above them and to their left the kitchen. In front of them stood a fireplace with a wide mantle and beyond that, the dining room and living room.

The house was quiet and still.

Marny tried again. "Hello. Mr. Tuttle. Molly. Here, Molly." But only silence answered.

He wandered into the kitchen. A dirty plate, crusted with food, sat in the sink. A mug half filled with coffee accompanied it. The countertop was mostly open and free of clutter. For a bachelor, Mr. Tuttle kept a neat home.

Marny walked into the dining room, Esther and William on his heels. Adjoining the dining room was the living room, furnished with beige sofa and chairs and a coffee table made of treated driftwood and glass. On the wall was a large weathered ship's wheel. But no Mr. Tuttle.

Through the living room and to the left was a door. It was slightly ajar, and through the opening Marny could see that it was a bedroom.

"Maybe you two should stay here, and I'll go see."

He thought Mr. Tuttle might still be sleeping. If that was the case, he was quite the sound sleeper, and they could quietly make their exit and walk around to the front door and try the doorbell. Marny didn't want Mr. Tuttle to awaken and find three strangers in his home and die suddenly of a massive coronary. Though that would not be surprising, given Marny's track record.

Marny walked across the carpeting, not making a single sound, and stood in the doorway. From there he could see the end of the bed and what looked like feet under a blanket. A hushed buzz came from the room, an air pump of some kind. He pushed the door open. Mr. Tuttle was lying on his back, covers pulled up to his chest. He had a plastic mask on his face with a hose extending from it, a CPAP machine. Apparently Mr. Tuttle suffered from sleep apnea.

Marny was about to step back out of the room when he noticed something dark about Mr. Tuttle's face, along the side of the mask. The shades were drawn in the room, muting the morning sunlight, and at first it appeared to be nothing more than a shadow...only it wasn't.

Taking small, slow steps, Marny walked closer to the bed, close enough that he could see what he didn't want to see, what he'd feared most. Mr. Tuttle was dead, a gunshot through his right eye. And next to him, also dead, was his dearly beloved Molly.

Chapter 22

MEMORIES ARE HAUNTING things, bold nightmares not satisfied to lurk in the world of dreams.

At least Marny's memories were. When he was nine, Billy Tillman moved next door. Billy was a year older than Marny and a good four inches taller and twenty pounds heavier. Billy was what the other kids called a deadhead, a punk. When he wasn't running around town, he stayed mostly to himself, listening to his Black Sabbath and AC/DC and Alice Cooper. His wardrobe consisted of black rock 'n' roll T-shirts and faded jeans. And his mouth consisted of cuss words and racial slurs and colorful descriptions of body parts.

His mom used to beat him something awful. Billy would never admit it, but when he'd show up in the woods with a swollen eye or fat lip and try to tell Marny he'd fallen down the steps, it was no secret what had really happened. Marny could see it in his eyes, hear it in the tone of his voice. The pain was there, the shame. He'd try to cheer up Billy, offer to play whatever he wanted and let him win, but on those days nothing seemed to help.

For three years straight Billy was Marny's only friend. He was the big brother Marny had always wanted. When Marny was eleven, Billy gave him his first cigarette; when he was twelve, Billy gave him his first dirty magazine.

A month later Billy was dead. Time caught up with him, and the payment on Marny's curse came due.

They were playing hide-and-seek in the woods behind their neighborhood, and it was Marny's turn to be It. Billy always found the best places to hide. No matter how long Marny looked, Billy would never come out, would never even make a peep to give him a hint. It was as if he enjoyed the time alone and didn't want it to end. On this particular Thursday, Marny had been looking for nearly a half hour, and the sun was getting low in the sky. Finally he gave up and hollered to Billy to come out; it was getting too dark and he was going home.

After a few minutes, Marny heard a rustle high in one of the trees, then a sharp snap and a yell. A quick moment and burst of cracking branches later it all ended with a thud. Billy had fallen from the tree.

Marny ran to where he'd heard the noise and saw Billy lying motionless facedown at the base of a white pine.

"Billy? You okay?"

He didn't move. Billy's hand twitched like it had a stutter in it. He nudged Billy's shoulder. "Hey, Billy. C'mon, man, you okay?"

Still nothing but the stutter in his right hand.

Marny rolled Billy over and immediately vomited on the ground beside him. A stick, a jagged branch, protruded a good two inches from Billy's left eye. Billy didn't move, but his right eye fixed on Marny. The older boy's lips formed words, but Marny couldn't hear what he was saying. He leaned closer and realized his friend was speaking gibberish. Saying something about giving the dog a bath and taking it for a walk. Only Billy didn't have a dog.

Leaving Billy there on the forest floor with that branch sticking out of his eye and the stutter in his hand and talking about the dog he didn't have, Marny ran home and told his mother. An hour later Billy officially died on the operating table, but the doctor told Marny's mom he was gone before he hit the ground.

∞

When Marny looked at Mr. Tuttle and saw that empty eye socket, he thought of Billy Tillman's eye, and the vomit surged up his throat. Fortunately he was able to control it this time and didn't soil Mr. Tuttle's carpet. As quickly as he could, he exited the room and glanced at Esther and William. They were in the middle of the living room holding hands.

"We need to get out of here."

Esther said nothing until they were on the patio with the glass door shut securely. "What is it?"

Marny stopped and inhaled long and slow. The smell of sea salt cleared his head. "He's dead. Murdered."

"By Gary?"

"I suppose."

"He knew we might come here for help."

Marny looked at her, anger clawing at his chest. "Really? Is that the kind of animal he is? He'd murder an innocent man while he slept just because we *might* go to him for help?"

William glanced at his sister as if giving permission to tell the truth.

Esther didn't hesitate. "You have no idea what kind of a monster he is. We thought we did, but it's so much worse."

"Oh, I have an idea," Marny said.

"Then it's wrong," she said. "Whatever you think he's capable of, it's a million times worse than that. You've never seen darkness like he has inside him."

Marny thought of Karl Gunnison and the hate that filled that man, the anger and violence that lurked just under his exterior like a beast hungry for its next unsuspecting victim. He'd always thought Karl was the father of evil, the king of hatefulness. How could anyone be worse than him?

Marny looked around, trying to develop a plan as quickly as possible. To their backs was the bay. The sun had fully cleared the horizon by now and the line between sky and ocean was vivid and straight. The waters moved peacefully, oblivious to the turmoil that brewed on land. Booker Island was out there as well as a few other small, uninhabited islands. To their left the shoreline was dotted with boulders and pebbled beach and, off in the distance, the town of Pine Harbor stirring from a sound night's sleep. To their right was Mr. Condon's house, the place of last night's nightmare. The Nova was still in the driveway, parked behind Mr. Condon's pickup, but there was no sign of Petey's patrol car.

"I need to get the keys to Mr. Condon's truck."

They headed across Mr. Tuttle's yard and into Mr. Condon's. The bungalow stood silent and lifeless. Memories of the previous evening replayed in Marny's mind. The sound of strangulation, Mr. Condon's tortured gurgles and gasps, Gary's voice, thick with venom. He didn't want to go in there, didn't want to face what he'd only imagined up to this point.

But they needed the keys to the truck. Marny had an idea, a place they could go to hide and collect their thoughts.

"Wait," Esther said. "What if he's in there?"

Marny had thought of that, the very real possibility that Gary would be waiting for them, ready to rain down violence and revenge, but their other choices were equally dangerous. They could go to the main road and walk to Pine Harbor, but that left them in the open, easy targets for an insane pursuer. They could make their way down the beach, but again, they'd be in the open, nearly begging Gary to locate them.

"I don't think he is," Marny said, and he meant it. Call it instinct or some kind of weird sixth sense—maybe William's abilities were rubbing off on him—but he didn't feel Gary's presence. "We'll take it slow."

The back door was unlocked. It opened into the kitchen, the place where Mr. Condon always greeted Marny with a "Well, hello, Mahny." There was no greeting this time, only silence and fear of what was to come. Esther put a hand on his shoulder and squeezed. Marny expected to see Mr. Condon seated at the table, face gray and swollen, Pete on the floor in a pool of blood, and the place a mess. But it looked like none of what they'd heard taking place last night had actually occurred. Nothing was out of place, nothing broken. No bodies. No sign of struggle or violence. It was as if he'd imagined the whole ordeal and would find Mr. Condon at the garage under someone's car.

"Esther?" Marny wondered if she saw the same thing.

She said nothing, but the tears in her eyes said it all.

"Gary did this, didn't he? He cleaned up after himself."

She nodded. "He knew the police would come looking for your friend."

Petey. The police had come, that's why Pete's patrol car was gone. And they'd most likely found nothing.

Marny walked over to the kitchen table and ran his hand along the surface. Three scratch marks, shallow ruts in the wood, were all that remained. Maybe Mr. Condon was still alive. Then Marny thought of Mr. Tuttle in his bed and the pointlessness of his execution and doubted Mr. Condon had made it out of the house alive last night.

"There is someone we can go to for help," Esther said.

She had Marny's attention.

"Our father."

Chapter 23

Come again? I thought you said you didn't know where your father was."

"I said I hadn't had any contact with him since he walked out on us."

"But you know where he lives?"

Esther was quiet for a moment. She took William's withered hand in hers and rubbed it. "A few years after he left, before Gary came on the scene, I heard my mom talking on the phone to her sister. I got enough from the conversation to find out that our father had moved to western Massachusetts, Franklin County. It was the last time I ever heard her mention him."

"And you want to go there and ask him to help you after all these years." Marny had his doubts this plan of hers would work. He wondered how this guy would react to his daughter and son—the son he'd walked out on—showing up on his doorstep with a stranger. "What makes you think he can help us, if he even will?"

"Our father was a Maine state trooper, loved his job. He must still have some sense of justice." She paused, looked at Marny, looked at William. "I can convince him to help us, I know I can."

Marny didn't miss the way she only referred to her father as "father." He knew there was a time when she must have called him Daddy, then Dad, but that bond had been shattered when he abandoned them for his own selfish gain, and she was left with the wounds.

"What makes you so sure? Western Massachusetts is a long way off. I don't want to go there for nothing." He turned to William. "And how about you, William. How do you feel about asking your father for help?"

William looked at Esther. "What do you think, Esther?"

She smiled and rubbed his hand. "I think he's asking you."

Looking at Marny with those big brown eyes, William shrugged. "Do you mind if we find your dad?"

Marny could tell by the look on William's face that *dad* was a foreign term to him, but he shrugged and said, "No, Marnin." That was it.

"Okay, let's find him then." Marny headed into the living room and turned on Mr. Condon's computer. "What's his name?"

"Harold Rose," Esther said. "Harold J. Rose."

Marny tapped the computer keys. It didn't take long to find the street address for Harold J. Rose of Monroe Bridge, Massachusetts. "There he is. Should we call the state police and find out if he still works there? Maybe he got a job with them when he moved."

Esther shook her head. "No. The fewer people who know this the better. Mr. Tuttle wound up the way he did because of association."

An image of Mr. Tuttle's empty eye socket flashed through Marny's mind. He'd met his fate while he slept not only because the long tentacles of Marny's curse had reached through Mr. Condon to him, but because of his association with Esther and William through Mr. Condon and Marny. It was a double whammy, more disastrous than any Marny could have imagined. If Esther and William's father would agree to help them, one curse to battle was enough. "You say that like it's happened before."

Esther turned to the window. "There've been others."

"Other murders?"

She nodded, and he didn't miss the tears in her eyes.

"Because of association?"

Esther shrugged. "I don't know why. He had his reasons, no

matter how twisted they were. In his mind, he was doing the right thing." She looked directly at him, and a single tear slipped from her eye and slid down her cheek. "You have no idea what kind of monster he is."

∞

Gary had made a calculated decision.

After taking care of the house and disposing of all evidence, after getting rid of the patrol car parked in the driveway, after erasing every track of his ever having been in the vicinity of the Condon place, he'd decided to leave for the night rather than wait for the three to return to the house. If he was going to see this thing through to the end, he'd need sleep. Besides, there was the chance that the cop had radioed in his last stop, and sooner or later his fellow officers would be out to look for him when he didn't answer their repeated calls.

Gary didn't want to risk being there when the police arrived, found nothing out of the ordinary, and left. And he made sure they'd find nothing suspicious.

He'd slept just fine at the Bayside Motel in Pine Harbor. The bed was firm and the room dark. He'd opened the window to let the sounds of the water waft over him and lull him to sleep. At 6:00 a.m. the alarm had sounded, and with it, the voice in his head.

Don't let him out of your sight. He must be protected at all times. He is your responsibility now.

It had taken Gary only thirty minutes to shower and dress. Then he was off to the house to wait for the three to return. When he arrived, he drove by the place two times to make sure the area was clear of cops or other visitors. Satisfied that he was alone and the house was empty, he pulled the Taurus into the driveway and said a prayer.

∞

Marny wrote Harold Rose's address on a piece of paper. "I really don't like this Gary guy."

"Not too many people do."

"Are you—"

His question was cut short by Esther's hand on his mouth. Her eyes widened, and Marny immediately saw the fear in them. She'd heard something.

William inched closer to his sister.

A second later Marny heard it too, the sound of tires rolling over asphalt. A car had pulled into the driveway. He got up from the desk chair and moved quickly to the front window. A car door shut. Peering around the window pane he saw Gary standing outside his Taurus, running his thumbs around the waistline of his pants. He looked around, then headed for the front door.

Marny pointed toward the kitchen and grabbed the piece of paper with the address on it as they passed the desk. Once in the kitchen he went for the keys to Mr. Condon's pickup, only they weren't there. He always hung them on the hook by the telephone.

Marny had another thought, a backup plan. "Follow me."

As they slipped quietly out the back, Marny heard the front door open. The garage was no more than ten feet from the house, connected by a breezeway. Mr. Condon kept the keys to the Buick, his Darla, hanging on a nail just inside the door. Marny grabbed the keys. "Hurry, get in."

Esther pulled up. "This?"

"You have another idea?"

The Buick didn't look like much on the exterior, but under her hood she'd been fully restored and was ready to hum. Marny slid in behind the wheel and cranked the engine. It sprang to life without protest. Gripping the wheel with one hand, he hit the garage door opener with the other. "Here we go."

The door lifted and let the morning light in. Gary had gone back out the front door and was sprinting down the driveway to meet them, arms and legs going like crankshafts on a steam locomotive. Marny had seen this show before. He threw the car into gear and stomped on the accelerator. The tires spun on the concrete, let out a high-pitched squeal, and finally found purchase. The car lunged forward.

Gary was there in no time, his face drawn up like a cinched burlap bag, murder in his eyes. He grabbed at the door handle as the car passed him, but missed and kicked the rear panel instead. Marny yanked the steering wheel to the left to avoid the pickup, and the car dipped off the driveway and into the side yard. Again the tires spun, unable to find their grip in the grass. His heart beat through his hands and into the wheel. In the back, William whimpered and began to cry.

By the time they made it out of the yard and back onto the road, Gary was in his car and turning it around. The chase was on, but they had the advantage: Marny knew these roads like the lines of his palm.

Chapter 24

MARNY'S FOOT GOT a little heavier on the accelerator.

He was a good two hundred yards down the road when he looked in the rearview mirror and saw Gary pull out of the yard. The front end of the Taurus bounced and swerved, then straightened and pointed right at them. The needle on the Buick's speedometer climbed closer to seventy. Route 1 wasn't far away, and from there Interstate 95 was only a short distance. Once on 95 they could head all the way down to Boston, then get 495 to Route 2 and take that to western Massachusetts. But first they had to shake Gary. Navigating the proper course didn't matter if they didn't lose the Taurus.

Stepping on the brake and yanking the wheel hard to the right, Marny jumped onto Little Pond Road and accelerated. Little Pond was an unpaved lane that wound and curved like a snake through the pine forest. In the mirror he could only see maybe fifty feet behind them at one time and couldn't tell how close Gary was, how much ground he had gained.

Up ahead a quarter of a mile Bog Road split off to the left. Marny took it and kept his foot on the gas as much as possible. The road straightened out at one point and shot through the trees like a runway. On either side stood pools of shallow water over-populated by cattails and pondweed. It was along this stretch that Marny caught a glimpse of the Taurus closing fast. It was now only a hundred yards back. Marny wanted to floor it, see what kind of speed the Buick had, but a sharp right was coming up ahead and he had to slow. Immediately after the curve he turned right onto a paved road known to the locals as Devil's Run because of the high number of fatalities recorded on it. No one knew the reason for the deaths. The road was not uncommonly treacherous or winding. There were no unmarked hairpin curves, no steep grades. It was not unlike any other rural road in Maine, save for the fact that it had claimed nine lives in the past year alone.

Local folklore reported that a group of school children were murdered along this road back in the 1920s, and now the spirits of the deceased kids roamed the woods and wandered onto the roadway, causing accidents. Eyewitnesses who survived their encounters with the lost children said they appeared confused, panicky. But this was not something Marny wanted to dwell on. He had his own theory that because of the reputation of the road, inexperienced drivers preoccupied with visions of bodiless school kids causing gruesome and violent wrecks got distracted. Self-fulfilling prophecy at its worst.

Another glance in the mirror told him he better not play it cautious; Gary was gaining again. In the backseat, Esther and William huddled together. Marny's eyes met Esther's, and in hers he found a weird mixture of fear and trust.

"Can *he* do something?" Marny said.

"Who?"

"William."

Gary was only fifty yards behind them now. The Buick was built for comfort, not performance.

Esther shook her head. "No. It doesn't work like that."

"Bummer."

The road curved to the left ahead, and beyond the bend a smaller paved road broke off to the left. Marny took it. He knew this road, lots of twists and turns and offshoots and driveways. This is where he would lose Gary.

He took each turn barely slowing, just on the edge of

out-of-control. The car's tires did their best to grip and hold the asphalt, but more than once he felt them slip. He wondered if each turn would be their last, if the tires would finally give up and allow the car to careen off the road and play pinball with the pines.

But despite the ferocity with which Marny drove, despite the myriad of roads, both paved and unpaved, Gary stayed with him.

Marny had one last idea, one final hope for shaking Gary for good. Passing on the next road, he hit the accelerator and the Buick's engine whined. Up ahead was a left that would lead them to Route 69, and that would lead them to Interstate 95. He needed to get to where people were, other vehicles, witnesses.

The road came up quick, and he almost missed it. The brakes moaned and the car slid on some loose gravel, but it held. Not far behind them, Gary came around the corner faster than Marny did, and the Taurus slid to the shoulder and onto some loose ground. Marny had to keep his eyes on the road ahead, but when he checked the mirror the Taurus was back on the road and moving forward again. Marny had managed to put a little more distance between them.

A mile down the road, 69 branched to the right, and Marny took it at nearly the same speed. Once on the open road the accelerator hit the floor and the speedometer pushed eighty. He hoped dearly that one of Maine's finest was waiting along the shoulder for someone just like him, a frantic gas station attendant in a classic car literally running for his life. This would certainly be a welcome time to see some flashing lights.

Seconds later Gary's Taurus appeared, fishtailed, and started after them. He wasn't giving up. William's words—*he won't stop until he gets what he wants*—screamed through Marny's head. This could turn into a test of fuel efficiency; whoever ran out of gas first was the big loser. For the first time since jumping into the Buick and leaving ruts in Mr. Condon's yard, Marny checked the fuel gauge. Three quarters of a tank. He knew the Taurus had more because he'd just filled it himself the day before. Unless Gary had gone on an excursion overnight, it would be barely below full.

If it came to fuel levels, they were the losers. He had to come up with another solution, a way to even the odds.

Marny kept the accelerator down, occasionally lifting it to cruise around slight bends. At last he saw the sign he was waiting for—Junction I-95. Less than a mile.

He took the ramp at full speed, nearly putting the Buick on two wheels. Esther let out a little scream from the backseat, then apologized.

When Marny hit 95 the road was clear and free. This stretch was never very populated.

Something bumped them from behind.

Chapter 25

THE VOICE WAS in Gary's head again.

It was loud, so loud, in fact, that it drowned out the sound of the engine and the noise of the tires on the road.

The boy is the reason you were put on this earth; he is your purpose for existing. You must protect him. You must. You MUST.

There was nothing Gary could do to silence it. At these speeds he had to keep both hands on the wheel. His foot shook on the accelerator but managed to hold it down. The Taurus may have seen its better days, but it still performed well. The way it had handled the back roads was impressive, but, of course, much of that had to do with Gary's driving ability. But the voice was not interested in his earthly gifts and talents. It was interested in only one thing—the anointed one.

This is your calling. Nothing else matters. Your life is not your own; it is the Lord's, and this is what the Lord requires of you. Do not fail Him.

Gary gripped the steering wheel tighter and pressed the gas pedal to the floor. The car responded well and pushed forward.

Sweat rolled down his forehead and into his eyes. It burned, blurring his vision. He took one hand off the wheel and wiped at his eyes, lost control of the car for a fraction of a second, and swerved left. He yanked the wheel back. The car jerked and pulled right and almost skidded off the shoulder of the road. At the speed he was going, almost ninety, even the slightest sudden movement could throw the vehicle out of control. Heart in his throat, Gary managed to regain control, but with the near miss a series of images skipped through his mind.

A large man in a black suit, towering over him. He holds the Holy Bible against his chest. His narrowed eyes are a piercing green, his snow-white hair is combed straight back. Thin lips, angular jaw. He is the image of holiness.

The boy is there too. He's in his wheelchair facing the man. The man holds the Bible in the air with his left hand and puts his right hand on the boy's head. When he speaks his voice resonates in a rich baritone.

"And you, my child, will be called a prophet of the Most High; for you will go before the Lord to prepare a way for Him. To give His people the knowledge of salvation through the forgiveness of their sins, because of the tender mercy of our God, by which the rising sun will come to us from heaven to shine on those living in darkness and in the shadow of death, to guide our feet into the path of peace."

The memories didn't last long, barely seconds, but they were enough to bring tears to Gary's eyes. He feared the minister, but at the same time he respected him. His words were words of truth. Gary knew that. He was called to protect the boy, God's anointed, the prophet of the Most High.

Gary gripped the steering wheel tighter and pressed on the accelerator. The Taurus sped onward until its bumper met the rear of the vehicle in front of him.

Chapter 26

The Buick lurched forward, and Marny's seat belt reflexively tightened against his chest.

In the rearview mirror the grill of the Taurus and the bull behind the wheel closed in again.

The bumpers met and the Buick jerked, tires skidding.

Marny put the accelerator on the floor and changed lanes without using the turn signal. They were at speeds nearing a hundred, and he felt like even the slightest alteration of course could send them into an out-of-control tailspin and topple the car end over end.

Gary followed into the left lane and closed in again.

Marny tried to keep his eyes both on the road ahead and on the mirror. Another bump like the ones before, especially at these speeds, and the outcome could be very bad. Right before the front bumper of the Taurus met the rear one of the Buick, Marny switched lanes again. In the side mirror he saw Gary slap the steering wheel and change lanes as well.

Ahead, no more than a quarter mile, was a handful of slower moving cars. Marny gained on them quickly, and with one hand on the wheel and the other on the horn—and with Gary on his tail—he navigated through the crowd, swerving, dodging. He thought maybe the moving obstacles would throw Gary off his course and put some distance between them, but his hopes were dashed when he checked the mirror and found Gary still behind, keeping pace.

Marny had to shake him; they couldn't keep this up much longer.

They passed a sign indicating that the exit for Route 1 was a mile ahead, and an idea hit Marny. It was a long shot, but quite possibly their only hope.

He glanced in the mirror at the backseat. "You two have your seat belts on?"

"You think we wouldn't?" Esther said.

"Make sure they're snug. And hang on."

Behind them Gary was still playing his tailgating game. Marny moved to the right lane and stepped on the gas. The speedometer pushed a hundred and five as the sign stating Route 1 was only a half mile ahead whizzed by in a green blur.

Marny could see the exit ramp on their side and the entrance ramp on the opposite side of the road. A pack of oncoming traffic was approaching on the other side heading northbound. A big rig and maybe five or six cars. He had only one chance at this, and it had to happen now. If he missed, it would be the end.

"Hold on," he said. "And you may want to close your eyes."

Just as the Taurus lunged forward again, Marny yanked the wheel to the left and hit the brakes, not hard enough to lock the tires but firm enough to grind the brake pads. But he didn't stop at the left lane; he let the Buick cruise into the median, moving at a forty-five degree angle to the roadway. They bounced along, tires slipping in the grass, hit the dip in the middle of the median, and came out on the other side.

Now they were traveling against traffic, and the big rig and his buddies were bearing down fast. The on-ramp was across the pavement.

Marny nearly stood on the gas pedal and hit the ramp just as the rig, air horn screaming, passed. Then it was to the brake again. The Buick screeched and slid and finally slowed. Fortunately, no one was coming the other way on the ramp, or they both would have been scrap metal.

He pulled the car to the shoulder and got off the ramp and onto Route 1 going south.

A check in the mirror brought relief, and he noticed he'd been holding his breath. He exhaled. Gary was nowhere in sight. William's face was buried in Esther's shoulder, and she still had her eyes shut tight.

Marny wanted to stop, to settle his frantic heart, to let his breathing slow and swallow the bile in his throat, but they had to keep going, to get as far away from Interstate 95 as possible. He'd have to find another way to exit Maine and head for Massachusetts.

"You can open your eyes now." His voice was hoarse.

Esther opened her eyes slowly and looked behind them. "You lost him?"

"I think. For now. We gotta keep moving, though."

"I think I wet myself."

He couldn't tell if she was joking or not, but for the first time in nearly twenty-four hours he smiled. "Thank you."

Her eyes met his in the mirror. "For wetting myself? Or *not* wetting myself?"

"You were praying, weren't you?"

She nodded. "I couldn't think of anything else to do."

"So thank you."

"You're welcome."

Up ahead a road branched to the left and headed for the coast. Marny took it. "You okay, William?"

He nodded. "That was pretty scary, Marnin."

"You're the king of understatement, buddy." He felt like a million pounds had been lifted from his chest.

"Did your father teach you to drive?" William said.

Marny laughed. "No. My mother."

"Did she teach you to drive like that?"

"No. She was a much better driver than me. She taught me to drive the right way."

"So where did you learn to drive like that?"

It was the most Marny had heard William talk since they'd met. It was nice to hear his voice. "That, William, was my own doing. Don't ever drive like that when you get older."

"I won't. Thank you for getting us away from Gary."

Chapter 27

MAINE IS A vast expanse of forest and wilderness, wild land untamed by mankind.

It took Marny nearly two hours to get out of the state. He stuck to secondary roads tucked into the coastline to avoid running into Gary. He had no doubt Gary hadn't given up the chase that easily, that he was patrolling Interstate 95 and maybe Route 1 waiting for his prey to show up. He didn't know where Marny was going, or at least Marny presumed he didn't, and that was to their advantage. Esther and William both slept. Their night under the stars coupled with the near-death experience of losing Gary had proved too much for them, and they'd finally given in to sleep.

They hit New Hampshire around ten o'clock, and Marny's grumbling stomach told him it was time to stop for food. He got back on Route 1 and pulled into a fast-food joint just outside Portsmouth.

Esther stirred in the backseat. "Where are we?"

"Breakfast stop. New Hampshire." He pulled up to the drive-through speaker. "You hungry?"

"Starved."

"Then we stopped at the right place. What do you want? They're still serving breakfast."

She gave him her order and one for William, and he passed it along to the voice. Esther climbed into the front seat, and minutes later they were on the road, headed west to Monroe Bridge, Massachusetts.

"How long do you think it will take to get there?" Esther said.

"Couple hours, give or take."

William still slept. Esther said she didn't want to wake him, he'd eat when he was ready. Right now he needed sleep more than sustenance.

Marny was quiet for a few minutes, going over all that had taken place in the past day. Part of him regretted ever getting involved. If he'd left that piece of paper lying on the lot at the garage, or if he'd merely read it, crumpled it, and thrown it away, Mr. Condon and Pete would still be alive, and so would Mr. Tuttle. And he wouldn't be on the run from some crazed monster with a hunger for violence and death. His curse had caught up with him again, and this time it had attitude...and a name: Gary.

"So are you going to give me the whole story now?" he said.

Esther lifted her eyebrows. "The story?"

"Yeah, what's going on here. You, William, Gary. William's gift or whatever it is. Faith. I think I deserve to know what I've gotten myself into, don't you?"

She turned to the side window, then straight ahead. "I suppose you do. Do you want the Twilight version or the Dracula one?"

"William's a vampire?"

She laughed. "Not that I'm aware of, though I'm sure there are things about him even I don't know. I mean do you want the sanitized version or the dirty one?"

"How 'bout the one that's going to tell me the truth."

"That would be the dirty one." She paused, as if collecting her thoughts or sorting through the memories or a little of both. "My father was my best friend. He was a dad then, and we did everything together. Like I told you before, he used to call me Squirt. We laughed a lot together. He told me once that from the day he found out my mom was pregnant he wanted a daughter, and the day I was born was the happiest of his life. He was content with one daughter he could dote on.

"Then, when I was ten, William came unexpectedly. My father didn't want any more kids, especially not a son, and especially not a crippled one. They didn't know William had cerebral palsy right away, but the deformities were enough. My father was repulsed. He and my mom fought all the time. He stopped hanging out with me and rarely came home after his shift until we were all in bed. When William was just four months old, I came home from school and found my mom crying. She said my father had left and he wasn't coming back." She looked at Marny with sad eyes and shrugged. "That was it. I never saw him or heard from him again. The last words we shared were days before that, when he snapped at me for wanting to help him with something on the car. I don't even remember what it was now. I do remember I was crushed. That wasn't my father; it wasn't the same man."

"He changed, huh? Did a complete one-eighty."

Again she checked the windows as if expecting Gary to come swooping out of the morning sky and land on the roof of the Buick. "Yeah. He did a real Jekyll-and-Hyde, and Mr. Hyde was never so heartbreaking. That's a tough thing for a girl to get over."

"Did you resent William?"

She shook her head. "No, never. William's been the best brother anyone could ask for."

"Because of his gift, his abilities?"

"No. Because of his heart. He knows how to truly love. That's where his gift comes from."

William did seem like a good kid. A little odd, but no more than any other eleven-year-old. "So when did Gary come on the scene?"

"Yes, Gary." She was quiet, contemplative.

Marny couldn't tell what she was thinking, or if she'd even answer his question.

After a few long seconds she sighed deeply. "Gary showed up when I was fifteen and William was five. My mom said he was her half brother. Her parents had divorced, and her father remarried. Gary was his son to his second wife. Apparently he'd strayed

113

from the family, spent some time traveling the country finding himself or something like that, and finally returned home to get his life back in order. He settled down in Maine, and Mom moved us in with him. From the get-go he tried to be a father figure for us. Really took a liking to William. He was okay, but he wasn't my dad, you know what I mean?"

"Your dad had fled the scene, but no one could replace him."

"Exactly. A year later things started going downhill with Gary. It wasn't anything obvious at first, just little stuff."

They passed a sign that said *Massachusetts Welcomes You* and a much smaller, handwritten sign next to it that read *Potatoes Ahead Mass-Hamp Farms*.

"Little stuff?" Marny said.

"Like I said, he really took a liking to William. Treated him as if he were his own son. For William it was great. At first."

"Sounds like there's more to this story."

She looked at Marny. "You know it doesn't have a happy ending."

"It's not over yet."

Esther turned around and checked on William. He was still sleeping in the back, resting against the door. "Things slowly escalated, and Gary's attention to William grew more and more obsessive. He wouldn't let him out of his sight, made him stay in the house at all times. Restricted the toys he played with. Wouldn't even let him walk up and down the stairs without a chaperone. My mom noticed it, she had to, but never said a word. I think there was a part of her that feared Gary. After she died and I turned eighteen, I thought about going out on my own, but I couldn't leave William with him. Something about Gary just wasn't right, and I felt I had to be there to protect my brother."

"Did he ever do anything to William that was, you know..." He hoped she knew what he was getting at.

"No. Never. His obsession with William wasn't like that at all."

"How do you know?"

"William would have told me."

"It's not exactly the kind of thing a young boy likes to talk about."

"He would. He tells me everything. I asked him once, and he said nothing like that ever happened, never even came close to happening."

There was silence in the car for a few minutes. The noise of the tires and the rhythmic *chunk-chunk* of the seams in the road were the only sounds.

Finally Esther spoke again. "After our mother died, that's when things really went bad."

Chapter 28

THE DAY WAS moving by quickly, traffic was light, and the road ahead was clear.

In Massachusetts, Marny got back on Interstate 95 and headed south to Boston. He was not conservative on the gas pedal. Once it got going, the Buick had a nice engine under its hood, and Marny was just fine with letting it do its thing.

"Did he ever hit you?" He hoped to God that she'd say no. The thought of that beast laying a hand on Esther made Marny's knuckles go white.

"Once."

The first time Karl Gunnison hit Marny it felt like he'd gone and broken his jaw. Karl was drunk from a six-pack too many of his Pabst and getting more belligerent by the minute. Marny was fifteen and about as tall as Karl, but not nearly as wide or thick.

Janie was in the cellar doing laundry when Karl started hollering for more beer. She came up the steps and told him he'd had enough, if he drank anymore he'd drown himself.

No one told Karl Gunnison when to stop drinking, especially when he'd had too many already. He got up in Janie's face, sticking out his chest, jabbing his fat finger at her. His face was deep red, and veins the size of fingers bulged in his neck.

Janie begged him not have another drink. She knew what happened when he got really loaded. Violence became his default behavior, then came the vomit and passing out. But the more Janie insisted, the angrier Karl got. At one point she stood in the doorway to the kitchen and told Karl she wasn't moving, that he could go back to his chair and watch the rest of the game. From where Marny stood in the corner of the room he could see Karl's fist close and muscles tense in his arm.

"Whoa, Karl," he said. "Let's just settle down, okay?"

Karl turned and looked at Marny like he wanted to rip off his head and use it as a bowling ball. "Stay outta this, Bustah. This ain't none a' ya business."

"She's my mom, and it is my business."

Karl grabbed Janie by the arm, his hand so large it wrapped completely around the upper part of her bicep. "She's my wife, she's my business. Now beat it." He yanked her around, and she yelped in pain like a beaten dog.

Marny stepped closer. "Get your hand off her." He was barely aware of what he was saying; he was acting on instinct now.

"Or what." Karl taunted Marny, using his mother as bait. He was in a mood to hit someone, and it didn't matter if it was Janie or Marny.

Through clenched teeth Marny said, "Let her go."

Karl leaned in so close Marny could see the veins in his blood-shot eyes and bulbous nose. "Or what, Bustah? You gonna do somethin' 'bout it?" He squeezed Janie's arm tighter, causing her to cry out and her knees to buckle.

Marny could stand it no longer and rushed him. He had no plan, no smooth move to engage Karl and break his hold on Janie's arm. With Karl as inebriated as he was, Marny's only hope was that his reflexes would be slowed and Marny would have the advantage.

He was wrong. Karl was quicker than anticipated, and his fist was up so fast Marny never saw it connect with his jaw.

But he felt it. Shock waves of pain vibrated through his skull, and he reeled backward and stumbled over the coffee table. The floor rose up to meet him, and the room went dark and spun in wide circles. Somewhere in the room Karl laughed. Marny tried to move his jaw, but it didn't work properly. Rubbing it did no good. He rolled over onto his back and stared up at the ceiling, watching it go round and round until the throbbing in his head stopped. By then Janie was kneeling over him, crying and going on about how sorry she was for upsetting Karl.

Karl didn't break Marny's jaw that time…but it wasn't the last time he hit him either.

Marny didn't want to know the details, so he didn't ask.

Esther paused, as if his question had stirred a memory she had to take time to suppress lest it crawl out of the past like a toothy specter and wreak havoc on her emotions. "I wasn't expecting it at all."

"You don't have to tell me."

"Yes, I do. I need to tell someone. If all this turns out bad, I need to know that someone knows our story."

Marny didn't say anything. He couldn't. It was like her last will and testament, that someone know the hell she and William had lived through. How could he deny her that one request? The road ahead was straight and smooth and thinly populated with other cars. Marny kept both hands on the wheel and his foot firmly planted on the accelerator. Only occasionally did he glance in the mirrors to make sure no Ford Taurus was gaining on them.

"Two years after my mother died I told Gary I was taking William and leaving. I was nineteen, and I could find a job on my own, an apartment, and support both of us." She paused, looked at her hands. Her mouth tightened and jaw muscles flexed rhythmically.

"Esther—"

She held up a hand. "Gary went nuts, started pacing and swearing. He stood in front of the door and told me if I ever tried to take William from him, he'd find us and kill me. I knew he was serious too, we both did, but I was tired of being pushed around by him. I told him I was leaving anyway, taking William and getting out of there, that he couldn't keep us prisoners."

"You were fed up."

"That's the understatement of the century. When I turned my back to him, he grabbed a handful of my hair and yanked me back hard. It shocked me more than hurt, and I lost my balance and stumbled backward. Even before I hit the floor Gary was there over me. He slapped me in the face, not hard enough to really hurt, but it stung and it scared the daylights out of me. After that he installed the locks on the door and the Plexiglas in the windows. He never left the two of us alone again. He usually has me with him because he's afraid I'll leave. He doesn't know I would never abandon William. And besides, I think he's afraid of William's gift."

William was still sleeping in the backseat.

"What exactly is William's gift?" Marny asked again. "Mind control, telepathy, telekinesis? What?" He was still sure there had to be more to it than Esther had let on.

"Something much more powerful, Marny. Like I told you before, it's faith."

Chapter 29

"Y ou're disappointed," Esther said.

"No, not disappointed, just, um, surprised." He could feel her smiling at him.

"You still thought he was some kind of superhero? That he could throw fire or leap tall buildings and catch bullets?"

Marny glanced at William in the mirror. He was an eleven-year-old kid with a withered hand and noticeable limp. He was still probably three or four years away from shaving. Marny was suddenly embarrassed and felt his cheeks flush. "Something like that."

"Like I said, what he has is something more powerful than anything some superhero could do."

Marny didn't understand. Faith seemed so passive, so timid, the stuff of little old church ladies and Sunday school teachers.

"And Gary—tough guy psycho—is afraid of faith?"

Esther looked at Marny for a long time. He could feel her eyes, yes, those haunting blue eyes, boring holes into the side of his head. She was sizing him up, figuring him out, wondering if he could really be such an idiot.

"Marny, faith is the most powerful force anyone can possess. With it men have called down fire from heaven, walked on water, healed the sick, raised the dead."

"So what, William's some kind of child faith healer?" He'd seen a documentary once about a kid down south who was a faith healer. He attracted huge crowds and had people falling all over themselves.

"This isn't about showmanship and being flamboyant. It's about belief. Simple, innocent belief. And love. Real love."

"And with faith he can do stuff like, what, miracles?"

"Stuff like that."

"Like what? Come on, Esther, spill it. I need to know the story here."

"He can do whatever God wills."

"Then why doesn't he just use a little faith to get rid of Gary? Believe him right into the grave." It made sense to Marny. If William was a miracle child, why couldn't he just believe some horrible death on the man who'd held him and his sister captive for four years? What Marny called a curse he could use as a blessing.

"It doesn't work like that. Faith only works when it's filtered through love. It's not a weapon. That's the part Gary doesn't understand."

"So that's why he wants William so bad? He thinks he's some kind of super weapon?"

Their conversation was getting stranger by the second, venturing into territory that was the stuff of paranormal phenomena and fringe science. Only it wasn't science, was it? Not according to Esther anyway.

She didn't answer his question, so he pressed further. "And science can't prove anything he does, give a logical explanation?"

"Science can't prove faith. The two operate in totally different realms."

"Natural and spiritual."

"You got it."

Marny was quiet for a while. He had to think, process, rationalize—somehow make sense of this miracle-working child in the backseat of Mr. Condon's Buick Riviera. His hands started to shake for two reasons. One, if Gary knew what William was capable of and if he thought it could be used for his own purposes, then Esther was right about what she'd said before. He wouldn't stop coming after them; his pursuit would be relentless. And two, if William was as special as Esther suggested he was, Marny had all the more reason to get out of their lives as quickly as possible. William may have been blessed, but Marny was cursed, and the fact that sooner or later those two forces would collide scared the cotton out of him.

A sign up ahead read *North Adams 12.* "We're going to be there soon," Marny said. "You ready for this?"

Esther shifted in her seat. "I don't have a choice. He's our only chance." She looked back at her still-sleeping brother. "William never even knew him. For him, it'll be like meeting a stranger."

"A stranger who walked out on you. Does William know why your father left?"

"I've never told him, but I'm sure he's figured it out. He's a smart kid."

Marny had to ask her something else and wasn't sure how to do it. He wanted to avoid implanting his foot in his mouth at all costs. "Esther, is William...you know, mentally..."

"Challenged?"

For the second time he felt his cheeks flush. "Yeah."

"IQ scores would say so. But he isn't. His brain works differently from ours; he sees and processes things differently. He's smarter than most people in a lot of ways. He's insightful, like he can look right through your external facade and see your soul."

"I guess it's hard to lie to him."

She laughed. "Impossible."

"No Santa Claus?"

"Never."

William stirred in the backseat. Marny heard him stretch and moan.

"Hey, sleepyhead," Esther said. "You're finally awake."

"I'm hungry, Esther. Is there any food?"

She unwrapped the breakfast sandwich she'd kept and handed

it to him along with the hash brown and his orange juice. "There you go. Might be a little cold, but it'll fill your belly."

"Thank you for buying the food, Marnin."

"You're welcome, William. Enjoy it even if it is cold."

"You guys should have something too," he said. "This might be the last time we eat for a while."

With that one statement by the miracle kid, Marny suddenly felt the weight of an impending storm growing closer. Droplets of sweat wet his forehead. He checked the rearview mirror, expecting to see dark clouds looming close or a blue Taurus on their bumper.

Chapter 30

HAROLD ROSE'S HOME was a modest rancher on the edge of the Monroe State Forest.

Marny and his companions arrived there after stopping at a gas station off Route 2 for directions. Harold looked to have at least three acres of land that butted up against the forest. The house was situated on the left side of the property, and nearby, not a hundred feet away, sat a small barn. It appeared to be newly constructed with an ornate cupola topped with a copper rooster weather vane at the peak. A Jeep Grand Cherokee was parked in the driveway, and from behind the house and out of view of the road a thick tendril of smoke curled toward the sky. Marny pulled the Buick into the driveway behind the Jeep and shut off the engine. They sat there in silence staring at the house, the open yard, and the column of smoke for a few long seconds.

It was hot outside, and with the engine off and windows rolled up, the temperature in the car quickly climbed.

Finally Marny turned to Esther. "Well, what do you think?"

She kept her eyes on the house as if she could see through the walls and watch the man she once called Dad. "Think about what?"

"Quantum physics."

She smiled.

"You still want to do this?"

"He's our only hope."

Marny wasn't as certain as she was. This was the man who had walked out on his family because his son had been born with a few defects. He'd abandoned them and never looked back, never attempted to reconnect, and apparently started a new life here in Massachusetts. If he was their only hope, they were all in a bucket of trouble.

Marny found William in the rearview mirror. The boy was leaning forward, studying the house and property. "What do you think, William? Any feeling about this place?" He was hoping William would use his gift to discern whether they were doing the right thing or not.

"Is this where my dad lives?"

"He's not our dad," Esther said. "He fathered us, but that doesn't make him a dad."

William's eyes continued to roam over the house and property. "And you think it's a good idea to go to him for help, Esther? To get us away from Gary?"

Marny shared William's concern. He didn't understand Esther's reasoning, what brand of logic she was using.

"I don't want to, but"—she glanced back at William—"for our sake I think we have to. He's our only hope."

Marny could tell she wasn't so sure about her declaration either but wanted desperately to convince herself that it was true. He turned and looked William right in the eyes and tried again. "William, do you have any feelings about this place or about your father?"

William remained silent for so long, his eyes taking in every tree, every shrub, every corner of every building, that Marny thought he hadn't heard him.

Finally he said, "No, Marnin."

"Okay," Marny said, "it's officially hot in here. Can we go check things out?"

They all exited the car and approached the house. Marny had the same feeling he used to get as a kid when he'd go to a haunted house at Halloween, a queer mixture of fear and anticipation.

On the way up the sidewalk William said, "Do you think he'll know who we are, Esther?"

"Oh, I'm sure he will." She put her hand on his shoulder. "You're pretty unforgettable, little brother."

Marny stepped up to the door and rang the doorbell. They waited, but there was no answer. He rang it again.

"Let's head around back," he said. "See if he's by the fire."

They rounded the side of the house, following a thirty-foot-wide strip of freshly mowed lawn that passed between the house and the forest. Around the back, in the left corner of the property, was a burn pile of twisted limbs and broken branches belching dark gray smoke into the sky. And before the fire, breaking a long, straight stick over his knee, was a man, his back to them. He was a big guy, at least six three, with broad shoulders and thick arms. His short, dusty brown hair was mussed and windblown. He wore faded jeans and a simple green T-shirt.

Esther held William's hand and had a strange look on her face. Marny couldn't tell if it was fear or remorse or regret or a little of each, but he immediately knew this man was her father, Harold Rose. And she was having second thoughts about this, wrestling with reason and logic. He almost expected her to turn and give the signal to abandon the mission, but she didn't; she held tight to William's hand, pulled her shoulders back, looked at Marny, and nodded.

Marny cleared his throat. "Excuse me."

Harold spun around, tense, and looked at Marny, looked at Esther, looked at William. He was an attractive man with chiseled features and deep-set dark eyes. Those eyes went to Esther, then to William again, holding on each for a few prolonged seconds.

Finally his shoulders relaxed. Without saying a word he turned back to the fire, broke a stick over his knee, threw it into the flames. He rubbed his hands together and said, "I was wondering when you'd show up."

Chapter 31

ESTHER WAS NOT prepared for the gust of emotion that buffeted and nearly knocked her over at the sight of her father.

"It's good to see you too," she said. She was sure the edge to her voice was unmistakable. Memories came storming in from as far back as she could remember. Good ones, special times, laughter, holding hands, playing catch, building models. Times when he was her dad and she was his Squirt. Tears pressed at the backs of her eyes, but she refused to let them come. Not here, not like this.

Harold turned completely around and faced all three of them. Esther noticed he kept his eyes on her, didn't even glance at William.

"It's been over ten years, Esther. I walked out on you and your mother. You expect me to just welcome you back and act like the past decade never happened?"

The tension was like a concrete wall between them. Esther pulled William forward a step. "You have a son too, you know."

Reluctantly Harold nodded at William.

William didn't say anything but kept his eyes on his father, studying him as if he were a rare insect under a magnifying glass.

Harold narrowed his eyes, tilted his head back, and put his hands in his pockets. "Why did you come here?"

"Are you still a state trooper?" Esther said.

"Nope. Retired last year. Now I make cupolas." He pointed to the barn's roof.

"And that pays the bills?"

He shrugged. "Between that and my retirement check each month I get by. People 'round here like cupolas."

"Is there a new wife?"

Harold ignored her question. "Why did you come here, Esther?"

"You didn't answer me. Did you replace Mom?"

Her attitude and questions didn't seem to faze him. He had been one tough cop. Hard to rattle. "I'm not married."

"We need your help."

Harold gave Marny a look that would mean bad news if he was in uniform, then said to Esther, "You get yourself pregnant or something?"

She rolled her eyes. "Not quite."

"Then who's he?"

"Marny. A friend."

Harold picked up a stick, broke it in half, and tossed it on the fire. "You've gotten along just fine for ten years. Why do you need my help now?"

Esther released William's hand. She pulled her shoulders back and tensed. "Do you even know what we've been through?"

If Esther hadn't been looking closely and if she didn't know this man standing before her, she would have missed the shadow of sorrow that flitted through Harold's eyes.

"I tried to stay out of your life. I know Angela...your mother moved you in with Gary. I know she died four years ago."

"Our life with Gary has been a prison. He's obsessive, possessive, and completely insane. Mom's death was no accident, and now he's after us. That's our life in a nutshell."

Harold was quiet for a long time. He put his hands back in his pockets and stared at the grass in front of him. "What do you mean he's after you?"

"That's why we need your help."

"Esther, what do you mean, he's *after* you? Does he know you're here? Is he dangerous?"

"I don't know," she said. "I mean, yes, he's dangerous. More so than anyone you've run into before, believe that. And I don't know if he knows we're here or not. I don't see how he could, but he's full of surprises."

"Why is he after you?"

Esther pulled William closer and put her arm around his shoulders, a motherly act. "He wants William."

"What's so special about him?" He didn't ask it with any kind of disgust or revulsion. It was simply a question.

She hesitated. She didn't want to give too much away. If she'd trusted this man at one time, she no longer did now. "He has something Gary wants."

"So what can I do to help?"

That was the question, wasn't it? What *could* he do to help? Gary was like a freight train barreling down the tracks toward only one destination: William.

Esther dropped her eyes to the ground. "We need you." It pained her to acknowledge that fact. After ten years of abandonment and hurt and fear and death, she'd come full circle back to the man it all started with, and she had to admit she still needed him.

"For what?"

"Protection."

Chapter 32

MARNY WASN'T COMFORTABLE with the way things were progressing.

Nor with *what* and *who* was approaching.

If Esther was right, and Marny had no doubt that she was, Gary was coming, and with him, he would bring Marny's curse in a new-and-improved package.

"Sorry," Harold said. "I can't help you." He turned back to face the fire.

Esther dropped William's hand and took a couple steps toward her father. "Can't or won't?"

Harold crossed his arms.

"You ran out on us once, abandoned us, and now you're willing to do it again without a thought. Just like that. Brush us off like some strangers knocking on your door looking to sell cheap windows."

Still Harold didn't respond.

"We're not strangers."

"Go away, Esther." Harold spoke as though he were addressing the fire. "Nothing good will come of this."

"Nothing *but* good can come of it."

"You're wrong. Take your brother and friend and leave. You shouldn't have come here."

"I'm not leaving."

"Go." Harold's voice rose a few decibels. "You don't know me anymore."

Marny cleared his throat. "Esther, maybe we should—"

Esther held up a hand to silence him. She took another step forward. She was almost close enough to reach out and touch her father, something she hadn't done in ten years. "I came to you because you were the only one I could think of who could help us. You. My father. Please, we need you. We have nowhere else to go."

Harold looked to the eastern horizon as if watching for the arrival of rain clouds. Maybe he could sense the same approaching storm that Marny could. He stood like that for a full minute, eyes shifting back and forth slowly, gears in his head churning, churning. He turned and looked at Esther, glanced at Marny.

"I have a cabin up in the Green Mountains, maybe a half hour from here. Not much, it's a hunting cabin, but it'll do. Sooner or later Gary will figure out that you came to me. It's not hard to find where I live, but there's no way he can know about the cabin."

Marny wasn't sure about that. A secluded cabin in the woods wasn't his idea of protection. Harold was a cop, trained in confrontation. But knowing what Marny knew of Harold Rose and his history of avoiding confrontation, the fact that he'd choose flight over fight was no surprise. He'd done the same thing ten years ago.

Harold must have noticed the look of uncertainty on Marny's face. "Look," he said. "I don't know this guy or what he's capable of. Let's go to the cabin, get our heads about us, come up with a plan. It'll buy us some time. If you want my help, this is what I got. I'm calling the shots."

Marny looked at Esther and was about to voice his concern about the seclusion of the place when she beat him to it. "Okay then," she said. "The cabin it is."

"Good." Harold brushed his hand through his hair. "Let me get some supplies and we'll get going."

Marny watched Harold cross the yard and disappear inside the house. He turned to Esther. "You sure you want to do this?"

"No. I'm not sure about anything right now. But Gary's coming. Can't you feel it?"

Of course he could. The storm. He was surprised she felt it too.

"What about you, William?" Marny said. "You okay with this?"

William shrugged. "I don't know, Marnin; how do you feel about it?"

"I asked you first."

He looked up at Esther. "How do you feel about it, Esther?"

"Answer for yourself, William."

William looked at the house for a long time, then looked north, toward the Green Mountains and Harold's cabin buried somewhere deep inside the forest covering them. It was too bad seeing into the future wasn't part of his gift. "I guess it's okay."

It wasn't much of an answer, but it was all they were going to get out of him at the moment.

Marny walked to the burn pile, picked up a stick, and tossed it into the flames. A sense of uneasiness chewed at his stomach, but then again, they had a killer stalking them; uneasiness came with the territory. "Do you trust him?" he said to Esther.

There was no hesitation in her answer. "I don't have any reason to. But we don't have much of a choice, do we?"

No, they didn't. The way Marny saw it, they had three choices: stick with Harold and flee to the mountains; keep running from Gary, which showed no end in sight; or go back to Maine and confront Gary on their own. None of the choices thrilled him. He didn't trust Harold. In Marny's opinion, any man who would leave his family because he was afraid of responsibility, afraid of a challenge, had proven himself untrustworthy for life. Running from Gary would only end badly. If what William and Esther both said was true, that Gary would keep coming, then there was no running from him, only prolonging an inevitable collision. The longer they prolonged it, the worse it would be. And as far as Marny was concerned, there was no confronting Gary on their own. Marny was no fighter, no handler of weapons. And he was certainly no hero, no matter what Esther thought. Their only chance would be William's gift, but Esther said it didn't work that way.

"What are you thinking?" Esther said. "Your face is one big question mark."

"I don't know. I just have a bad feeling about this whole cabin thing. Makes me uneasy being hidden away in some woods, no one knows where we are, with a man none of us trusts."

"He's our only hope."

"Yeah, you said that before."

For Marny, of course, there was a fourth choice: leave Esther and William with Harold and return to Maine. This wasn't his concern, not really, and now that he'd gotten them to help, his services were no longer needed and he could bow out of the picture. That had been his plan all along, hadn't it? He didn't need to stick around and put himself in jeopardy anymore. He'd done his duty. Besides, it'd be best for them if he did make like Harold and flee. If he stayed, eventually things would turn bad.

But there were two problems with that choice. One, he'd grown somewhat attached to Esther and William. Actually, more than somewhat. His feelings for her had escalated. He didn't want to leave her; he wanted to spend as much time with her as he could. And two, whether he wanted to admit it or not, he *was* involved now, and Gary knew it. Marny had done his part to tick Gary off both at the house and on the interstate, and the monster wouldn't soon forget that. When he was finished with Esther and William, he'd come looking for Marny with a thirst for revenge. Confrontation would find him no matter where he hid.

He's our only hope. Marny supposed Esther was right. They really didn't have a choice now. Harold had weapons, he had experience with types like Gary, and he had a plan of sorts. It was more than Marny could offer.

Marny nodded. "Okay. I'm with you."

Esther smiled, and he could see the relief in her eyes. And that's exactly what he wanted to see.

The storm door of the house slammed shut. Harold emerged around the corner of the house carrying a large duffel bag over one shoulder, a rifle case over the other, a cooler in one hand, and another duffel bag in the other. "You ready?"

Chapter 33

For Marny, memories were unwelcome guests, tinkering with the locks on the door of his emotions.

Billy Tillman's parents moved to Mississippi where his grandparents resided, said they couldn't stand living in Maine, too cold. Marny knew they weren't just talking about the weather. A couple weeks later the Williamsons moved in next door, and Marny found himself with another friend, Sarah, age eleven.

Sarah was what Marny called a know-it-all. Too smart for her age, she knew everything about everything, or at least acted like she did.

It didn't take long for Marny's curse to catch up to her.

It was February 13, and it had already snowed a good two feet. Add that to the two feet of white stuff already on the ground, and you had no school and a day of fun in the snow. With the flakes still falling by the bucketful, Marny and Sarah bundled up and high-stepped into the hardwood forest next to Sarah's house to build a fortress. They'd been learning about the French and Indian War in school, and Marny wanted to construct a replica of Fort Necessity. Sarah said that was a stupid idea because George Washington surrendered the fort to the French. She said something about scouting the area out for a better location and wandered off into the woods.

Marny got to work on the fort, building the walls high and

thick and clearing the snow out of the middle. He didn't think about Sarah again until the sun dipped in the western sky and the shadows got long and thin.

Sarah was gone, nowhere to be found. Her parents and Janie and Karl scoured the woods, calling her name over and over, and soon the neighbors were involved in the search. The police were called and an official search party assembled, but with night falling and the temperature with it, there was only so much they could do and too much ground to cover.

Marny lay awake all night listening to the wails of Mrs. Williamson next door. The whole neighborhood could hear her. Mr. Williamson and Karl were out most of the night. Their voices echoed through the woods like the bugle calls of a funeral dirge. Marny kept thinking if the soldiers of the French and Indian War could find a way to survive the cold winter nights, so could Sarah.

One day passed, then two, then three blended into four, and eventually the search was called off. The dark clouds over eastern Maine had dumped another two feet of snow. Karl said he overheard Chief Munson say that Sarah probably wandered off, got lost, and was now buried in the snow. They might not find her until the spring thaw.

Spring did eventually come, and with it warmer temperatures. The snow melted slowly and in spurts, as it does in Maine, and mid-May Sarah was found. She'd tunneled under the snow from the edge of the woods back toward the house. At some point the tunnel collapsed, trapping her, and there she'd perished.

She was no more than fifteen feet from the house.

Marny felt the weight of responsibility for Sarah's death, as though he'd somehow caused it or even enabled it—like he and death were in cahoots, planning, conspiring the demise of anyone who came into contact with him. And he hated that feeling, wanted to run from it, hide, shake it any way he could, but it was a shadow that clung to him wherever he went, a constant reminder of the price people paid for associating themselves with Marny Toogood.

∞

When Harold reappeared, weighed down by all his gear, Marny felt that same burden again, felt the shadow clinging to him, the ominous presence of storm clouds inching closer. And for an instant, the briefest moment on a clock, he wanted to run, just jump in the Buick and tear off, never looking back. He had no idea where he'd go. Not back to Maine, that was for certain. He'd head west, maybe Idaho or Nebraska. Maybe even as far as California, head for warm weather where the sun was bright. He could start over there and maybe lose the curse and its ill-fated shadow for good.

But one look at Esther and William and he knew he couldn't go. In spite of his growing sense of hopelessness he had to stay. He couldn't leave them alone with Harold on the run from their crazed Uncle Gary.

So when Harold said, "You ready?" Marny looked at Esther and nodded.

"I think we are," she said.

They threw the gear into the back of Harold's Jeep and climbed in. Esther sat up front with her father, and Marny and William took the backseat.

Nobody talked much during the trip. Harold commented a couple times about local landmarks and their significance in New England history. He told a story or two about homes he'd visited while on patrol, responding to reports of domestic violence. Esther said little other than to acknowledge that her father was talking. William said nothing.

Twenty minutes into the trip, in the heart of the Green Mountain National Forest, William, who up until then had been looking out the side window with apparent lack of interest, reached his hand over and found Marny's. He rubbed the top of it, then wrapped his fingers around Marny's fingers.

William turned his head toward Marny and said in a low voice, "Everything will be okay, Marnin. Do you believe that?"

Marny didn't say anything. All he could think about was little Sarah Williamson's perfectly preserved face, frozen in fear.

Chapter 34

GARY WAS CONVINCED the voice would never stop now, never give him another moment's peace.

He'd lost them. Again.

The stunt the punk pulled, cutting across lanes and dodging oncoming traffic, was incredible and stupid. He could have gotten them all killed. If his timing had been off even a second, the Buick would be nothing more than a ball of twisted metal. Gary didn't care about the girl and her gas station friend, though; he only cared about the anointed one. His life was more precious than both of theirs combined, more precious than even Gary's.

The voice reminded him of that.

His life is precious, he is so precious. He is God's chosen. You must never forget that. Protecting him must be your primary concern, no exceptions. He is more valuable than any other.

Gary's usual tendency would have been to hit the steering wheel and curse and do something out of anger and desperation, but this time he controlled himself. He didn't want to give the voice more of a footing in his mind. The next exit to Route 1 was just a mile up the road. He'd take it and circle back to Condon's place. It was no use going after the stranger now; he could be anywhere with the boy. This region of the coast of Maine was a spiderweb of back roads, small town avenues, and city streets, and Gary had no idea where they were headed.

And of course, the voice was there again, reminding him of what he already knew.

The boy's life is more precious than your own. You must be willing to lay down your life for his. The good shepherd lays down his life for the sheep. You must protect him fully, even if it requires the giving of your own life.

"I'm willing," Gary said. "You don't know how willing I am."

He glanced at the speedometer and lifted his foot from the accelerator, allowing the car to slow. He was doing eighty in a sixty-five. Getting pulled over by a Maine patrolman would only complicate matters. He had to play it safe until he found out where they were headed.

He found the exit, took the off-ramp, circled around, and got back on I-95 headed north. With nothing but open highway stretched before him, Gary had time to meditate. He thought of his time in seminary, those four years he'd spent studying God's Word, church history, and theology; four years preparing for a life of service. He'd immersed himself in his learning, intent on satisfying his father and somehow paying penance for his great failure. He was going to be a minister, a preacher of God's Word, someone others looked up to, admired, honored, respected.

Seminary proved easy for him. He was a bright and attentive student, focused and determined, but soon after landing his first job as an assistant minister at a small church in rural Ohio the voice began. Within days it had escalated to such a level of near hysteria that Gary could no longer focus on his duties at the church. He became withdrawn, moody, and forgetful. Eventually the elders voted to dismiss him, and he found another position at a country church in northern Texas. But this time he only lasted six months. The next church was no different. The voice had grown too loud, too urgent, for him to ignore. It haunted him every moment of every day, reminding him of the failure he'd been, the tragedy that had happened on his watch. There was no escaping it.

Thinking he was going insane, Gary fled the ministry and the voice. He wandered the country for several years, skipping from town to town, finding work in diners and fields, making his way across the states. But the voice was always there, taunting, belligerent, giving him not even a moment's reprieve. He knew now that the voice was not only hounding him, but it was also redirecting him, guiding him into a new ministry, a new calling—one of much more importance.

Finally he'd landed in Maine. He could go no farther east. He thought about heading north to Canada, getting out of the country altogether, but then he met someone who miraculously silenced the voice in his head.

What he didn't know at the time was that the cessation of the voice was only a temporary pardon. It would return, and when it did, the message it would bring would alter the course of his life as nothing else could.

Gary massaged the steering wheel. He mourned for the life he'd lost, the mistakes he'd made. He was a failure of the worst kind, and here, now, he was still trying to prove himself, still trying to make things right.

The only redeeming aspect of his life was the boy. The anointed one gave Gary purpose. Without the boy he was nothing, had no reason to continue living.

He had to find the boy, he had to retrieve the lost sheep, and he wouldn't stop looking until the day he dropped over dead.

At Condon's house Gary walked in like he owned the place. At once he noticed the computer. He clicked the mouse, bringing the screen to life, and saw a Google map. They were headed to Massachusetts for help. To the home of Harold Rose.

The voice did not like that.

You must protect the anointed one. You must give all to see that he is kept from harm. No evil should befall him. He is in your care; he is your responsibility.

Gary jotted down the address on a piece of note paper, folded it neatly, and placed it in his pocket. He had to obey the voice and go to Massachusetts.

Chapter 35

The Jeep trail working its way up to Harold Rose's cabin was as windy and torturous as any amusement park roller coaster.

The vehicle bounced and banged and jolted and jerked for a good three miles before slowing on a level tract and finally grinding to a halt in a patch of loose dirt.

Harold shut off the engine, but Marny saw no cabin. An eel of uneasiness squirmed in his stomach.

"We hike from here," Harold said.

They exited the Jeep and stood in silence as Harold unpacked the gear. They were surrounded by towering oaks, birches, and maples, all in full leaf and forming a perfect canopy seventy, eighty feet above. Around them, squirrels chattered and chipmunks grunted. Cicada buzzed and birds whistled their summer melodies. There was no sign of civilization whatsoever. If there ever was a hinterland, this was it, and it made Marny anxious.

"Hey, you gonna help or what?" Harold pointed at the cooler.

"Uh, yeah, sure." Harold was an intimidating man, but Marny had learned long ago in his dealings with Karl not to let intimidation rule the day. "Wait." His hand hovered over the handle of the cooler. "How do we know we can trust you?"

Harold narrowed his eyes and pushed out his chest, a move Karl had mastered and used daily. "You don't. But the way I see it, it's me or you're on your own. You choose." He picked up both duffel bags and his rifle case and started walking away. "You want to come with me, this is the way. 'Bout a half-mile hike. No one's forcing you to."

Marny looked at Esther, seeking direction. He was willing to do whatever she wanted, but he hoped like crazy that she would choose to hike back down that mountain and find another way to confront Gary.

When Harold had hiked a good fifty feet ahead, Esther shrugged and said, "He's our only hope, Marny. You know that."

And as much as Marny didn't trust him, he did know it. It was nice to think they could confront Gary on their own, but he knew it would be futile, a death wish even. Gary had already proven himself a formidable foe, but there was something else about him, something evil and otherworldly. What drove him was not of this realm; that was becoming more and more apparent. At the thought of that, the hair on Marny's neck bristled, and he once again had the ominous feeling that something was approaching, a storm of some sort, dark, baleful, relentless. Whether it was Gary himself or whatever malevolent force drove him Marny couldn't tell, but it was closing in fast.

Marny nodded, forced a weak smile, and picked up the cooler.

The trail up the mountain was steep and rugged, not well-traveled. Surprisingly, even with his twisted leg, William kept pace and avoided stumbling. Marny, however, proved he was no sure-footed mountain man. More than once he tripped on a rock or lost his footing and went down, and each time Harold offered not even a glance.

Marny fell farther and farther behind until Harold was all but out of view. Esther and William stopped and waited for him. Up ahead, Esther sat on a fallen maple whose root system jutted into the air like so many tangled arms of a school of octopuses. The tree had been ripped from its earthy home by some wild and powerful force, but it had not gone easily. Clumps of dirt clung to the roots, and a crater the size of a small car was left where the mighty tree once stood.

When Marny reached the tree, Esther crossed her arms and said, "Nice of you to join us. Are you doing okay?"

Marny put the cooler down and drew in several deep breaths. "Yeah. This thing's heavy." He looked up the trail and didn't see Harold. "You think we're going the right way?"

She shrugged. "I figure there's only one trail going up. Kinda hard to get lost. You want some company?"

"Company would be nice."

He picked up the cooler and started up the trail again. Esther and William fell in beside him.

"So, back at Harold's house, you said your mother's death was no accident."

"Gary killed her."

She said it so matter-of-factly Marny thought at first he'd heard her wrong.

"He killed her?"

"Well, not directly. He didn't pull the trigger, but he might as well have."

"I'm not following you."

"He abused her daily. Never physically, I never saw him lay a hand on her, but plenty of verbal and emotional stuff. He was so...possessed by something...hate, fear, I don't know, and so obsessive with William."

"So much for brotherly love."

"Half-brother. I think somehow that exempts him from treating her like a real sister."

"Lousy excuse, if you ask me."

"You got that right. She stayed there because she felt it was best for us. Gary provided everything we needed. But she could only take so much of it. I think after *he* left"—she motioned up the trail, toward Harold—"she kinda fell apart emotionally. And she was vulnerable to begin with. I loved my mom, but she wasn't a strong person."

"She did a pretty good job raising the two of you despite the odds against her."

"She was a great mom; don't get me wrong. Everything she went through...I don't know if I'd have held up any better. Or ended any differently. One evening we were all watching TV. During a commercial break she got up to go into the kitchen"—she glanced at William, who met her look and nodded his approval for her to continue—"and a couple minutes later we heard a gunshot. We searched the house up and down but didn't find her, didn't find anything. Finally I checked the pantry closet, and there she was."

Esther was quiet as she stepped in even rhythm with her labored breathing. By the casual way she spoke of the incident Marny could tell she'd emotionally detached herself from it, built a wall for safety and isolation. If that wall ever came down, there would be lots of tears and anger. He wondered if William hid behind the same wall. The boy seemed unfazed by his sister's retelling of their mother's suicide.

"I always wondered what happened after something like that." Her voice was low, thoughtful. "I mean, with the mess. It doesn't just clean itself up, you know. Someone's gotta do it."

With that she'd put the period on her recollection, and Marny knew she'd speak no more of it. "I'm sorry that happened," he said. It sounded trite and small, four meaningless words lost in a sea of sorrow and hopelessness, but it was all he could think of to say.

Esther gripped William's hand with both of hers and held it close to her chest. "So am I. William's my rock now. He keeps us both going."

They came to an area where the trail narrowed and inclined sharply. Rocks jutted from the ground, forming a natural staircase of sorts. Marny went first, digging his feet in and pushing off each rock. After just a few steps his quadriceps burned and the cooler felt like it was full of leaden blocks.

Finally, with rubbery legs and a heaving chest, he reached the crest and a clearing.

But there was no cabin.

Chapter 36

A<small>N AUDIENCE OF</small> pale-skinned birch and thick maples encircled the area, standing silent, watching.

The clearing was small, no more than forty by forty. Harold stood in the center, feet spread a little wider than shoulder width, arms hanging loosely at his sides, the duffel bags on the ground next to him. His mouth was bent into something between a grin and a grimace.

Marny released the cooler and straightened his back. He was still breathing heavily, and the brisk air of the higher elevation felt good in his lungs. Esther and William arrived, and he heard their labored breathing behind him. Harold, though, appeared neither wearied nor out of breath. In fact, he appeared so relaxed it seemed abnormal. Something wasn't right, and it put the hair on Marny's arms on end.

"This is it." Harold's voice was even and low, controlled and professional. A cop voice.

Marny looked around. "Where's the cabin?"

Harold said nothing. His eyes shifted between Esther and Marny, and he worked his jaw as if chewing on the inside of his cheek. He reminded Marny of an outlaw in the Old West, standing in the middle of the street, trigger finger itching, six-shooter on each hip, begging someone to feel lucky.

Esther came around to the side of Marny, William holding her hand. "Where's the cabin? You said there was a cabin." She too must have noticed Harold's suddenly odd behavior.

"Harold." Marny took two steps forward, toward the man Esther used to call Daddy. "You said—"

Without a word Harold reached behind his back and retrieved a handgun, swung it around, and pointed it directly at Marny.

Marny stopped and backed up a step, both hands now raised. "Whoa, wait a minute."

Harold was calm, in police mode. He'd been trained to take charge of a situation, to intimidate, to control. He pointed the gun at William, then motioned to his right. "You, over here."

Esther jumped in front of her brother. "No. Wait."

"Out of the way, Esther," Harold said.

"What are you doing? He's your son."

Harold flinched as if someone had sprayed water in his face. "He's not my son. He's a freak. A monster."

"No."

"Get away from him, Esther. I don't want you involved in this." He took a step forward, bringing the pistol that much closer.

Marny was no expert on handguns, but he knew enough to know that big and black wasn't good.

"No. I'm not leaving him. How can you do this?"

Marny took a step toward Esther. "Maybe—"

"Shut up!" Harold trained the handgun on Marny again. It was as steady as ice. The black hole of the barrel stared at him like a lifeless eye. "This doesn't concern you, boy." He motioned to his left. "Get over here and get down on your stomach."

With both hands still raised, Marny hesitated.

"Now!"

He moved a few steps to his right and lowered himself to the ground.

Harold turned back to Esther and William. "Now, over here."

Esther held William tightly, not letting go of him. "Whether you want to admit it or not, he's your son, your own flesh."

"Look at him. He's a freak. Step away from him, Esther." Harold was back to being a cop. "Do it now."

"He's my brother. He's all I have."

"You have me now," Harold said.

Marny saw where all this was going. His curse had found them—skipped right over Gary and tracked them through the Green Mountains, up this trail and to this clearing—and now it was eager to satisfy its appetite. And Harold was about to feed it William. It had to end here. The curse, the death, the constant looking over his shoulder. This is where Marny would take his stand, put it all on the line. He wasn't about to stand by and watch the curse claim another life, not William's.

William pulled away from Esther.

"No," she hollered and lunged for his hand.

But before she could take hold of him he was out of reach, headed for Harold with that hitched limp of his.

Harold took a step back and leveled the gun on William. "Over there." He motioned with his left hand. For the first time Marny saw what looked like fear in Harold's eyes. The man was scared of William, afraid of his deformities. His own son repulsed him enough that he feared even contact with him.

William didn't stray from his course, though, and continued hobbling directly at Harold, that same disinterested expression on his face he always had.

Harold took another step back. "Stop." His lips peeled back from gray teeth, and he jabbed the gun at William.

Marny saw his opportunity and scrambled to his feet. He made a dash for Harold with every intent of tackling the larger man and occupying him long enough for Esther and William to escape down the mountain. It wasn't much of a plan, but it was all he had.

But Harold's training had not been forgotten. He swung the pistol around and pointed it at Marny. There was hatred in his eyes, death in the curve of his mouth.

The gun discharged.

When Marny was nine, he stepped into the arc of a swinging

baseball bat. The impact of bat on his skull was so great he thought his head had exploded. He never felt his feet leave the ground, never felt the ground rise up to meet him, never felt the dirt on his back. One second he was looking up at the clouds doing circles in the sky above, the next he was swimming in a dark, warm liquid.

This was a thousand times worse. Marny never even felt the impact. He saw the flash of the barrel, then he was on his back in a world of darkness. His head was in a vise. In the far distance he heard another shot and a woman scream.

Then everything faded away.

Chapter 37

THE CONCUSSION OF the gun had ricocheted around the clearing and pushed Esther back a step as if it had a substance all its own.

Now silence reigned.

Esther's first thought was that the pistol was loaded with blanks, Harold's attempt to frighten or intimidate them. But then Marny's head had snapped violently and he'd gone down so hard. In an instant she knew what had happened, but she was paralyzed with shock. Marny lay on his back on the ground, motionless, and of course she feared the worst. But she couldn't move. Her feet were stuck to the ground with those nails of panic.

Before her mind could fully register what was taking place on that mountaintop, Harold, her father, the man she once adored, swung the gun around and pointed it at William.

An involuntary scream escaped her throat. She heard it as if she were outside herself, watching these events as a spectator in some gruesome game of survival. The gun went off again, and this time it was her little brother being driven backward by a bullet. His chest caved and his head went forward as he was pushed back and crumpled to the dirt.

A few silent moments passed. Harold stood like a granite image, arm extended, pistol still aimed at William. His face remained twisted into a devilish grimace and painted deep red with hate and disgust.

Esther couldn't breathe. Her brain no longer sent signals to her diaphragm to contract and relax, contract and relax. Finally her involuntary response kicked in and she gasped for air, began to shake. She couldn't cry, couldn't talk, but now she found she could at least move.

She ran for William and dropped to the ground next to him. He didn't move. His chest didn't rise and fall. A large red stain had overtaken the front of his shirt, and in the center of it, a hole. Her eyes saw it, there was no doubting it was real, but her mind refused to accept it. She put her hands on William's face and found her voice.

"William. William. God, please no. William."

But there was nothing. His cheeks were already pale and going cold. Esther looked back at Harold, who was just now lowering the gun. Their eyes met, and in his she found something darkly terrifying. This was not her father, not the same man who played catch with her in the backyard, not the man she laughed with and took walks with. Not even the man who'd walked out on her. This was a monster of the worst kind.

Harold blinked several times in succession, and the color slowly drained from his face. His eyes shifted between Esther and William. It was as if the realization of what he'd done had triggered the transformation of Mr. Hyde back to Dr. Jekyll. He blinked again, then looked at Marny.

Esther tried to say something, tried to question him or yell at him or curse him, but a lump had taken residence in her throat and brought with it a wave of tears. She sat back on her haunches and began to cry.

Harold shoved the gun into his waistband and moved toward her. "Oh, no. C'mon, Esther; we don't have time for this."

She waved him off with shaky hands, but he was insistent. He reached down and took hold of her arm. "Get it together, Esther. We need to get going."

Esther ripped her arm away from him and screamed something unintelligible, animal-like. Her world had been forced inside out and tumbled upside down. The foundation had crumbled, and the walls were quickly following.

Harold squatted beside her. "Esther, listen to me. We need to move now. Back down the mountain. Out of here. Come *on*."

Numbly, thoughtlessly, Esther stood. Suddenly she was freezing. She took one last look at William and Marny, then headed back down the trail, her feet mechanically finding footholds, her legs moving as if controlled by a puppeteer. She noticed nothing other than Harold's form in front of her; he carried the cooler and duffel bags. Her peripheral was black, bleak, dead space. Occasionally Harold spoke, but she couldn't make out what he was saying.

When they arrived back at the Jeep, Harold opened the back door and ordered her in. Esther climbed onto the seat and let her head fall back against the headrest. Her legs should have been tired and achy from the descent, but she felt nothing.

Harold leaned in close. He held something in his hand. "Esther, I'm going to give you a shot to help you relax. Don't fight it. This is for your own good."

She was in no mood to resist. She didn't care. If he was about to shoot acid into her veins, she would welcome it. She felt a slight pinch, then Harold shut the door. Seconds later, warmth spread over her body, and she grew very tired. She slumped to her side on the seat and allowed her eyelids to close.

The sleep, the escape, was welcome. Maybe she would wake up and find all of this was a nightmare. Maybe she wouldn't wake up at all.

Chapter 38

LIGHT OVERCAME THE darkness.

With his eyes still closed, Marny was suddenly aware he was lying on his back. A rock pushed into his left kidney, but he didn't care. The inside of his eyelids was a light shade of gray. In spite of the rock he was comfortable. Warm. A soft breeze washed over him, and above he could hear the excited chatter of squirrels and the drone of cicadas.

A hand touched his face and pushed back his hair.

Then a child's voice. "You can open your eyes now, Marnin."

William.

It came back to him then. He'd been shot. Harold had pointed the pistol directly at him and squeezed the trigger. He remembered the blast of light, the brief feeling of weightlessness as his body lifted off the ground, then the impact of earth with his back.

He should be dead, shouldn't he?

"You're okay now, Marnin. You can open your eyes."

Okay? No, he wasn't okay. He should be dead. Marny's eyes moved behind closed lids. He tried to open them, but the light was too bright. They fluttered and shut again. He lifted a hand and placed it over his eyes. He parted his fingers slowly, letting light in a little at a time and easing the transition.

Above him, leaves moved in unison as a breeze played through them. The sky was a pale blue, no clouds. A flock of birds took off from a high branch, crossed the sky, and disappeared into the foliage.

William was there, bent over him, looking intently at the side of his head. His little hand combed through Marny's hair. "How do you feel now?"

Marny heard his question, but it didn't make sense. How did he feel? He'd just been shot in the head at fairly close range and, oddly, he felt fine.

He pushed up from the ground, expecting pain to hit his head like a sledgehammer, but it never did. He didn't even have a headache. The side of his head was tender to touch and his hair was still a little sticky with drying blood, but he felt no wound. The skin was intact.

That's when he noticed two things that stole the air from his lungs. One, the front of William's shirt was stained with blood, and in the center of the stain was a hole the size of a dime. And two, Harold and Esther were gone.

He reached for William. "William, your shirt. Are you hurt?"

William looked at his shirt, put his hand up under it, poked his finger through the bullet hole and wiggled it. "I'm fine now, Marnin."

Marny reached for the shirt and lifted it. William's chest was covered with dried, flaky blood, and in the center, an inch to the left of his sternum, was an entry wound the size of a nickel, healed over like it had happened weeks ago. Marny lifted his hand and touched the side of his head again. "William, what did you do?"

William shrugged and diverted his eyes, clearly uncomfortable with the attention. Marny knew what he'd done. He'd healed both of them. His gift. His superpower or whatever it was.

"Are you okay? Your chest?"

William patted his chest and smiled. "I'm fine now."

Marny held William by both shoulders. "Where's Esther?"

William looked to his left, down the mountain. Worry lines formed on his brow. "Harold took her. I'm worried about her, Marnin."

154

Marny usually found hiking a relaxing activity, but after being shot and left for dead, this journey was anything but tranquil.

It took him and William the better part of an hour to make it down the mountain. The Jeep had done its job well, handling the rough terrain and making excellent time up the steep slope.

They mostly walked in silence, concentrating on their footing and breathing. More than a couple times they slipped on the loose ground and would have gone down if not for the steadying hand of the other. Once Marny asked William about his gift, his special powers, but William didn't answer. He only watched the ground before him with mild indifference and quietly limped his way along the path.

At the bottom of the mountain the service trail met a paved road. Marny sat on a fallen tree, rubbed his thighs, and tried to make sense of what had just occurred on the mountaintop, how death had been foiled.

But death was always on Marny's mind. Not just his own, but the deaths of the others. Those who shouldn't have died but did because of him.

His memories carried him back to high school and weekends on the farm with Adam Bitfield.

Marny had met Adam in the ninth grade. They were both fifteen and in that awkward stage between the teen years and adulthood. Problem was, they both thought they were more adult than they were.

Adam's father, John, was a potato farmer and owned one of the largest farms in the southern half of Maine. Usually Adam referred to it as Spud Kingdom, but on those rare days when his father (the Spud King) was in a mood, his fuse short, his tongue sharp, and his hand looking for something to hit, Adam called it Spud Hell.

That Saturday in September was one of those rare days. Marny rode his bike the eight miles to the Bitfield farm and dropped it outside the barn. He usually found Adam in there, either working or thinking. Adam liked to think. Said he wanted to be a philosopher once he got away from the Spud King. Only today it was no kingdom. It was hell.

Marny found Adam in the corner of the barn with a six-pack of Michelob, a fat lip, and a bruised right eye.

"What happened?"

Adam took a swig of beer and shrugged. He was working on his second can. "Old man was in a bad mood this mornin'. Woke up on the wrong side of the bed, I guess. Wanted someone to take it out on."

Marny knew there was always more to it than that. Adam downplayed his father's outbursts, but word in town was that the farm was in financial difficulties and that John Bitfield was about to lose everything.

"You okay?" Marny leaned in for a better look at Adam's wounds. "That lip looks nasty."

Another swig of the Michelob. "Looks worse than it feels. I think it's so swollen it's numb now." He touched it lightly and looked at this hand. "Bleedin's stopped at least."

"You wanna do something?"

Adam swirled the beer in its can. "Old man wants me to take the bush hog out and mow the north field. I better get to it before I get a matchin' pair a' these shiners. You want to come?"

Marny had nothing better to do. "Sure."

"Great. I could use some company." Adam grabbed what was left of the six-pack and stood. "Over there in the cooler is another one a' these." He held up the cans. "Grab one and let's head out. We'll take our time and drink our way through the field."

Unlike Karl Gunnison and John Bitfield, Marny was not a drinker, but he figured a few wouldn't hurt so he could keep his friend company. After all, when misery came at the hand of the Spud King, it almost demanded company.

They got on the tractor and Adam fired it up, then leaned over to Marny. "If you don't mind, I'd like to do more drinkin' than talkin'." He tapped his lip. "Not really in the talkin' mood, know what I mean?"

Marny nodded. "Sure. Anything you want, Adam."

"Besides, once this thing gets goin'"—he pointed at the bush hog behind the tractor—"it's so loud you can't hear yourself think."

Adam popped the tab on a can and handed it to Marny. "Here, wash your worries away."

By the time they reached the north field, Adam had downed another full can and was working on his fourth. He was already a little sluggish with the tractor's controls.

"Here we go." Adam held up his can and started up the bush hog. The sound of the rotating seven-foot blades was like that of a chopper going full blast.

There was no pattern to the way Adam mowed the field. Usually he was careful to steer the tractor in straight rows and cover every inch of ground, but today the tractor weaved right and left and missed whole stretches of field. While Adam guzzled his beer, one can after the next, Marny only sipped at his. He wasn't particularly fond of the taste and knew too well the effect it had on people.

About an hour into the job, one six-pack gone and Adam working on the other, his friend could barely stay on his seat, could barely lift the can to his mouth, and what little he said made no sense at all.

Marny was about to tell him he'd had enough and suggest they go back when Adam suddenly lost his balance and tipped left. As he fell, he jerked the steering wheel in the same direction, pulling the tractor into a hard left turn. Marny lost his hold and fell to his right, landing hard on the ground.

Marny righted himself and looked under the tractor, through its wheels, just in time to see the mower bump over Adam.

By the time Marny chased down the tractor and stopped it, there wasn't much left of Adam for the coroner to examine.

∞

William inched closer, bringing Marny out of the past. He leaned his head against Marny's arm. "Where do we go from here, Marnin?"

"Back to Harold's house, I suppose. It's as good a place as any to start."

"Start what?"

"Looking for Esther. We're not leaving her with that jerk."

William was quiet for a few beats; he twisted his hands, his good one rubbing the withered one. "He's not my father, Marnin."

Marny put his arm around William. The kid may have been gifted in math or science or human psychology, he might have special powers to manipulate the laws of nature, but he was still a kid, and finding out that the father who walked out on you because you were a "freak" refused to believe you and he even shared the same blood would be a bitter pill to get down at any age. "He *said* you're not his son. There's a difference. But for the record, he may have fathered you, but you're right; he's not your father, not really. He's a jerk who tried to murder us. Who *did* murder us."

William said nothing. Marny could tell he was deep in thought, his mind churning with questions that had no answers at the moment. Questions of origin and purpose and wrongs never made right. Questions no eleven-year-old should have to wrestle with.

"We'll find her, William," Marny said. "We'll find Esther."

Across the road the woods seemed to have fallen into a deep slumber. No breeze stirred the leaves; no wildlife foraged for food. The legions of cicadas present on the way up the trail could not be heard here. The road was silent too.

Marny stood and walked onto the pavement. Faded blacktop stretched in both directions and disappeared behind the dense, lifeless woods. "You have any idea where he'd take her?"

William shrugged. "Back to his house?"

Marny put his hands in his pockets and went back to the fallen tree along the side of the road. "Maybe. But I'm thinking that would be too obvious. He'll want to take her somewhere different, probably far from here. Maybe back to Maine. A place familiar to him. To both of them."

"I remember Esther talking about the house we used to live in before Gary came. She really liked that house."

"Do you remember it?"

"No, Marnin. I only remember Gary's house."

"Did she ever mention the name of the town?"

"Comfort."

Marny patted William's knee. "You think he'd take her there?"

William thought for a bit, his eyes scanning the woods on the other side of the road. For a moment Marny thought the boy had seen something there, something unseen to the average eye but spotted by some extrasensory ability William had been hiding from him. Finally he said, "Yes."

"Why?"

William shifted on the tree and found Marny's eyes. His irises were striated with the richest shades of brown Marny had ever seen, and in them was an innocence this world did not know. "Because it's the last place he was happy."

The sound of rolling tires approached from around the bend and broke the tranquility of the woods, reminding Marny that civilization was not that far away. A full-sized, extended-cab pickup came into view, passed them, then slowed and pulled to the shoulder. Through the rear window Marny could see the driver, a woman, holding a cell phone to her ear. The white reverse lights came to life, and the truck rolled backward. It pulled alongside them and stopped; the passenger side window slid down.

The woman behind the wheel was in her midthirties, attractive, with shoulder-length brown hair and dark green eyes. She leaned to the side and eyed William, then Marny. "You guys okay?"

Marny realized how William's bloodied shirt must look to the driver. "Uh, yeah. Actually we are. Got into some trouble along the trail up there, but we're both all right. It looks worse than it is."

"Looks pretty bad."

William's shirt did look bad. Most of the front was stained crimson.

"Yeah, I know. I fell and knocked my head. You know how head wounds bleed. We used William's shirt here as a bandage until the bleeding stopped."

"William, huh?" The woman nodded at William. "How are you, sweetie?"

William didn't answer. He simply lifted his good hand and gave a little wave.

The woman looked ahead, then back at Marny. "Well, if you're headed this way, I can drop you off somewhere. You think you need a hospital?"

"No. I'm fine, really. You know where Monroe Bridge is? We have a friend who lives there."

She smiled and nodded. "Sure do. Hop in."

Chapter 39

THE HOUSE WAS everything he expected it to be.

Gary pulled the Taurus along the side of the road and shifted into park, but he didn't shut off the engine. First, he double-checked the address he'd gotten from the computer in Condon's house. It was the correct house, Harold Rose's. And it was completely Harold: remote, unassuming, and dangerous. But more than the house, he was interested in the Buick parked in the driveway. His hunch was correct. Esther had taken William and her new friend to seek help from her long lost daddy. There were no other vehicles on the property, which meant Harold had taken them elsewhere.

Gary tightened his jaw and bowed his head. Immediately the voice was there.

The good shepherd is willing to lay down his life for his sheep. To him, nothing else matters but the safety and protection of the sheep.

"I'll find him. I'll take care of it." His voice sounded oddly weak to his own ears, not the voice of one certain of success. Was his faith wavering?

He shifted the car back into drive, drove a hundred or so feet up the road past Rose's place, and parked behind a stand of birch trees, out of the home's line of vision. Grabbing the rag from the passenger seat, he exited the car and made his way along the edge of the property to the rear of the house. Carefully, so as not to be seen and mistaken for a common burglar or peeping Tom by any passing motorists, he moved from window to window. No one was home.

At the back door, Gary wrapped the rag around his hand and, as he'd done at Condon's garage, put his fist through the window. The glass made a popping sound when it broke. He waited a full minute before entering to make sure the house was indeed clear and that there were no alarms triggered by his intrusion. It was a minute of silence. For an ex-cop, Harold Rose was not as cautious as he should have been.

The door opened easily, and Gary quickly found his way through the house to the study. At the desk he scanned the papers in full view, looking for anything that might signify where Harold had taken William. Nothing but bills, auto insurance papers, and a calendar book. One by one he then went through the drawers and emptied them of their contents. Harold had kept every form and receipt and manual imaginable, but nothing that spoke of a destination, a hideaway, an alternate residence.

His last hope was the file cabinet in the corner of the room—one of those metal, four-drawer jobs that always hid the answers to questions in the movies. In the top drawer he found file after file of nonsense. Electric bills, propane bills, credit card statements. Nothing he could use. The second and third drawers were more of the same. Harold Rose was quite the pack rat. The bills and statements went back some ten years. In the bottom drawer, though, he found a stack of newspaper clippings.

Gary lifted the stack out of the drawer and took it to the desk. He wasn't worried about Harold returning home and finding an intruder sitting in his office. No, Harold was long gone by now, and there was nothing Gary could do about that except find out where he was headed, where he was taking William, God's anointed.

It took but one article for Gary to realize what this stack of newsprint was. Invisible spiders climbed up his arms and over his back and neck. Page after page, article after article, the stories recounted the work of the serial killer known as the Maniac.

A decade ago, a lunatic ravaged the Down East region of Maine, killing twenty-three people in two weeks.

Gary scanned one article, then the next, looking for any clue. He was about to give up when his eyes caught a line in the last story: *Lieutenant Harold Rose of the Maine State Police said that local and state law enforcement officers are working closely with federal investigators but that they currently have no credible leads. He said the frustration levels of all who are involved are rising steadily.*

There was a photo of Harold in his uniform, looking directly at the camera, a mixture of fear and anger tightening his face. The caption read: *Lieutenant Harold Rose stands over the body of the latest victim of the Maine Maniac, seventeen-year-old Emily Rooter.*

Gary dropped the clipping and ran his hands through his hair. He was trembling. Rose was taking them back to Maine; it had to be the case. He'd be familiar with that area. Comfortable. He'd feel in control. And he had a house there. When Angela died, the house would have gone to Harold.

He stood from the chair so quickly it nearly toppled over backward. He was about to stuff the articles into a folder to take along with him when he heard the crunch of tires on the gravel outside.

Chapter 40

THINGS ARE RARELY as they seem.

When the pickup pulled into the driveway of Harold's house and stopped next to the Buick, the home appeared to be empty, still.

The driver, who had earlier introduced herself as Cheyenne, kept the engine running and said, "Here you go, guys. Doesn't look like anyone's home."

Marny forced a smile. "He must've just run out for some groceries. Maybe to the hardware store. He should be back soon. We'll just let ourselves in, and I'll take care of this head of mine."

"You sure? I can run you by the hospital now. It isn't but twenty minutes away."

Marny opened the rear door of the truck. "No, that's okay. Thanks for the lift. I'll be fine."

Cheyenne shrugged. "Well, it's your head. I wish you'd let me help, though."

"Really, we're okay," Marny said.

She nodded to William and grinned, but her smile was anything but genuine. "You take care too, William," she said. "Nice meeting you."

William said nothing. His eyes found Marny, and in them was panic. What did he know about their new friend that Marny didn't?

"Well, okay then," Marny said, stepping out of the truck. "I guess we'll be all right on our own now."

William followed him out, and Marny shut the door behind them.

The passenger window rolled down, and Cheyenne leaned toward it. A thin smile tugged at the corners of her mouth. "You guys didn't think it would be this easy, did you?"

A tingling started in Marny's fingers and crept up into his hands. William pushed closer to him; he put his arm around the boy's shoulders.

The truck's engine still ran; Cheyenne had yet to shift it out of drive. A red danger light went berserk in Marny's head. This woman was no stranger. Her happening upon them along the side of the road was no accident.

He thought of making a run for it, heading for the house, but Cheyenne would run them down before they could get off the driveway. Maybe they could turn and bolt for the barn where Harold crafted his one-of-a-kind cupolas. But what good would that do? They'd be trapped.

Cheyenne lifted a handgun and pointed it at Marny. "The thing I don't understand," she said, "is how are you two even standing here? Harry said he took care of both of you."

If it was a question intended for an answer, Marny wasn't playing along. Though Marny had some questions of his own. "Are you working with Harold?" It was obvious she was, but Marny wanted to hear her say it. There was a lot you could tell by the tone of someone's voice and the body language that accompanied what they said.

But Cheyenne wasn't playing along either. "You can't run, you know; it's no use. You won't get far now."

"How did you know we'd be by the road?"

"Shut up."

"How did you know we'd been shot?"

The gun wavered in Cheyenne's hand. Her arm was getting tired. Sooner or later she'd have to change positions, either get out of the truck or scoot over to the passenger seat. Either way, she'd have to take her focus off Marny and William, and that's when Marny would make his move. He had no idea what he'd do. He was making this up as he went along.

"I said shut up." Cheyenne's eyes grew more intent. She nudged the gun toward Marny. "You, we really don't have a need for. You have a big mouth. But the kid we can use."

Marny's eyes went to Cheyenne's finger an instant before it depressed the trigger. He wrapped his arms around William, and they both hit the ground as the gun went off. Another shot sounded, but this one was followed instantly by the pop of breaking safety glass. The windshield.

Marny's head spun, processing all it could in a matter of seconds. Had he been shot? He'd felt no impact. No pain. What about the glass? Was it the windshield?

A third shot rang out, this one close, and Marny flinched. He moved over William to shield him. That shot was followed by a series of more distant cracks coming from the direction of the house.

Suddenly the pickup's engine revved loudly and the tires spun in the gravel. They found traction, and the truck lurched forward, the engine roaring. More gunfire erupted from the house. The truck picked up speed and smashed into the house, busting through the exterior wall. Its rear tires continued to spin, pistoning the truck back and forth. The front tires were caught on the home's foundation.

Marny climbed to his feet and pulled William up with him. "The car. Get in."

More gunshots sounded. The truck's tires continued to spin.

Marny jumped in behind the wheel of the Buick, and William slid onto the passenger seat beside him. Marny felt his pockets. No keys. He fumbled with the ignition. He hadn't left them there. He patted his pockets again.

"William, can you do something? Please?"

William reached for the ignition, but before his hand could

make contact and supernatural power flow from him into the car's starter, the car door swung open and something hard nudged the side of Marny's head.

"Get out."

Gary.

Chapter 41

THERE WAS NOTHING sweet about returning to *this* home.

Esther stood on the sidewalk, now cracked by weeds pushing their way up between the slabs of concrete, and stared at the house she once loved. The sun was far enough down in its arc that it hid behind the treetops; here in the woods darkness came early.

Despite the thin film of grime that coated the windows and the moss that had begun growing on the shady side of the roof, the house was in surprisingly good condition.

Harold wrapped his hand around Esther's arm and guided her up the steps. Her head was still a little foggy from sleep, and it felt like someone had scooped out her brain and filled her skull with concrete. She'd awakened in the car to find they were back in Maine, back in their old town of Comfort, back at their old home on Cranberry Road. The house was on a remote stretch of the road, out of view of any others. It sat on three acres of land, mostly wooded.

On the porch Harold said, "You remember this place?"

The question was absurd, but everything about this day was absurd. What had she been thinking? She must have been out of her mind to hope Harold would help them. And now her miscalculation had cost William and Marny their lives.

Esther grabbed her head with both hands. She couldn't think

about this now; it was too much to process at once. William was gone, and Harold was asking her if she remembered this house?

"Of course I do," she said. Her words sounded slurred to her ears.

He turned and frowned at her. His face was hard, and his cheeks appeared gaunter than they had earlier. If he felt any remorse at all for taking two lives, he wasn't showing it. "What do you remember?"

"You killed William."

"About the house. This place."

"You shot a child."

Harold looked away and swallowed hard; his Adam's apple bobbed in his neck. "He's no child; you know that."

"He *is* a child. My brother."

"He's a monster," Harold said. "A freak. I put him out of his misery."

"He isn't in misery. He loves life despite the hell we've been living." She was talking about William as if he were still alive, still in Massachusetts waiting for her to come and rescue him. But he wasn't. He was gone. Dead. She'd seen it with her own eyes.

"I wasn't the only one. Angela, your mother, she was disgusted by him too. She was afraid of him."

He was lying; Esther was sure of it. Trying to defeat her psychologically, beat her down and into submission so she wouldn't struggle against whatever it was he had in store for her. Their mother had loved William, cared for him, adored him even. She would never say such a thing, especially not to the man who walked out on her because of her precious baby boy.

"You're a liar," she said. "And a coward. You ran out on your responsibility."

Harold dug in his pocket and removed a key. "That may be, but right now I'm in charge, and we're playing by my rules. Now what do you remember about this house?"

There was a point to his question; there had to be. Esther decided to play along. She thought it best to stay on his good side. "The last memory I have is walking out of here, off this porch, with two suitcases stuffed full. I tried to change Mom's mind, tried to convince her to stay and raise us herself. I was convinced you'd come back sooner or later, find us gone, and never try to find us again. I fell right here"—she pointed at a spot on the porch right above the first step—"and cried. I thought you'd come back sooner or later, that you and Mom had just had an argument and when the dust cleared and everyone settled down you'd be back and make things right. That things would be the way they used to be before…"

"Before the freak came along?"

"He isn't a freak."

Harold put the key in the door and turned it. The dead bolt clicked, and he pushed the door open. He started to go inside, but Esther stopped him.

"Wait. The last *good* memory I have is playing ball with you. I'd stand here on the porch and you'd be in the yard. You'd throw me the ball and I'd jump off the porch and catch it. We'd do it until my legs wouldn't work anymore. Do you remember that?"

For a moment Harold looked as if he might cry. His chin dimpled and his mouth tightened. His right eye twitched. Then just as quickly the hardness returned, the mask of indifference. "Of course I do. Now come on, inside."

"What if I don't want to?" She wasn't making a stand there on the porch; she was merely testing him, peering into his soul.

He shrugged. "I can make you, Esther. You know that. Now let's go."

She crossed the threshold from porch to foyer and was immediately swept into tears by the sudden rush of memories that flooded her mind. She'd spent years putting this behind her, trying to forget. The good memories only served to usher in the hurt and pain and abandonment that followed. She didn't want to relive any of it. And now here she was.

Harold put his hand on her shoulder, but there was nothing soft about it, nothing fatherly or comforting. "That's it, girl. Let it out." His voice was flat, mechanical. "It'll all be over soon."

Chapter 42

MARNY KNEW THIS day would come sooner or later. Eventually his curse would backfire and turn on him. It would have succeeded already if not for William, but Marny doubted the wonder boy would be able to do anything this time. Kinda hard to heal a head that's been blown off.

Marny climbed out of the car and for the second time that day put both hands in the air. A habit he didn't want to get used to.

Gary stood before him, red-faced and panting. Sweat dotted his forehead and cheeks. In his eyes was the look of hunger, of death. He held the handgun at shoulder height, the barrel pointing right at Marny's forehead.

And for the second time that day Marny found himself staring at the black, soulless eye of the reaper bringing death.

But death was no stranger to Marny. It had been following him his whole life, and now it had turned its gruesome claws on him. Strangely, he wasn't afraid of the gun trained on him, wasn't afraid of the monster holding the gun. A part of him was actually relieved. The world would be a safer place without Marny Toogood in it.

Gary's lips parted and the muscles in his shoulder tensed.

Marny shut his eyes. If this was how he was going to go, he didn't want to watch. At least it would be quick.

"Wait." It was William's voice. "Don't do it, Gary."

Marny opened his eyes. Gary's eyes were on the boy.

William shuffled his feet. "We need him."

This was certainly an odd turn of events.

Not until the barrel of the gun pointed at the ground did Marny lower his hands. He swallowed hard and wiped his palms on his pants. He was alive, yes, which was certainly better than being dead, but he wasn't entirely comfortable with where things stood. He and William had fallen into the hands of a madman, a monster. Things would get ugly, and Marny couldn't count on anything better being on the other side. He didn't have the super faith of William. He didn't even have common faith.

Gary blinked slowly and stared at William, who came around the car.

"We need him, Gary," William said again. "*I* need him."

Gary pulled his shoulders back. He seemed to be thinking about that, weighing the pros and cons. The gun moved at his side, and for a moment Marny thought he'd lift it and fire before William could protest again.

When William came the whole way around the car, Gary's eyes went to the front of the boy's shirt. "William, are you okay? The blood."

William lifted his shirt and showed Gary the scar. The blood was still there, the deep red a stark contrast to the boy's pale skin. "I'm fine, Gary. There's nothing to worry about."

"Did Harold do that?"

William nodded. "Yes."

Over at the house, the truck's wheels were still going around. Having torn up the grass, they now dug deep ruts in the soil. The rear of the truck fishtailed slowly back and forth in the ruts.

Gary pointed the gun at the pickup. "Who is that woman?"

"I don't know," Marny said. "Said her name was Cheyenne. I think she was working with Harold."

"Where did she pick you up?"

Marny turned his head north. The mountains on the horizon looked small and insignificant from this distance. So removed from the violence that had taken place there just hours ago. "Back there. Harold took us to the mountains and"—he glanced at William—"shot us. He took Esther."

Marny expected Gary to question the shooting part, but he acted as though being shot and healed was all part of a normal day. Nothing out of the ordinary there.

"She didn't say where she was from or how she found you?" Gary's voice was rising in tempo and volume.

Marny shook his head. "No. We assumed she was just passing through and felt like being nice."

Gary stared at the truck for a long time, then at the mountains north of them. "There was nothing nice about her."

"Yeah, no fake," Marny said. "She was about to shoot us. Who is she?"

The way Gary's mouth dipped at the corners said he didn't know. "One way to find out."

He turned and headed for the truck. Marny and William followed.

At the pickup, Gary opened the door. Cheyenne fell out and landed on the ground. A deep gash above her eyebrow leaked bright red blood, and a gunshot had ripped the base of her neck. Gary reached over the steering wheel and deflated air bag and shut off the engine. The wheels slowed and eventually stopped. He knelt beside the woman and felt for a pulse, then slapped her cheek. There was no response. Gary slapped her again, harder. Cheyenne moaned a little and her eyes fluttered. Gary grabbed a handful of her hair and lifted her head off the ground.

"Who sent you?"

Cheyenne spasmed, gasped for air, fluttered her eyes again. Her mouth opened and closed like a fish on dry land looking for water.

Gary leaned in close. "Who are you? Who sent you?"

But she was too far gone, had lost too much blood. Her life was rapidly pouring out of those head and neck wounds.

Gary released Cheyenne's head and let it fall to the ground. He placed his hand on the woman's cheek and whispered something

Marny couldn't understand. He appeared to be a priest bowing over a dying parishioner, administering her last rites. Then, loudly enough for Marny to hear, Gary said, "Those who oppose the Lord's anointed shall be judged with hellfire forever and ever. The choices you have made in this life will follow you into the next, and your judgment will be harsh." His voice softened. "May God have mercy on your soul."

In one quick motion, before Marny could register what was happening, Gary lifted the handgun, placed it against the woman's right eye, and pulled the trigger. The concussion of the gun nearly knocked Marny off his feet. William grabbed his hand and squeezed.

Gary placed his hand on Cheyenne's chest, whispered something again, then stood. "We need to get out of here." There were tears in his eyes.

Marny tried to speak, tried to ask where they were going, why he had shot the woman, what the prayers were for, but his throat wasn't working.

As if he read Marny's mind, William asked, "Where are we going, Gary?"

"Back to Comfort." He looked at his watch. "We should be able to make it by late afternoon."

"Why?"

"Your chest, William," Gary said. "He tried to kill you. Sooner or later he'll find out he didn't succeed, and he'll keep trying until he does. You're a witness now, and he needs you out of the way."

William acted as if Gary's statement was old news, nothing surprising, as if being targeted by a psycho ex-cop was just part of a normal day. "I'll need a new shirt," William said. "And some water."

Gary nodded toward the house. "Five minutes. Go wash up. We'll stop somewhere on the way and get you a shirt."

Marny glanced at the gun in Gary's hand, then squared his shoulders. "Why does Harold want William dead?"

"Five minutes," Gary said.

174

William took Marny's hand. "Let's go wash up, Marnin."

In the house, Marny faced William. "What's this all about, William? Why does Harold want Esther, and why did he try to kill us?"

"Maybe just because he doesn't like me. I don't know." William's eyes said he was telling the truth. He might be a wonder boy, but he wasn't omniscient.

"Does Gary know?"

William's eyes shifted back and forth, studying Marny's, as if in them the boy had found a secret long held and never revealed, a secret that would explain the curse, the deaths, the storm clouds that had followed him since birth. "I don't think so."

William headed for the kitchen and stripped off his shirt. Marny ran the water and put his head under the faucet. After drying off, he went to Harold's room, dug through the dresser drawers, found a clean T-shirt for himself and one for William. He returned to the kitchen and tossed the shirt to the boy.

"Here. This will do until we can get you something that fits."

William slipped the shirt over his head. It was an extra large and hung nearly to his knees.

"We could call the police now, you know. Get out of this whole mess."

William shook his head. "Gary won't let that happen, Marnin. We have to go with him."

"What will we find in Comfort?"

Without hesitation William said, "More death."

Chapter 43

Memories can be terrible things to deal with.

Esther walked through the house room by room letting the recollections come one by one. At first she'd resisted, not wanting to relive the good or the bad. Both were painful, in different ways of course, but equally so. Eventually, though, she grew tired of fighting and let the images and sounds return like ships that had sailed so long ago and were just now returning, some bringing loved ones missed but not forgotten, some loaded down with boxes containing the remains of those who did not survive the journey.

In the living room she stopped. Most of the furniture was still exactly as they had left it all those years ago. A film of dust covered everything, but once she looked past that, she was swept back to more than a decade ago, before William came on the scene. There was giggling and joy, nights spent playing games and watching movies. The smell of popcorn was in the air. Harold was her daddy then, a kind man who loved to laugh and doted on Esther's mother.

Pushing back tears, Esther left the living room and walked upstairs to the bedrooms. Funny, she still remembered which steps creaked and which ones didn't, as if she'd never left the place, as if the past decade were a mere handful of minutes and she was a child again. At the top of the steps, off the hallway, were four doors, three bedrooms and a bathroom. The door to her room was closed. Her mind told her not to open it, but her heart begged to relive better days.

She opened the door, and the flood of tears that followed took her by surprise. She walked to the center of the floor and sat on the braided rug. It was here that she used to bring William when he was just a baby and lay him on his back on a blanket and play with him, speak baby talk to him. She loved to make him smile. The thought of William was too much for her, and, rolling to her side, she broke down in sobs.

The sound of a ringing phone reached her from the first floor. She sat up and wiped her eyes. It rang again. Why would Harold have phone service here? Did he still use this house for something? Esther ran her sleeve across her face, mopped up the tears on her cheeks. After another ring Harold answered. He was in a distant part of the house, probably the kitchen, and she had difficulty hearing what was said. She didn't want to move for fear she would make a sound and alert him of her eavesdropping.

"She's here," Harold said. "I have her."

There was a pause, then she heard "at the house" and "we'll be ready."

A chill slid down her back like a sliver of ice. There was something about Harold that scared her. Yes, he was a jerk for abandoning her when she loved him so much. Yes, he was a murderer. But there was something even more than that, a darkness that she now knew had driven him to do those things, to commit those crimes. She could see the devil in his eyes, prompting him, controlling him, and it scared her. With that kind of blackness in his heart there was no telling what he was capable of.

She had no idea what that phone call was about, but it didn't sound like Harold was inviting old friends over for a welcome home party. She needed to take action. She knew that fleeing the house and trying to outrun a man bigger, stronger, and fitter than she was a lousy option, but it was the only one she had. She'd rather run and take her chances in the thick Maine forest, among the trees and rolling terrain, than stay and face whatever it was

Harold had in store for her. At least there she had the *possibility* of escape. And if he caught her, she'd kick and scream and fight to the death.

Esther scrambled to her feet, fled the room and down the stairs, trying to make as little noise as she could. Her only advantage would be the element of surprise. Apparently he didn't expect her to run, or he would have been keeping a closer watch.

Skipping the last two steps, Esther bolted for the storm door, pushed it open, and found herself on the porch. The door slipped from her hand, and the pneumatic closer pulled it shut faster than it should have. The door slammed. Esther didn't wait to see if Harold was on her trail; she jumped from the porch and made a dash for the back of the house. The forest was there, a forest she knew well from her childhood, and if her memory of the land was as good as her memory of the house, she might just have a chance at losing him.

It wasn't until she was fully behind the house that she heard the front storm door slam shut again.

"Esther." His voice seemed to surround her, coming from every direction at once. "Come back, Esther. It's no use to run. You know I'll catch you."

Esther fled his voice but could not flee the memory that it stirred. They used to play hide-and-seek in the backyard. Esther was always the hider, Harold the seeker. She found some wicked good places to hide too, and more than once thought she'd finally outsmarted her old dad before his voice would catch up to her.

Come out, come out, Squirt. It's no use to hide. You know I'll find you.

She did know, and despite the fact that he was her daddy, her playmate, a fear would grow in her, a fear of being found, a fear of her father.

That fear was back again, a thousand times stronger, and it pushed her beyond the line where yard met forest and into the safety of the evergreens that greeted her with open arms.

Chapter 44

WHILE WILLIAM CHANGED and Gary went to work disposing of Cheyenne's body in the barn, Marny took a quick tour of Harold's place.

To any stranger visiting it would appear to be a rather normal home, not the dwelling of a cold-blooded murderer. The furniture was new and polished, the rugs vacuumed. In the bathroom there were no mildew stains or odd smells. There were three bedrooms on the first floor. One was Harold's—nothing special, just a bed, dresser, nightstand, and plasma TV on the wall; one was an office; and the other was an exercise room furnished with a universal gym, a treadmill, and a stair-stepper. No wonder Harold showed no signs of fatigue after climbing the trail to the top of the mountain.

There was something odd about the house, though, something missing. There was no warmth to it, nothing that made it a home, that connected Harold to anyone or any place. It was as though he'd moved into a show home and done nothing to make it his own.

In the office Marny walked over to the desk and found a stack of unpaid bills. Most were addressed to Harold J. Rose, but two on the bottom of the pile were addressed to Julia C. Powers. Cheyenne? If so, she was with Harold, his live-in. That explained how she came across them by the side of the road. Maybe Harold had called and asked her to hike up the mountain and dispose of the bodies.

Next to the bills was a pile of old newspaper clippings. He picked one up, read it, and was not prepared for the prickles that crept over his skin. He picked up another, then another. With each one the prickling deepened and spread. They were all about the Maniac.

Marny remembered the murders well. He was a teenager at the time. The papers divulged some of the details, that the victims were all young, teens and twenties, and that the bodies were drained of blood and dumped by the side of the road. All the victims had one thing in common: their blood was type O. At the time the police thought they were related to some local cult. Maine, with its deep wilderness and remote areas, was no stranger to such doings. The serenity and seclusion of the endless forests attracted people from all walks of life. And if Marny remembered correctly, the police also thought at one time that the Maniac could not have operated alone. Unless he was a phantom, it would have been logistically impossible. Nevertheless, it was a killing spree such as Maine had never seen before.

And ground zero for the Maniac's activity was the tiny town of Comfort, Maine. Eleven of the murders took place within the town limits. Quite a jolt for a town of only a couple thousand.

Coming out of the office with the clippings in hand, Marny found William standing in the living room, looking out the window.

"Do you know about this?" Marny asked, showing William the news articles.

William's eyes ran over the headlines, showing no sense of recognition or emotion. "I was a baby, Marnin."

"But do you know anything about it? Is this why we're going back to Comfort?"

William went back to watching the outside world. "Harold took Esther to Comfort."

"William, look at me."

William turned his head and met Marny's eyes.

"What do you know about these articles, about the Maniac? You said in Comfort there would be more death."

"Esther told me about Harold, that he was a policeman on the case."

"And what about the 'more death' part? Was Gary involved in these killings? Is he the Maniac?"

William looked outside again. "I think Gary wants to kill Harold."

"Why?"

"Because Harold wants to kill me, Marnin."

"Why?"

"I don't know. Maybe just because he hates me. He thinks I ruined his life. And he's afraid of me."

"But he thinks he did kill you. Let's just get out of here and never go back to Maine again." It sounded like a good plan on the surface, but hearing himself say it aloud put a rock in the pit of Marny's stomach. Esther was in Maine, at least both William and Gary believed so. He couldn't leave her with Harold. She might be Harold's daughter, but Marny now knew what he was capable of, and this new Harold didn't seem like the type to let family bonds stop him from more violence.

William shook his head. "He knows we're alive."

"How?"

"Cheyenne told him, Marnin. Didn't you notice she was on the phone when she pulled the truck over to pick us up? I think she was talking to Harold."

"You don't know that."

"I think so. Do you remember what she said when she pointed the gun at us?"

Marny thought back, tried to replay the scenario in his mind. So much had happened in such a short period of time. The shooting, the resurrection or whatever it was, the hike down the mountain, Cheyenne picking them up, then everything with Gary. His mind garbled the images and words and nothing made sense to him anymore. William's ability to recall and his attention to detail impressed Marny. "No. Help me out."

"She said there was no use running, that we wouldn't get far now."

Marny remembered. William was right, of course. Cheyenne must have called Harold and told him the murderous plot hadn't succeeded.

Outside, Gary emerged from the barn and headed for the house.

"We better go," William said.

Moments later Gary's heavy footsteps crossed the kitchen floor, and he appeared in the archway between the kitchen and living room.

William faced him. "We're going to Comfort, aren't we, Gary?"

Gary's eyes flitted between William and Marny. "Yes."

"You're going to kill Harold, aren't you, Gary?"

Again the nervous eyes. "Yes."

"And then you'll kill Esther and Marnin?"

Gary's eyes met Marny's, and in them Marny found something wild and foreign, a distant quality that spoke of hunger and hurt. He knew the answer before Gary had time to voice it.

"Time to go." Gary turned and exited the house.

Chapter 45

ESTHER WAS WELL into the forest, concealed by low-hanging boughs of pine, by the time she heard Harold hit the tree line.

She didn't stop, though, no way. She wanted to put as much distance between herself and her murderous father as possible.

Not looking back even once, she ran until her legs could carry her no longer, then collapsed by a fallen tree. The trunk was covered with moss and surrounded by jack-in-the-pulpits and fern. Stilling her labored breathing, she listened but heard nothing.

Her lungs burned and her diaphragm worked overtime to pull oxygen in and replenish her starving cells. Sweat matted hair to the back of her neck. Her feet ached.

She listened again. This time she heard the faint sound of footsteps. Pine needles softened the forest floor, so no leaves crunched to signify how close Harold was. He could be thirty yards away or thirty feet.

Slowly, inch by inch, Esther raised her head over the bulk of the fallen tree and looked in the direction of the footsteps. Harold was there, a good forty yards away. She couldn't see his face through the pines but caught glimpses of his body from the waist down. He walked carefully, pausing briefly between steps to listen. He was trained in hunting fugitives; she had no training in how to run like a criminal. Whatever advantage she had or thought she had was gone.

As Harold grew closer, Esther's heart beat faster and harder, so hard in fact that she was certain Harold would hear it. He was now thirty yards off and gaining ground by the second.

She was trapped. If she made a run for it, he would see her and catch her for sure. If she stayed put, he would eventually stumble upon her, for he was headed in her direction. She needed a diversion, something to throw him off her trail.

She wished William were here; she could use some of the faith that came so naturally for him. Instead, Esther did the one thing that came naturally for her. She prayed. She knew she was asking for a miracle, the kind of thing that folks rolled their eyes at when it happened in a movie. She was asking for an easy out.

But Harold was now twenty yards away, and the easy out wasn't there yet. Panic overcame her, and she almost threw herself up and surrendered. She no longer trusted herself to peek over the trunk, so she sat as still as she could and listened to Harold's footfalls grow closer and louder.

He stopped. She didn't know if he'd heard something or had seen her, but his progress halted. For a long time, minutes that felt like hours, he didn't move. Had he heard the sound of her breathing? Or her heart clomping in her chest? Was he waiting her out, letting her make the first move?

Esther's legs began to cramp. She didn't know how much longer she could remain motionless. Something had to give.

Finally Harold moved, one step, then another, but he moved away from Esther, to his right. It was a trick, she was sure of it. He'd either seen or heard her and was now baiting her, luring her out into the open. But as his footsteps faded she grew more confident that it was safe to peer over the trunk again.

Harold was nowhere in sight. Her prayer had been answered. But this was still no easy way out. She had to go for help.

She could backtrack and return to the road then follow it into the town of Comfort and find a policeman. But what would she tell them? That her father, Harold Rose, *the* Harold Rose they all knew and admired, was trying to kill her? No way. They'd call him, and then she'd be handed over to the man who was trying to kill her.

Which led to another thought. How did she know he wanted to kill her? Yes, he'd shot William and Marny. He'd proven he was capable of murder, but that didn't mean he wanted to murder *her*. That phone call could have been anything.

Doubts wrestled in her gut, causing her to waste precious time. She needed to be running, opening the space between her and her father.

So she ran. She pushed through the pines and jumped fallen limbs and whole trunks. Ahead, over the ridge in the distance, was a pond, and beyond the pond was a house. The Karstens lived there. She used to go to school with their daughter, Susan. They would remember her and help her.

Stealing a glance over her shoulder she saw nothing but pines, both standing and fallen. No Harold. She wondered how long it would be until he caught up with her. After all, she knew sooner or later he would.

Come out, come out, Squirt. It's no use to hide. You know I'll find you.

Chapter 46

IN THE TOWN of Pickering, Massachusetts, midway between Harold's house and the Maine border, Gary slowed the car and Marny saw a shimmer of hope.

The town was not much more than a couple of faded-asphalt streets, a hardware store, a fast-food joint, and one strip mall that looked like it hadn't been touched since the sixties. It was here that Gary wheeled the Taurus in front of a Goodwill store. He turned to Marny and William in the backseat.

"We'll find William a shirt that fits here." He paused and glared at both of them, a silent warning. "No funny stuff. Don't talk to anyone. Five minutes and we're out."

They got out of the car, and Marny suddenly had the urge to run, to grab William and get away from Gary once and for all. Pickering was a small town, but there were homes and businesses. Surely they had some form of a police force. Somebody would help them. But it wouldn't be once and for all, would it? His curse had finally fully matured and was a mammoth of a beast standing right in front of him. There was no way around it or through it. If they ran, it would pursue them like a hound on the scent of fresh blood.

In the store William headed straight for the back where the children's clothes were. The T-shirt rack was in the center, in easy view of the front door and the Taurus parked outside. Gary hung by the door, keeping an eye on them.

Again Marny thought about escape. They could slip out the back and put good distance between themselves and Gary by the time he crossed the length of the store and found his way out the back exit.

William turned his back to the front of the store and busied himself with fingering through T-shirts. "We can't run, Marnin. He'll catch us." He kept his voice low, barely above a whisper.

Marny feigned interest in a particular shirt, pulled it off the rack and held it up. "How do you know?"

"He won't stop until he does."

William pulled a shirt from the rack, a blue one with the Miami Dolphins logo on the front.

Marny threw a casual glance Gary's way. The big man was still by the door, hands in his pockets, watching them. Turning back to the shirt rack, Marny said, "William, I'm lost here. What's going on? Why does Gary want you so bad?"

"Gary thinks God has chosen him to protect me. He thinks I'm special. He won't let himself fail; he'll do anything, even kill people, to make sure he doesn't. We can't get away from him, Marnin."

As much as it made no common sense in the real world, in a perverted, twisted way—in Gary's world—*that* made complete sense. It explained Gary's obsession with William, his relentless pursuit, his protective compulsion, his cold willingness to kill. He was crazy, nuts.

"William," Marny said, "can't you do something? Use your gift to get away from him?"

William was quiet. He held up the Dolphins shirt and sized it against his torso. It was a perfect fit and the color looked good on him. At three dollars it was a steal. "It doesn't work like that."

"Yeah, I've heard that before. Why?"

William turned up his face, and his eyes had never looked more sincere. "Because that would be selfish." He said it like it was the most obvious answer in the world and why hadn't Marny figured that out on his own.

"Well, I'm not going to sit around and wait for him to kill me. Listen to me; we'll play along for now, but when we get to Comfort, we're gone."

"What do you have in mind, Marnin?" William's eyes were now wide, expectant.

What did he have in mind? Last night on the island (was it really just last night?) Esther had asked him what his plan was. He didn't have a plan. He told her he wasn't the planning type. And still he had no plan.

"Nothing yet." There was no use lying to William; he'd see right through it anyway.

William held up the shirt. "I want this one."

"Miami, huh?"

"Yes. I like dolphins."

"Okay then, the dolphin shirt it is."

They paid for the shirt and joined Gary at the entrance. Together they left, Gary in front. A police cruiser was parked a few stores down, and the officer stood on the sidewalk talking to someone, jotting notes on his steno pad. Marny stopped and took hold of William's arm. If he ran for the cop, made enough noise and commotion, Gary would be forced to flee. He wouldn't want a confrontation here in public view.

Marny glanced at the officer, glanced at Gary. Gary's eyes were wide and fiery, his mouth a thin line. He'd seen the cop too and read Marny's intent.

Marny tightened his grip on William's arm and took off toward the cop, hollering and waving his free arm. "Help! Help us!"

The officer dropped his steno pad, turned, and reached for his weapon. The woman he was talking to backed away, stumbled over her bags.

Marny, dragging William along, continued to holler and wave his arm.

What happened next seemed to play out in slow motion. The

cop's eyes went from Marny to something over Marny's left shoulder. Before he could draw his weapon, a shot fired; the cop folded in on himself and was pushed back by some unseen hand. Another shot sounded, and a spray of blood burst from the man's head. Marny stopped and covered his head with his free arm, pulled William close to him, and went down on the sidewalk. Another shot; the woman gasped and crumpled to the pavement.

Then Gary was there, full speed again, cursing. He walked to the cop, rifled through his utility belt, and grabbed the handgun and extra clips. After shoving them into his pocket, he groped at Marny's arm. "C'mon. Let's go. Get up."

Marny stayed down, but Gary was having none of it. He grabbed Marny by the arm and lifted him from the ground as if he were a toddler. His hand found the back of Marny's neck and squeezed. Pain shot down Marny's back.

"Get in the car now or you're next," Gary said.

Marny and William stumbled toward the car. People began to gather. In the distance someone hollered.

"Move!" Gary shouted into Marny's ear.

At the car he opened the back door and shoved Marny in, then William. Gary got in behind the wheel, threw the car into reverse, then into drive, and laid down rubber getting out of the parking lot.

When they were back on the road Gary found Marny in the rearview mirror. His face was red and sweaty. "That was stupid. Really stupid. Don't ever try to be a hero again."

Chapter 47

THE KARSTENS LIVED in a two-story log home on the fringe of nowhere.

The house sat at least a mile from the road, with its only access a dirt lane that was only passable with a four-wheel-drive vehicle. From what Esther remembered, that's the way they liked it: private. Susan was a little odd, mostly kept to herself. Esther was her only friend. As a child she'd been to their house twice, once for Susan's tenth birthday and once to say good-bye before she, William, and their mother went to live with Gary.

When the house was in view, Esther pushed ahead harder, crossing from forest to clearing without slowing even a step. The image of the home, those deep mahogany, tightly fitted logs, so orderly, so sturdy—so much like a fortress—brought a surge of relief over her, as if in this manic world where her father was a murderer and everything she knew no longer made sense, there was something of logic, something outside her plight, something oblivious to the murky waters she found herself trying to stay afloat in... something of hope.

With the exception of the house appearing a little more weathered, the property hadn't changed a bit. The same two pickups were parked in a gravel driveway. There was no landscaping to speak of, except what nature had to offer at no charge: trees and grass, a shrub here and there. A row of metal garbage cans, lids bungee-corded in place to keep the bears from rummaging, lined the rear of the concrete foundation.

When she got within thirty feet of the house, a dog started barking from inside. Seconds later Mr. Karsten appeared on the front porch, hands in his pockets. He was a large man with broad shoulders and a barrel chest. Thick graying beard. Flannel work shirt with sleeves rolled to the elbow and jeans, despite the warm weather. He was a lumberjack and looked every bit the part.

Esther stopped at the bottom of the porch steps. She was shaking, and her lungs were working double time.

Mr. Karsten eyed her, then glanced around the clearing, cocked his head to one side. "Ya lost, miss?"

Inside the house the dog kept barking, a steady yelp that could have set time for a musical piece.

"Mr. Karsten?"

Mr. Karsten squinted his eyes and nodded. "That's me."

She glanced around the clearing and had the sudden fear that Harold would burst from the woods, pistol in hand, firing away. "I need help. He's after me. Please, can I come in?"

From what Esther remembered, Mr. Karsten was not a sympathetic man; at least he'd never appeared to be. He wasn't a friendly man either, but he wasn't ignorant. He took his hands out of his pockets, ran his steady eyes over the clearing, and motioned for Esther to come up on the porch. "Well, come on then, girl. Let's get ya inside."

Inside Esther was immediately welcomed by a lanky Redbone Coonhound who couldn't keep his tongue off her. She was also greeted by Mrs. Karsten, a thick, plain woman with straight gray hair pulled back in a ponytail. She recognized Esther at once and smiled warmly. "Why, Esther Rose, dearie, what's wrong? What's the matter with ya?"

The interior of the house was cluttered with flats of canned and dry food, but it was clean. Apparently the Karstens were pack rats, but they gathered and stored with some semblance of order. They would be well prepared for the coming nuclear winter or economic depression.

The dog nudged Esther's hand, wanting her to pet him.

"Nosey, you stop that," Mrs. Karsten scolded.

"He's after me. He's coming. You have to help me."

Mrs. Karsten smoothed Esther's hair from her face, a motherly, endearing gesture. "Who, dear? Who's after ya?"

"Do you remember my father, Harold Rose?"

"O' course I do," Mr. Karsten said. "The state troopah."

"Did you know he left us and moved to Massachusetts?"

Mr. Karsten nodded. "We heard that. Right around the time a' the killin's."

The killings. The Maniac, the serial killer. Esther remembered hearing about him. Harold had been on that case. She recalled her mother talking about how much the case was stressing him out, wearing on his nerves, and that's why he was acting the way he was.

Esther swallowed hard and fought back the tears. "Do you remember my brother, William? He would have been just a baby when my father left us."

Mrs. Karsten stepped forward. "I talked to your mother once about him. He was…handicapped, right?"

"Yes. Cerebral palsy." She paused, caught her breath, glanced out the window, but there was no Harold. She knew of no other way to say it other than straight out. "William's dead. Murdered."

Mrs. Karsten's hands went to her mouth. "Lord!"

Mr. Karsten clenched his fists. "How? How did it happen?"

Esther looked him right in the eyes. She hoped that by seeing the clarity in her own, the honesty, the goodness, he would believe her. "My father killed him."

Neither of the Karstens said anything for a long moment. Nosey nudged Esther's hand with his nose and whined.

Finally Mrs. Karsten said, "Your father, he was a police officer, a nice man from what I remember."

"Did you see him do it?" Mr. Karsten said.

Esther nodded. A few stray tears slipped past her eyes and tracked down her cheek. Her hands trembled.

Mrs. Karsten walked over and stood next to her husband, put a hand on his shoulder. "Dearie, do ya know what you're sayin'?"

"Yes. I know exactly what I'm saying. And now he's after me. He's going to kill me next." The words poured out now, like water over a dam flooding the plain below. Either they would believe her and offer help, or they'd think her crazy and call the police. This was her last hope.

"He kidnapped me and brought me back here, to our old house. I got away. This was the only place I could think of to go. Please, you have to help me. Please."

Again they were both quiet. Mrs. Karsten's hand tightened on her husband's shoulder. "Dearie," she said, "do ya know what you're accusin' your father of?"

"O' course she does," Mr. Karsten said. He looked out the window, then at his hands. "I believe her. I never did like that man. Somethin' 'bout him didn't sit right with me from the first time I met him. And when he left durin' those killin's…that was the stuff of a coward." He met Esther's eyes. "I believe ya."

Nosey's ears perked, and he cocked his head to the side and stood motionless as a marble statue.

"What's the mattah, boy?" Mr. Karsten said.

At once Nosey ran for the window, his gait more of a glide, and erupted into a fit of barks.

Chapter 48

THEY RODE IN silence for a half hour.

In the back of the Taurus William had worked his hand across the seat and found Marny's. He held on tight as if the window would suddenly open and Marny would be sucked out. Gary kept glancing in the rearview mirror at Marny, shooting him looks that wielded daggers and clubs and poison-tipped arrows.

And Marny remained motionless, still stunned from the barrage of violence Gary had rained down on the small town of Pickering, Massachusetts.

It was Marny's fault. His curse was in a feeding frenzy now, like a ravenous wolf that had gotten the taste of blood and wanted—*needed*—more. Sooner or later it would satisfy its lust, but how many would be left dead in its horrid wake? Marny wished it would turn on him and just be done with it.

The image of blood spraying from the cop's head, his eyes wide with surprise, mouth open, kept tramping through Marny's mind, as did the way the woman slouched to the ground, almost in slow motion, that red stain spreading on her chest. And each time, the images dumped a little more guilt on him. If he'd just done what Gary said, if he'd just gotten into the car and let Gary drive away, if he'd stopped trying to be the hero Esther thought he was, that cop would be going home to his family tonight. His children would run to him, their arms open. His wife would give him a hug and a kiss and ask him how his day was, and he would say that it was uneventful as usual. A few traffic citations, a suspected shoplifting incident. Nothing more. He would eat dinner with them and tuck his kids into bed.

Instead, because of Marny, his wife would get the phone call no officer's wife wanted to receive. She'd be making funeral plans.

And the woman, she was most likely a wife, a mother. Mommy would not come home this evening; there'd be no dinner on the table, no good-night kisses.

Because of Marny.

As if he could read Marny's mind, or maybe only read the anguish on his face, William squeezed Marny's hand tighter.

The car slowed and pulled to the shoulder of the road. They'd gotten off the main route a few minutes back, and this secondary road was forested and appeared deserted. Gary shifted the car into park and shut off the engine. His eyes found Marny in the rear-view mirror.

Marny's heart thudded in his chest, and his hand closed around William's.

Gary tossed the keys onto the passenger seat and opened the door. He got out of the car and walked around to Marny's side. Marny looked up and down the road. Not a house in sight, not even another car.

Gary stood by Marny's door, both arms hanging casually at his sides. Behind him, across the road, the deep forest seemed to creep closer and box the car in. There was no escaping. For a moment Marny thought the bigger man was going to put his hand through the window and strangle him right there in the backseat. Instead he opened the door, snatched a handful of Marny's shirt, and yanked him out of the car.

"Get out here," he said. His voice was strained and raspy, laced with hate.

Gary was a big, thick man. His forearms were the size of Marny's thighs. Marny was no match for him one on one. Gary turned Marny around and grabbed his shirt in the back, between the shoulder blades, so he could control him like a dog on a leash. He pushed Marny forward, toward the woods. "Walk."

Marny stumbled and tripped over his own feet, but he was able to remain upright as they tramped through underbrush and a carpet of fallen leaves. About thirty feet into the woods, with the road now barely visible, Gary pushed Marny against the rough bark of a tree, face first. Gary's hand found Marny's neck and tightened. He had such strength that Marny knew if the man wanted to, he could squeeze the life out of him right there. Swift and easy. Instead, something hard nudged his head.

The pistol.

Gary's mouth was next to his ear. "I've had enough of you."

Rage is a dangerous yet liberating thing.

Gary held the gun to the punk's head and pressed the barrel against his skull.

Off its leash, rage could be devastating, could destroy one's soul in a matter of seconds. It was a monster on a rampage, acting without thought, fueled by instinct and desire and hunger. But tethered by self-control, rage freed the emotions, was a vent for the deepest seated frustrations and annoyances of a man. It was anger given permission to act without pause, but only within the confines of set moral boundaries.

What Gary experienced was the monster brand of rage, unleashed and unharnessed. He was out of control, and it scared him.

He wanted to shoot the punk, put a bullet in his head, not only because he was a threat to the safety and security of William, but because Gary genuinely did not like him. He hated him, in fact. The punk had forced Gary's hand, pushed him into killing the cop and a woman.

Gary pressed the side of the punk's head against the tree. His face was turned toward Gary, and there was fear in his eyes. No, more than fear—there was terror. This is what it looked like when someone saw their life flash before their eyes, when they saw the end of all things upon them and they were about to enter into eternity unprepared.

Normally, the thought would have sickened Gary. He didn't relish taking lives; he did it only because it was the only way to protect William. Normally. But what Gary felt here, the rage that had unhinged his moral restraint, was anything but normal. He could feel his pulse through his palm and all the way into his trigger finger. He imagined pulling that trigger, feeling the gun jump in his hand, feeling the relief that comes with venting rage, with satisfying an unbearable itch. He wanted to do it.

He *would* do it.

He leaned in toward the punk's ear and whispered, "May God show no mercy on your soul. I now usher you into the endless corridors of eternity."

But before he could squeeze off a round and quench his hunger, a voice stopped him.

"Don't do it, Gary. You can't."

Gary turned and found William by his side. The boy was like an angel. The very sight of him held such power over Gary. He was Gary's purpose for being, his reason for existence.

"Why?" Gary asked. "Tell me why."

"Because I need him."

Gary shook his head. The boy didn't need him. He needed Gary and only Gary. *He* was the boy's protector, his shepherd. The good shepherd. "No, you don't. You don't need anyone except me."

"I need Esther too, Gary. You know that."

No, he thought he needed them, but he didn't. Gary knew what was best for William, what he needed and didn't need.

"You don't need anybody but me."

Gary repositioned his hand on the punk's neck and pushed his head against the tree again. He was ready to do it, despite what William said. He didn't need this punk. Not at all.

But what stopped him this time was not William's voice but his touch. The boy rested his hand on Gary's side, just above his hip. "Gary. Please, I need him. He has to help us get to Esther."

Right now Gary didn't care about Esther. Harold could have her. For that matter, he didn't care about Harold either. Sooner or later their confrontation would come, but it could be later. This was the first time William had ever intentionally touched him, the first time he'd voluntarily made contact. It was a breakthrough Gary had never imagined. He looked down at William's hand. He'd touched him with his withered one, his special one.

Heat like warm water spread out from William's hand and radiated through Gary's body. His entire body relaxed as if soothed by the trained hands of an accomplished masseuse. The gun suddenly felt like it was cast from the densest iron, and he almost dropped it.

William's eyes were relaxed and calm; he showed no emotion. "He can't die, Gary. Please."

But Gary no longer thought about the punk and whether to kill him or spare his insignificant life. He thought about William and his withered hand and the touch of the anointed one. He wanted more of this; he *needed* more of this. It was like a drug that hooked its user on the very first dance.

William pulled his hand away, and immediately the warmth dissipated.

Gary did drop the gun this time and reached for William's hand. "No. Don't let go." He was frantic, desperate to restore the touch, the feeling. The drug had a hold on him already, and within seconds he had suffered withdrawal. He groped at the air for the boy's hand.

William yanked his hand away and stepped back. He tripped over a branch and landed hard on his butt.

Gary realized then what he had done. He'd gone too far. He'd let down his guard and crossed the line. He'd given in to his emotions and offended the anointed. Grief washed over him like a wave of nails, pricking at his flesh and leaving open, raw wounds. He fell to his knees before William and rocked back and forth.

"I'm sorry. I'm sorry. What have I done?"

William climbed to his feet and brushed off his pants. The dolphin on his shirt was twisted to one side.

Gary reached for the boy, then pulled his hands back. "Are you okay? I'm sorry."

"I'm fine, Gary. We should probably get back on the road, though."

Gary retrieved the gun, stuck it in his waistband. He stood and faced William. Shame overtook him. The shame he felt so long ago. But there was no condemnation in William's eyes.

"Yes. We will," Gary said. He stole a glance at the punk, who was still hugging the tree.

William walked over and touched the punk's back. "It's okay now, Marnin. We need to get to Maine. There's not much time left."

They trudged back through the woods, Gary first, then William, then Marny. At the car Gary waited until the punk and William were in the backseat, then got in behind the wheel. He said nothing to either of them. He'd been shamed because of his failure. But with every shaming came an opportunity to regain honor.

And he would regain his very soon. But for now, he needed to move. After what happened back there in the town, the cops would be on his trail soon enough.

Chapter 49

THERE ARE TIMES for talking, and there are times for running. Mr. Karsten appeared to move faster than his size would allow. At the window he peered around the frame, then cursed. He turned to his wife.

"Lydia, show Esther the cellah." Then he turned to Esther. "You stay quiet down there, and I'll handle this."

Mrs. Karsten led Esther out of the living room and into the kitchen, where she opened a door that led to a wooden staircase to the cellar. The walls on either side were covered with pegboard, and on pegs hung a broom and dust pan, extension cords, hand tools of all kinds, and some iron skillets. Mrs. Karsten hit the light switch on the wall, and a hanging bulb illuminated at the bottom of the steps.

"When ya get down there, the switch for the rest a' the cellar will be on the wall on the right." She put her hand on Esther's back and rubbed. "It'll be okay. Ya just stay quiet and let my Chris handle it. Okay?"

Nosey was there too, looking up at her with thoughtful eyes. He blinked once, chuffed, then went back to the window and resumed his barking.

Esther nodded. Fear had so clutched her in its grip that she could not speak. Her hands and feet felt numb and heavy. Her throat had swollen shut so she could not even swallow.

Down the steps she went, into the bowels of the house. Mrs. Karsten closed the door behind her, and Esther heard it lock. She didn't like the sound of that. She didn't know the Karstens except what she remembered from her childhood friendship with their daughter. For all she knew they were the ones Harold had received the phone call from back at the house, the ones he was later meeting. This could all be a trap.

But she had nowhere else to turn. And besides, she was here now, nothing she could do about that.

At the bottom of the stairs she found the light switch on the wall and flipped it. Three fluorescent tubes stuttered to life and lit the entire cellar area. It was cluttered but, like the first floor, not unclean. Everything seemed to have its place. There was a fishing boat supported on cinder blocks, stacks of plastic containers lining one wall, an extensive workbench and tool collection lining another. Over to the left, around the staircase, were the furnace and water heater, and farther back the washer and dryer.

To Esther's left she found what she was looking for: a way out. Two doors, French style, opened to the outside.

Above her, on the first floor, a knock sounded on the front door, and Chris Karsten's heavy footsteps pounded across the wood flooring and shook the crossbeams.

Esther moved quickly to the double doors. She checked the lock and disengaged it. She would wait, see how things went upstairs.

Nosey barked continuously until Mr. Karsten shouted, "Lydia, keep that dog quiet."

The front door opened. Esther could hear clearly what was said.

"Sorry to bother you folks. I'm Harold Rose. I used to live down the road a bit and recently moved back into the area. My daughter, Esther, has gone missing, and I was wondering if you'd seen her. Early twenties, brown hair, slight build."

"Nope. Haven't seen no one 'round here." Mr. Karsten's voice did not sound relaxed.

"I see. Maybe you don't understand... she's ill, mentally. She has delusions, paranoia, bouts of psychosis, manic depression, you name it. She's not well at all and has a tendency to wander."

"Maybe *you* don't understand. I said we haven't seen no one 'round here. No one."

There was a pause in the conversation. Esther's mind swam in circles. She wanted to open the door and make a run for it while Mr. Karsten had Harold preoccupied. But then she'd be right back where she was, on the run in the woods with nowhere to go. And if Mr. Karsten succeeded in getting rid of Harold, then her father would still be back on her trail. She decided to wait and see what the outcome of the confrontation brewing upstairs would be.

Harold cleared his throat. When he spoke he sounded different, authoritative. He used his cop voice. "I know she's here. I don't know what she told you, but you can't believe her. She's ill. She comes up with crazy ideas. Now I'd like my daughter back."

"Mister, are ya deaf? I said there ain't no one here. Now I'll ask ya to leave."

"I was hoping we could avoid this."

Feet shuffled quickly.

"Lydia!" Mr. Karsten's voice came out high-pitched and strained.

Mrs. Karsten screamed. Nosey began his barking again.

Then there was a series of grunts and thuds and curses. The two men were wrestling, fighting. Glass broke. Wood splintered. More thuds and curses. And through it all Mrs. Karsten screamed and Nosey barked.

A gunshot erupted and seemed to shake the entire house.

Mrs. Karsten cried out like a woman in labor.

"Where is she?" Harold sounded out of breath.

More screaming from Mrs. Karsten.

Another gunshot sounded, like a crack of close thunder, and the screaming ceased. Esther jumped, and above her something hard hit the floor.

Esther fumbled with the doorknob, turned it the wrong way.

Nosey snarled, and the click of nails moved across the floor. A sharp yelp, followed by a third gunshot, then nothing.

Finally Esther got the door open, slipped through it, and ran for the forest. Halfway across the clearing she looked over her shoulder, back at the house.

Harold was at the window, watching her.

Chapter 50

For the second time that day Esther hit the tree line running. And for the second time the trees welcomed her freely. They did not judge, did not reject, did not wish violence and destruction upon her. But behind her the man who did was on her trail once again.

Without looking back, Esther pushed through the forest, deeper and deeper until she no longer knew where she was. She dared not stop, dared not even pause to catch her breath. She had been given a head start and needed to use every second of it.

She came upon a slope, a sharp decline in the topography of the forest. At the bottom was a creek, not five feet wide. Down she plunged, her legs trying desperately to keep up with the pull gravity had on her body, her hands dancing from sapling to sapling, keeping her on course. The ground rose quickly to meet her, and at the bottom she nearly stumbled but caught herself on a thickly barked white pine. A quick glance over her shoulder revealed what she had hoped to see: no Harold.

Here she paused for a few seconds to catch her runaway breath and ease the burning in her chest. Her legs throbbed with lactic acid and begged for rest. But she had to keep moving. Harold's voice from the past rang in her ears.

It's no use to hide. You know I'll find you.

For a brief moment she again entertained the thought of giving up, letting Harold take her. After all, he was her father. Surely he didn't have thoughts of murder concerning her. But he'd so easily taken four lives already, five counting poor Nosey. What would one more be to him?

Deciding Harold's intentions were not honest or fatherly, Esther once again made her legs move, *willed* them to move. She had to keep running, keep gaining ground, until...until what? When would she be safe? How much distance was enough distance?

In an instant, all her questions were answered.

"Esther!"

There would never be enough distance.

Harold's voice tore through the stillness of the forest, a harpoon lancing her through the heart and dragging her back toward that ship of despair and desolation.

Esther turned her head, caught a glimpse of her father on the ridge, a hulking, evil figure, and promptly tripped over a decaying stump. She went down hard, but the bed of pine needles cushioned her fall.

Another glance back showed that Harold was on his way down the slope, gaining ground quickly.

She scrambled to her feet and took off. Tears of panic pressed on her eyes, blurred her path. She screamed to relieve the pressure building in her chest.

A rocky outcropping sat just ahead, like some cancerous graying wart. Reaching it, she dodged behind one of the boulders and found a broken tree limb, about three feet long and as thick around as her arm. She huddled down in a nook and waited. She could run forever and never lose Harold. He'd always be there, just on her tail, and would eventually catch her anyway. Her only hope was to make a stand. She knew a stick was no match for a handgun, but if she caught him by surprise...

Trying in vain to settle her breathing, she crouched low, stick held shoulder high. Harold's footsteps came into hearing distance and slowed. She could distinguish each individual footfall, soft and even, coming closer, closer, until they were just on the other side of the boulder.

"Esther." Harold's voice was thick and gruff. "You know you can't hide forever. You know I'll find you."

Esther crouched lower, afraid he'd catch a glimpse of her head or shoulder peeking out from around the rock. He started walking again, toward where she was hidden. She had to time this perfectly.

When Harold's footsteps sounded like they were only feet away, just around the corner of the rock, Esther uncoiled her legs, trunk, and arms and came out swinging blindly. Surprisingly, the limb caught Harold across the side of the head and knocked him sideways. He stumbled and lost his footing.

Seizing the moment, Esther swung again, aiming for Harold's head but catching him along the shoulder. She had to keep swinging, keep beating him back, until she needed to fight no more. Until he was either dead or unconscious.

She swung again, this time a weak blow to the back of his head. He fell forward and rolled over.

Esther saw her opportunity, lifted the limb, and brought it down with a high-pitched grunt. But Harold was quick and blocked the blow with his left forearm. Then with his right he reached and grabbed hold of Esther's ankle. He pulled hard and brought her down. The limb slipped from her hand.

Keeping his grip on her ankle, Harold rolled toward Esther and managed to get his free hand on her wrist. In one quick, practiced motion, he twisted her arm behind her back and flipped her onto her stomach. Before she could struggle or fight back he was on top of her, his knee in her back between her shoulder blades. He wasn't even breathing hard. Esther gasped for breath, but the knee pressed so heavily she couldn't expand her chest to draw in air. Harold twisted her arm higher up her back, sending searing pain through her shoulder and down her arm. She was sure he'd rip it from its socket.

Harold adjusted himself and grunted. A second later Esther felt something sharp sting the back of her shoulder.

The last thing she remembered was feeling terribly tired.

Chapter 51

E VENING WAS ON its way, and with it, darkness.
When Gary and Marny and William arrived at Harold's
house on Cranberry Road in Comfort, Maine, the sun was on its
downward slide. Fragments of muted light filtered through the
trees like dust. The pines stood tall around the house, like giants
with outstretched arms, shielding the clearing of light and has-
tening darkness, welcoming it, bidding it come near and fellowship.

Marny got out of the car and shivered. Something about the
place frightened him. On the outside it appeared to be a rather
normal house. Two stories, a large front porch, windows, door,
that sort of thing, but there was an odd aura about it. This was
not home sweet home, not a place where laughter was heard, not
a place where families lived and loved and grew older together.
The house seemed to loom over them, to have breath of its own. It
seemed to be watching them.

William came alongside Marny and took his hand.

"You remember this place?" Marny asked.

"No." William stared at the house like it was a giant from a
fairy-tale land.

"I don't like it. Feels…weird. You feel it?"

William nodded. "We're going to need you in there, Marnin."

That was an odd comment. "Need me? How?"

"You're the key to all of this," William said. His eyes were still on the house. "They think it's me, but it's not. It's you."

Gary came around the car and climbed the steps to the porch. He stood there staring at the front door. There didn't appear to be anyone home. The windows were dark and shut. In Maine, everyone opened their windows in the evening.

"Hate to break it to you, buddy," Marny said, "but I'm nothing special. If anything, I'm a curse you should be staying away from."

William turned his head and drilled Marny with sad eyes. "You're not a curse, Marnin. You're a blessing. You just don't know it yet. But I think you will."

Gary tried the front door but found it locked. He peeked in one of the windows, cupping his hands around his eyes, then tried the door again. He took three short steps back, then two large steps forward, and kicked the door right beside the knob. The frame splintered and broke, and the door swung open.

The house seemed to exhale, and a warm, musty breeze blew through Marny's hair.

Gary turned and motioned for Marny and William to follow him, then disappeared inside.

The sun was mostly hidden by the pines. The tops of the trees stood black against the rich blue backdrop like the silhouettes of so many serrated knives.

Before they entered the house, Marny turned to William. "Do you know what's going to happen in there?"

William shook his head. "No, Marnin. But I have a bad feeling about the place."

"Yeah, so do I."

"You'll be tested in there, Marnin. More than you've ever been."

"That's not encouraging."

When he stepped over the threshold from porch to foyer, Marny felt as though a million spiders had descended from the ceiling and now crawled over his skin, under his clothes, through his hair.

Gary flipped a light switch, and a small table lamp flicked on, casting the foyer in a dull orange glow. Inside it was a common house, nothing special. No strange antiques or oddities of any kind. No shrunken heads or goat skulls hanging from the walls. The furniture was not contemporary, but not terribly old either. It was just a house, nothing more, nothing less. To their right, a staircase rose to the second floor. To their left, the living room, everything coated with a light sheet of dust. Straight ahead a hallway extended to a dining room on the left, beyond the living room, and a kitchen at the end. The light of the lamp barely reached the kitchen, but what little of it that did revealed a white linoleum floor and white cupboards.

The light switch in the living room was just around the corner. Marny found it easily, and two table lamps sprang to life. The room was large and furnished nicely. Lots of chairs. It was obvious that at one time the Roses enjoyed entertaining friends. Laughter had once resonated through the house, but whatever was once here was long gone. The place was like a mausoleum now, stone cold and dead.

"I don't like this place," Marny said.

Gary stood in the archway between living room and foyer. "He's here. I can feel him."

"I don't feel anything," Marny said.

William hung on to Marny's hand. "He's right, Marnin. Esther is here too."

Suddenly that warm, musty breeze was there again, blowing through the house despite the closed windows. It rushed down the hall and into the foyer, slamming the front door shut.

Marny pulled away from William and ran for the door, yanked on the knob, but it wouldn't open, wouldn't even rattle. It was as if it'd been nailed shut. "It must be jammed or something."

Gary came over and gave it a try. But still the door would not budge.

That's when Marny noticed the doorframe. The place where the wood had splintered and broken was now whole, like a wound that had healed over the course of weeks, maybe months. It showed no sign of any kind of damage.

Gary inspected the door, the frame, the hinges. His face was somber and flat. He ran his hand over the wood, knocked on it, turned the knob. Nothing.

On the second floor a floorboard creaked; another moaned. Pipes rattled and clanged, and then came the sound of running water.

Chapter 52

They were not alone in the house.

Marny stayed at the bottom of the steps with William as Gary climbed them cautiously, one at a time, back to the wall. The second floor was darkened by the hidden daylight, and the water continued to run. More floorboards popped and groaned. Gary stopped midway up and drew his pistol. He waited, motionless, listening. Holding the gun out front with both arms extended, he continued his ascent.

Marny and William exchanged a quick glance. Someone was up there. The water thing was obviously a lure, a trick. Marny was glad Gary was going up to check it out and not him.

At the top of the stairs, Gary turned and looked at Marny, then William, but said nothing. He wiped his brow with one hand, then disappeared around the corner. They could hear his footsteps pad down the hallway, then stop. Seconds ticked by, and nothing happened. All was quiet except for the continuously running water.

It started as a trickle at the top of the staircase. A thin line of water pushed over the edge and dropped to the second step, then the third and fourth and continued down step by step until it reached the bottom and pooled around Marny's feet. Through his shoes he could feel the water was cold, frigid actually. He bent and touched it, rubbed his fingers together, then wiped them on his pants.

"I'm going up," he said to William.

"That's probably not a good idea, Marnin."

"Probably not, but I need to see what's going on up there."

The water had picked up a little now; the stream was as wide as a man's hand and coursed down the middle of the staircase.

Marny released William's hand. "Stand over by wall, out of the water, okay? Don't move. I'll be right back."

William nodded.

Staying to his right, along the wall, Marny took the steps slowly, careful not to touch the water. There was something about it, a quality he didn't like. It was too cold to come from the pipes this time of year. Maybe in the dead of winter, but not in June. He would just get to the top and take a peek around the corner. See if he could locate Gary.

Three quarters of the way up the water increased to take up most of the width of the steps. Marny could no longer avoid getting his shoes in it. It splashed up around the soles and wetted the tops, soaked through to his socks and numbed his feet. He turned to see if William was staying clear of the water puddling on the floor, but he wasn't there. Marny stepped to the other side of the stair and leaned over the railing, scanned what he could see of the first floor.

"William."

The rattling of old pipes started in the walls again, this time louder than before. It grew in volume until it sounded like the pipes would burst.

The water continued to cascade down the steps, steadily increasing in volume and strength. It now covered Marny's shoes and splashed up to his knees. He gripped the railing with both hands and struggled to keep his footing. The numbness had spread from his toes to his feet to his ankles.

Then the steps were gone, folded down on themselves to form a slide, just like the ones in Marny's dream. Water poured down like a mountain spring, forceful now. Marny quickly lost his footing and went to his knees. He tried to hold on to the railing, but a second later his grip gave way and he slid down the ramp on his belly. Water engulfed him and left him disoriented and flailing about. His hands and arms lost feeling; his vision blurred.

At the bottom he was met with a jarring stop and banged his head on the banister. The flow had suddenly stopped, and he now lay on his back in a pool of water, gasping and sputtering. He rolled to his side and coughed. His head ached. Slowly, his clothes dripping with the oddly cold water, Marny pushed himself up and climbed to his feet. The stairs were back to normal, the upstairs quiet. No water, no footsteps, no creaking floorboards, no rattling pipes. Water had pooled at the bottom of the steps and worked its way into the hallway and living room. It was already starting to recede, as though the floor was soaking it up.

But this was not the same house. Marny shook his head, smoothed back his hair. Something was definitely wrong. The foyer was different, the hallway, even the staircase. Had he hit his head that hard? Within seconds the water was totally gone and the floor dry, as if the whole staircase thing had been a dream.

"William." If he could find the wonder boy, that would add credibility to what he saw, but there was no answer. "William." Still nothing.

Marny walked to the living room and stood in the archway. He hitched in a breath. No, this was in no way Harold's house. It was *his* house, Marny's. The sofa, the chairs, the Barcalounger situated in front of the TV, the braided rug, and the coffee table with the broken leg. This was the house Marny lived in as a kid with his mother and Karl.

Behind him a voice said, "Hey, Bustah, you gonna do somethin' or just stand there like a meathead?"

Chapter 53

THE FIRST ROOM Gary came to was a bedroom.

The bathroom where the water ran and ran was beyond that. A steady stream exited the doorway, meandered down the hallway, and rounded the corner at the steps. The light was on in the bathroom, an odd white light that looked more like natural sunshine than anything that originated from a bulb. It flickered almost imperceptibly, like the slight variations of candlelight.

He stopped at the bedroom, gun out in front. The door was closed. He should check every room, clear the second floor before heading back downstairs. He placed one hand on the glass doorknob, then quickly snatched it away. It was covered with frost.

An involuntary shiver rippled through his body. The temperature in the house had plummeted. His breath clouded as soon as it left his mouth. It was nearly summer; where had this sudden drop in temperature come from? It wasn't unlikely for Maine to get an unexpected, fast-moving cold front from Canada, even in June, but this was ridiculous.

But he knew where this arctic chill came from, didn't he? It was the sign of death. Death had entered the house and brought with it the cool winds that beat from the wings of the soulless.

At the door, one hand on the knob again, Gary whispered a prayer of protection, fished the cross from under his shirt, and kissed it. He turned the knob and opened the door all the way.

He was not at all prepared for what he found. The place was set up like a funeral parlor. The carpet and walls were burgundy. The windows on the far end were covered by thick drapes, allowing no light from the outside world to penetrate the gloomy space. A single chandelier hung from the middle of the ceiling, crystal and ornate. Its soft light cast an ominous glow over the room, as if it were in a losing battle with the darkness. Straight-backed chairs lined the walls, and at the far end, in front of the windows, stood a casket. It was black and glossy with brass trim and perched on a pedestal. But there was something strange about it, something not quite right. Its size... it was smaller than a standard casket, more like a child's.

Gary took one step into the room and forgot about the arctic temperatures in the hallway. This room was warm and muggy, and the smell of old wood and dust was in the air.

When he stepped over the threshold, the door slowly closed and clicked shut. But Gary barely heard it; he was so intently focused on the casket. Something about it was familiar. As he drew closer, taking each step slowly and deliberately, the gun in his hand felt heavier and heavier, and he finally released it and let it fall to the carpet. He had no need of it in a place like this. Death was already here.

Halfway across the room he noticed the flowers surrounding the casket. There were only a couple arrangements, and they were both made entirely of lilies.

Lilies.

Why did he know lilies?

Again, that feeling of familiarity overcame him. He looked about the room again, feeling as though he'd been there before. But he'd never been to Harold's house.

Something caught his eye that brought memories back in a rush. Behind the casket, behind the flowers, folded and propped against the wall, was a wheelchair.

He knew that chair. He knew the boy who once occupied it.

He'd reached the casket by now and stood before it. Though the temperature in this room had to be near eighty, his hands and feet felt cold and tingly. The cross resting against his chest, over his heart, felt heavy, almost too heavy to hold, as though he were suddenly supporting an anvil around his neck.

Gary lifted both hands and rested them on the casket. The wood was smooth, polished to a high sheen.

He had to do it. With shaky hands Gary lifted the top half of the split lid. His breath caught in his throat.

Landon. His little brother.

Gary took a step back but couldn't pull his eyes from the boy. Landon was only eleven when he died. A tragic accident. Gary's fault.

The memory came back then, like the playing of an old movie. He'd been charged with caring for his younger brother, who suffered from cerebral palsy and had been chair-bound since he was old enough to sit. Gary's father, the Reverend Morris, had said Landon was special, chosen by God to bear this unique blessing. He said Landon was anointed, that he had God's hand upon him and that his faith was of the purest kind, the kind that would change the world. Because of that, he needed special care and protection. And it was Gary's duty to fulfill God's call by protecting God's anointed.

For three years Gary never left his brother's side. But he too was only a child, just three years older than Landon.

That day came roaring back with teeth and claws flashing. The Reverend Morris had to go out on visitation, had to see the widow Luella Wingert and administer Communion. He'd charged Gary with Landon's watch, as he did every time he left on visitation.

"Son, you watch over God's anointed, care for him as you would for yourself." He patted Gary on the shoulder and gave it a little squeeze. "As John the Baptizer was for our Lord, so is your calling for your brother. We all have our duties to perform, and yours is among the highest. Your brother will bring healing to the world. He will point them to Christ. Do your service as unto the Lord."

And then he was gone, and Gary was alone once again with Landon, his brother, his crippled, chair-bound brother. It wasn't that Gary didn't love his brother; he did, more than anything. And it wasn't that he was jealous of the attention his father showed Landon, especially after their mother had died; he wasn't. In fact, Gary truly believed there was something special about Landon. The boy was innocent and kind, never spoke a harsh word, never showed even a shadow of selfishness. He was special; he was anointed.

For Gary the problem was that he too was only a kid, just fourteen. He wanted friends, he wanted to go out on his own and explore the forest and run through fields, maybe join the baseball team, go camping. But he could do none of that. He was charged with watching Landon, his little brother, the anointed.

But there was one thing Landon liked that Gary also enjoyed. Fire. Once a week Gary would roll his brother to the burn pile at the back of the yard. He would leave Landon there while he collected the garbage for the week and piled it high. Gary was careful not to sit Landon too close; a stray spark could be disastrous.

On that day, the day the Reverend Morris went to visit the widow Luella Wingert and administer Communion, the wind was especially lively. It came from the north and brought with it cooler air and a rugged attitude. As he always did, Gary pushed Landon to within ten feet of the fire, ignited what was there, and left to gather the rest of the garbage from the kitchen and back porch.

When he emerged from the house just minutes later, the fire in the burn pile was already as high as a man, whipping about angrily in the wind. And Landon was on the move. He'd managed to get his withered hands around the tires of the wheelchair and had inched closer to the fire.

Gary dropped the trash bags and bolted for his brother. Halfway there a gust of wind ripped through the fire, throwing flames toward Landon and momentarily engulfing the boy. Fiery arms encircled him and groped at his clothes, his face, his hair. Gary's heart thudded in his chest like a sledgehammer on concrete. The flames ignited Landon's shirt and trousers. Gary was still a good fifty feet away; he pushed his legs harder, urged them to move faster, ripped off his shirt as he ran. It was amazing how quickly the fire took to Landon's clothes. Within seconds the boy was covered with flames. His arms flailed about, and his weak screams echoed across the clearing.

Gary reached his brother in full sprint and threw himself at the chair. It tumbled sideways, spilled Landon onto the ground. Gary pounded on him with his T-shirt, tried desperately to smother the flames. It took what seemed like hours for the last of the fire to be extinguished, and by the time it did Landon lay motionless and charred. He was only eleven; his lungs weren't strong to begin with.

Back in the room in Harold's house, the funeral parlor, Gary looked at his own arms and the burn scars that covered most of them. They had faded over the years, but the tight, smooth skin was a constant reminder of his failure.

Landon in the casket, however, showed no sign of the cause of his death. His skin was smooth and supple, the skin of a child. Gary wanted to touch it. He needed to prove to himself that this was real, that the boy in the casket was really his brother. He lifted a hand and hesitated, returned it to his side. He pulled in a slow breath and lifted his hand again.

Landon's eyes opened, rolled around in their sockets, then found Gary.

Chapter 54

IT WAS IMPOSSIBLE, wasn't it?

Marny didn't want to turn around, didn't want to face the truth of where he was. He couldn't be back in the old house. He was in Harold's house; he'd come here with Gary and William, looking for Esther.

"Bustah, I'm talkin' to ya," Karl said.

Still Marny held his ground. His head was a little foggy from the fall and hitting it. He felt his clothes; they were dry. Had he imagined the whole thing? Had he hit his head and blacked out? This was all a dream; he was sure of it. The whole thing was a dream. He was still lying at the bottom of the staircase, unconscious. But that had happened *after* the whole water down the steps thing, after Gary had ascended those steps and disappeared, after William had gone missing. Maybe he was still lying on the ground up on that mountain with a gunshot wound to the head, teetering between life and death, and his brain had concocted all of this. He grabbed his head with both hands. His mind spun in circles, doubling back on itself. Nothing made sense.

Behind him, Karl didn't give up. "Hey. Don't ya ignore me. Turn around and face me like a man."

Slowly Marny turned and faced his stepfather. Karl seemed larger than he'd been the last time Marny saw him, but that couldn't be. It had to be this house playing tricks on him, the lighting maybe.

Karl squared his shoulders and jutted his chin. "Ya in my way, Bustah. The game's gonna be on soon. Why don'tcha make yourself useful and get me a beer."

The numbness was back in Marny's feet and hands. He knew this scene, knew how it would play out. He'd run through it countless times in his mind. He had to get out of there; he couldn't go through it again.

Karl stared at him with narrowed eyes. When he squinted like that, his small, wide-set eyes almost disappeared in his head. "Well, watcha waitin' for?"

He came at Marny, but Marny didn't move. This wasn't happening. It was part of his imagination, a memory his brain had dug up and replayed in an attempt to jump-start itself after the concussion he'd received from hitting his head on the banister. Or after receiving a bullet to the head. That was the only explanation that made sense.

Karl pushed past Marny, bumped his shoulder, and knocked him off-balance. He smelled of beer and body odor. He was real—too real. This was no concoction of images and sounds that had been hidden away in the neurons of Marny's gray matter.

Before he sat in his Barcalounger, the brown one with the tear in the armrest, Karl looked at Marny and raised his eyebrows. "Well? You gonna get me a beer or not?"

Marny didn't say anything.

Karl snapped his fingers. "Hey, Bustah. Ya there? Ya deaf? A beer. How 'bout it?"

No matter what he said, this scenario would have the same ending, and it put a lump the size of his fist in Marny's throat. Nothing could change the outcome, or could it? Could Marny stop the inevitable? He had to try. It was time to stand up to the curse that had followed him his entire life and had stolen the lives of so many loved ones.

Karl sat, and Marny turned away from him.

"Don't ya turn your back on me, boy." Karl's voice boomed throughout the first floor.

Marny headed for the staircase, first at a walk, then a run.

Behind him Karl screamed and cussed, demanded he return and fetch him his beer. But Marny was already halfway up the stairs. This time no water poured down them, and they did not collapse on him.

At the top he knew exactly where to go. He headed for his mother's bedroom. She sat on the bed, combing her hair. When he saw her he almost burst into tears. She looked exactly like she had that day, the day she...

"Hello, Marny." She smiled at him, a warm smile, *her* smile. But it quickly faded. "What's the matter?"

Footsteps thundered up the stairs. Karl was on his way.

Marny panicked. "Mom, you need to get out of here. Go. Out the window or something. Just get out of here."

She smiled again. "Oh, don't be silly. Out the window? Why in the world would I go out the window?" She didn't get it, the danger, the nightmare that was on its way.

"Mom, please, just *do* it."

Karl's footsteps reached the top of the stairs and started down the hall. Marny jumped up and went to shut the bedroom door.

"Marny—"

But Karl was there quickly and blocked the door with his foot. Marny leaned against it, but Karl pushed the door open and grabbed him by the shirt. "You'll pay f' this, ya lobstah." He shoved Marny against the wall, then went for Janie.

Fear shadowed her face and twisted her mouth.

"Woman, your son is outta control." Karl reached her and grabbed a handful of hair. He yanked her head back. "Since he's too stupid to get me my beer, ya can do it for him, show him how it's done."

He pulled her up by her hair and dragged her toward the door. Marny tried to stop him, but Karl was built like a bulldozer and deflected every one of Marny's assaults. Finally he jammed his elbow into Marny's stomach, doubling him over. Nausea radiated through his abdomen, caused the muscles to cramp and spasm.

It was happening just as it had five years ago. In Marny's attempt to change the past, he'd re-created it. He couldn't escape what the past had already written.

He struggled to his feet and reached the hallway just as his mother and Karl neared the top of the stairs. Karl still had a grip on her hair. Her eyes were wild with fear, and she was crying.

"Now, get down there and show ya lazy, stupid son how to get a beer from the fridge. It ain't that hard."

He gave her a shove, and she clumsily stumbled down a step, lost her footing, tripped, and plummeted head first. Over and over she tumbled until she rested at the bottom, one arm pinned under her body, her head bent at an odd, sickening angle. There was no expression on her face, no light in her eyes.

Karl cursed and casually descended the steps. At the bottom he pushed Janie's limp body out of his way with his foot and hollered up to Marny. "Ya wanta take care a'this?"

Marny ran down the steps, but there was nothing he could do. There was no need to check for a pulse, no need to try to revive her. He knew how this ended.

Chapter 55

DARKNESS CAN HAVE a weight all its own.

Esther opened her eyes against darkness so heavy she thought at first she was under a blanket. Her mind swam in some murky, distant water, confused, disoriented. For a moment she thought she was back in her house, in bed. Not Gary's house, but *her* house, where happiness once lived and she was a carefree child. An only child. Her bed was so warm then, so soft. Sleep came easily and soundly, a welcome gift at the end of a day filled with play and laughter and lots of smiles. And her dreams were always pleasant and populated by flying horses and beautiful princesses.

She tried to roll over but was scolded by a sharp pain in her shoulders. That's when she noticed that her hands were bound behind her back. Her feet were tied too. And her mouth was taped shut.

Her eyes were open fully now, and an ache settled in her stomach. The room was dark, but not completely. As her eyes adjusted she noticed the candlelight that danced on dirt walls. The floor and ceiling were dirt as well. Thick beams lined the walls and supported the ceiling. Was she in an old mine?

Memories started working their way to the front of her mind. She'd arrived at the old house with Harold. She'd run from him. The Karstens, the poor Karstens. And Nosey, the friendly Coonhound. Gunshots, screaming, cursing. Then Harold was on the move after her again, and he'd caught her, but not before she'd taken a stick to his head. The sharp prick in the arm, the sleepiness that overcame her.

Harold had drugged her. Her father had abducted and bound her. How twisted was that?

Rather than fear, a great sadness overcame her. What had her father become? The man who was once her hero had betrayed her.

From the corner of the room she heard the low thrum of voices. She didn't have a good view of the entire space because she was on her side in the corner behind a generator of some sort.

She listened, tried to make out what the voices were saying, but it was useless. They sounded as if they were speaking a foreign language. She tried to right herself, but that too quickly proved futile. Her shoulders were too sore. She must have been lying there on her side, shoulders pulled back like that, for hours. Besides, even if the stabbing pain wasn't there, she couldn't get the leverage to sit with her arms behind her back. All she could do was scoot.

Slowly, so as not to make any noise, she inched around by pulling her knees up, then extending them. Each movement sent waves of pain through her shoulders. Sweat quickly broke out on her brow. It was warm in the room, and the air was heavy and musty.

She didn't remember any mining operations near their house in Comfort. Harold must have taken her somewhere else. Maybe a different part of the state. She remembered the phone call she'd overheard. Harold said he would meet the caller *at the house*. Maybe it wasn't a mine shaft after all; maybe they were in the root cellar of an old home or a bomb shelter from ages past.

Finally Esther maneuvered enough to peek around the corner of the generator and see the source of the voices. A group of bodies were gathered in the corner in a tight circle, all facing each other. It reminded her of a football huddle. But these players didn't wear uniforms, and there was not a blade of green grass to be found. The huddle seemed to pulsate in time with the chant. She couldn't make out what they wore; their clothes were too dark and the light so dim. Along one of the walls was a wooden table, and on it sat three candles. On the opposite wall was a wooden door.

From her vantage point Esther couldn't make out how many bodies were there—seven, eight, maybe nine?—nor if they were male or female. There were no skulls in the room, no goblets for the drinking of blood, no cauldron filled with a strange boiling liquid, yet it seemed somehow a cultic scenario. Her stomach squirmed, and panic now clawed at her chest.

She had to get out of there. Whatever was about to take place couldn't be good.

Esther closed her eyes and prayed. God was her only hope now. He always had been. She needed a miracle. With William and Marny gone, no one even knew she was with Harold. But God knew, and as odd as it seemed, that brought some measure of comfort and hope.

The chanting stopped, and she heard the dry shuffle of feet. Esther opened her eyes and found someone standing over her.

It was her father.

Chapter 56

MARNY DROPPED TO his knees beside his mother. This was something he'd never got to do the first time. He straightened her neck, then placed his hand on her forehead and stroked her hair. With the other hand he shut her eyelids. The life was gone from her, taken by the brute in the Barcalounger. And just as it had happened the first time, Karl acted as though he didn't care one bit, as though Janie's life was nothing more to him than a beer can that, once empty and used, could be crushed and tossed to the side.

Anger blew through Marny like hurricane winds. He got to his feet and clenched his fists. If this was history replaying itself, then there was something he could do now that he hadn't the nerve to do the first time. This time he didn't care. His curse had caught him again, exacting another payment for whatever he'd done in life to deserve all this.

But that was the question: What had he done to deserve it? Be born? That was it? Where was God in all this? Where was Esther's and William's faith? Forget that. This was Marny's time to do the right thing. He crossed the foyer with deliberate steps, fully intending to round the corner into the living room, walk right up to Karl, knock the pathetic beer can from his hand, and make hamburger meat of his face. He was going to kill him.

But when he turned that corner there was no living room. No

Barcalounger, no beer cans, no Karl. Marny was back in Harold's house. He spun around and found the foyer empty. His mother was gone too. The floor was dry, the steps intact. Had he indeed imagined the whole thing? From the time he first heard the creaking second-floor boards and rattling pipes?

But where was William? Where was Gary?

The image of Karl and that confrontation was still so fresh in his mind. The feelings were raw nerve endings, scraped with a sharp edge. Karl was never convicted for Janie's death. It had been his word against Marny's, and Karl swore she merely slipped and fell. There was no proof otherwise and plenty of reasonable doubt that Karl intentionally pushed his wife, the wife he loved and cared for and now cried for, down a flight of stairs.

But justice is no respecter of men and is rarely fooled. Sooner or later it comes knocking. For Karl Gunnison it came sooner, a week after the acquittal. He was putting in overtime working the gillnet on a trawler when he got tangled in the net, fell overboard, and in an accident as freakish as they come, got sucked into the boat's propeller. His remains were never found, and it was presumed what was left of him became lobster food—a horrible but fitting ending to a life that brought others so much pain and sadness.

Marny shook the memory and walked back into the hallway. "William?" As before, his voice sounded small in the house, lonely. He said the boy's name again, louder.

Down the hall William appeared in the kitchen doorway. "I'm here, Marnin. Look what I found."

Marny rushed down the hallway and pulled William close. "Where were you? I told you to stay in the foyer."

"The water was getting too bad, so I came in here."

Marny knelt in front of William. Despite all that had happened and being shot and chased and winding up in this bizarre house, William still appeared calm, innocent. "You saw the water? It was there?"

He nodded the confirmation Marny needed, confirmation that he wasn't going plumb mad.

"Yes, Marnin. The water was real. It was cold, so I came in here to get away from it."

"What's happening here, William?"

It appeared to be a normal kitchen. White cupboards and countertops, white tiled linoleum floor. White appliances.

"The house is alive, Marnin. It knows us. Don't believe everything you see or hear, okay?"

"Okay, buddy. Let's get out of here."

Marny reached for William's hand, but the boy pulled it away.

"Wait. Do you believe in God, Marnin?"

Marny wasn't sure this was the right time for such a question. He reached again for William's hand, but again William pulled it away.

"Do you?" the boy asked.

"Yes, of course I do. Now—"

"Do you believe in Jesus?"

Jesus. What did this have to do with anything? "I don't know, I guess. Now come on, we need to get out of here."

"Do you or don't you, Marnin?"

His mother did; Marny knew that much. And when he was a kid he'd said a prayer with his mother, asking Jesus into his heart. Wasn't that enough?

"Sure I do. Now let's go."

But William wasn't finished. "Do you trust Him?"

Behind William the oven turned on, and all four burners suddenly sprang to life. Blue flames rose inches above the stove top.

"William, we need to go *now*."

William didn't take his eyes off Marny. "Do you trust Jesus, Marnin? You're going to need to trust Him to get us out of this."

"Yes. Yes, I do."

Marny heard a dripping then, not like the high-pitched dripping of water, but lower, thicker, the splash of something more viscous, like…

Blood oozed out of the cupboards all around the kitchen and

plinked onto the countertop below. Just a slow drip at first, like that of a leaky faucet, then steadily increasing.

William held his ground and kept his gaze on Marny. "Esther is here, Marnin. She's in this house."

"How do you know?"

"I'm her brother. I can feel her."

The blood was picking up its pace now, streaming out of the cupboards and pooling on the countertop. The oven and stove continued to burn their flames.

"William, are you sure?"

William nodded. "But you won't make it out of here without trust. You need to have faith, Marnin."

So they were back to the faith thing. Marny didn't have faith; he knew he didn't. And he didn't trust God or Jesus, not really. What had They ever done for him? Death had followed him his whole life and had stolen anyone who was ever dear to him. Where was God in all of that? Marny was convinced that no amount of faith could have stopped those deaths.

Now the blood was spilling over the edge of the counters and puddling on the floor below, turning the white linoleum a deep red. The pipes had taken to rattling and knocking on the walls again too. It sounded like every pipe in the house had joined in on the chorus.

Near the sink, on the wall, hung a telephone in its cradle. Marny crossed the floor, avoiding the pools. "I'm calling for help." He grabbed the phone from the jack and put it to his ear, but there was no dial tone, nothing but silence. He slammed down the phone. "Listen to me, William. If we're going to get Esther, we need to move now. Where do you think she is?"

William hesitated, clearly not satisfied with Marny's response. He pointed to a door in the corner of the kitchen. "Down there."

Chapter 57

THE MOUTH MOVED, lips formed words, and the corpse found a voice.

"Why did you leave me there, Gary?"

It was Landon's body in that casket, but the voice that came from his mouth was not that of Gary's brother. Landon was low functioning and rarely spoke, and when he did, his words were barely intelligible. No, the voice that came from the boy in the casket was William's.

William. The anointed. The *other* boy Gary had been charged to protect.

And had left downstairs.

But right now Landon had his attention.

"Why did you leave me there, Gary?"

It was the question everyone had asked him. He was fourteen; he needed to be consoled, comforted, told it wasn't his fault. He needed his mother; she would have understood. But she was gone too. Instead, all he got were questions and more questions. Why did you start the fire on such a windy day? Why did you leave it unattended? Why did you leave Landon there alone? Why didn't you put the brakes on the wheelchair?

Gary had withdrawn into a cave and pulled so far back that no light could reach him. His relationship with his father deteriorated into nothing, two empty shells coexisting in the same house but having no bond. The Reverend Morris continued his duties as minister at the church, but his heart was never in it. For months after Landon's death he'd insisted the boy would live again, that God would raise up his anointed, but when a year had passed and Landon's body had not climbed from the grave they'd placed him in, the Reverend Morris lost all hope.

And though Gary had withdrawn, though he'd distanced himself from his father and convinced himself that he hated the man, deep down, down where the heart and soul unite, he longed to gain his father's approval once again.

Landon's eyes never wavered from Gary's. "Why did you leave me, Gary?"

Gary didn't answer. He'd answered that question a thousand times as a kid, and every time it was the same: "I don't know."

"Why *did* you leave him?" A man's voice.

It was the voice Gary heard in his head every day. His father's voice. The voice of the Reverend Morris.

Gary turned and found his father standing in the far corner of the parlor. The man was tall and thin, old. His white hair perched atop his head like a half-made bird's nest. His suit hung on him like a boneless body. The Reverend Morris had died three years ago, and though his funeral was attended by many, Gary was not among the mourners. But he was here now.

The Reverend Morris stepped closer. "Son, it was your calling, your charge, your duty. You were his John the Baptizer, preparing the way." His voice was frail and raspy. He sounded tired. "You had one purpose in life...to protect God's anointed. How could you fail in such a colossal manner?"

Gary wanted to run to his father and throw himself at the man's feet, beg him to grant him another chance. Gary would make things right with William.

William. Again Gary remembered he'd left the boy downstairs with the punk. Guilt pricked at his conscience. He'd been so drawn by the water, by the sound of someone on the second floor, he'd lost focus and abandoned William. Just as he'd done to Landon all those years ago. He needed to get downstairs.

Behind him Gary heard the crackle of fire. He spun around and found flames climbing the drapes behind the casket. Paralysis overtook him, and he watched, helpless, as fire completely consumed the drapes. It licked at the ceiling and quickly spread to the carpet. He needed to get out of there. He needed to move now, but his legs wouldn't work. Inch by inch he turned his feet until he faced the doorway.

His father stood between him and the closed door, hands clasped in front, head tilted to one side. "You disappointed me, son. You let us all down. The whole world. He was an innocent lamb in your care. What a disappointment. What a failure."

In an explosion of spontaneous combustion, the Reverend Morris burst into flames. He showed no sign of pain. "What a disappointment."

Gary yelled and lifted one leg, then the other. The room was rapidly becoming an inferno.

"What a failure."

He needed to get to William. He needed to protect the anointed one. He'd failed once; he would not fail again.

Screaming like a man on fire himself, Gary willed his legs to move and ran for the door. He reached down and scooped his gun off the floor, met his father in three steps, and put a round in the fiery man's chest. The Reverend Morris stumbled back and fell. Gary hit the door at full speed, splintering it from its hinges. The door gave way, and both it and Gary landed in the hallway where the temperature had dropped even further.

Chapter 58

SURPRISES OFTEN LURK behind closed doors.

The door was shut and locked from the kitchen side by a brass sliding bolt, which seemed kind of odd to Marny. If Harold had taken Esther down into the cellar, how could he have locked the door from the other side?

Not wanting to spend any more time than they had to in the kitchen with the cabinets that dripped blood and the pipes that shook the walls, Marny and William headed for the door. Marny threw the lock and turned the knob. The door opened smoothly, revealing a wooden staircase that descended into a dark cellar. There was a light switch on the wall to their right, so Marny flipped it. As far as they could see from the top of the steps the cellar was empty. Just concrete floor, concrete walls.

They both took a step down, then two. The door slammed closed behind them, nearly knocking Marny off-balance. He heard the bolt slide back into place.

Panic seized him, and he reached for the knob, tried it, shook it, pushed on it. Nothing. They were trapped.

Marny turned to William. "You sure your sister's down here?"

William glanced down the steps, then back at Marny. "She's down here somewhere, Marnin. I can feel her."

Marny could too. He didn't know if it was his imagination or not, but he felt a strange certainty that Esther was down there.

He'd formed a bond of sorts with her and realized now that it was more than a bond of friendship. He truly cared about her. He'd go through hell to rescue her—which may be exactly what awaited them at the bottom of the steps. "I do too. I feel her."

"We have to save her."

"Yeah. I guess it's my turn."

Down the steps they went. As Marny's head cleared the first floor he saw that the cellar was not empty after all. Stacks of boxes lined the far walls, some three rows deep. And other things were there as well. A dust-covered treadmill. A ten-speed bike. Skis. Snow shovels. Even a canoe. Behind the stairs, in the middle of the floor, were the furnace and hot water heater. Normal stuff. Things of life. Nothing unusual and nothing that said Esther was or had been there.

The cellar was quiet too. No pipes rattled, no blood dripped, the steps did not turn into a mountain spring.

"Well, William, what do you think?"

Without saying a word, William walked over to where the boxes were three rows deep against the wall. He lifted one and sat it on the floor behind him. Then another and another.

Marny went to help him. "What are you doing?"

William stopped. He had a box in his arms. "Looking for my sister, Marnin."

"And you think she's in one of these boxes?" Marny was being facetious, but he didn't like the sound of what his question implied.

William eyed him evenly. As usual, his face showed no emotion. "I think she might be behind the boxes."

Each row of boxes was higher than the row in front of it. The third row reached almost to the ceiling, but was flush with the wall. How could anyone be behind the boxes?

It didn't take them long to get through the first and second rows. Most of the boxes were light, and some felt like they were empty. Marny grabbed the box off the top of the third row and stopped. He stared at the top of a wooden door.

"William, buddy, do you see that?"

"It's a door, Marnin."

"Yeah, I know what a door looks like, but where does it go?"

The only place it could go was back outside. Part of that sounded very appealing to Marny. They could get out of this awful house and farther from Gary. But it would take them no closer to Esther. Maine was a big state, and if she wasn't in this house, Harold could have taken her anywhere.

They removed the rest of the boxes to reveal a wooden door with large, iron hinges and a latch lock.

Marny wiped his palms on his pants. "Only one way to find out." He lifted the latch and pulled on the door. It opened with a sigh of almost human quality, like it had been holding its breath and finally exhaled.

On the other side were no steps leading out of the cellar and back to ground level. Instead, a dirt tunnel stretched before them, long and straight. Some light from the cellar filtered in, but only extended fifteen feet before the darkness swallowed it.

Marny turned to William. "You don't happen to have a flash-light, do you?"

Chapter 59

To ESTHER, HAROLD loomed like an ancient hunter over his prey.

He wore a black pullover and dark blue jeans and rested his hands on his hips as if he had grown impatient with her and was ready for things to proceed. He squatted in front of her and ran the back of his hand over her cheek but said not a word. His eyes were dark and lifeless, a shark's eyes. This was not her father, not even the same man who had brought her back to this house. Something dark and malevolent indwelt him, and it was that *thing* that stared at her now through Harold's eyes.

He stood again, turned to another of the men. "Take her to the room and prepare her."

A smaller man stepped forward and smiled at Esther. He too wore a black shirt and jeans.

He bent at the waist, cut the bands around Esther's ankles, then put a hand on her shoulder. His touch was cold and his eyes colder. His jet black hair contrasted with his pale, almost lucent skin.

"Come now, let's get you up." He pushed Esther to sitting, then helped her to her feet.

Esther got a better view of the room. It was about fifteen by fifteen and empty save for the one table and candles, generator in one corner, and a refrigerator next to it. Thick power cords led to the doorway, then disappeared. There were six men besides

Harold, and all of them appeared to be drugged or in some sort of trance. They all had the same black, empty eyes.

The smaller man took Esther by the arm and led her to the door. "Come, I'll show you the way."

They left the room, walked down a short, darkened hallway, and entered another space of similar size. This room had a single bed against one wall and a table on the other side, upon which sat more candles. The bed was made up with dark brown sheets and had a single pillow on it.

The man motioned toward the bed. "Please, lie down."

Esther hesitated.

The man smiled, an empty grin that showed no real emotion. "It's okay. I can assure you, no one here wants to rob you of your innocence."

She sat on the edge of the bed.

He fished in his pocket and pulled out a pocket knife, the same one with which he had cut the bands around her ankles.

"Now, here's how things will work." His voice was soft and melodic, almost feminine, but Esther found no comfort in it. "I'm going to loosen the cord around your wrist, and then I'll remove the tape from your mouth. Don't try to escape and don't scream. You won't get anywhere and no one will hear you. We're many feet underground and far from any exits." He paused and ran his thumb lightly over the blade of the knife. "And besides, I'd hate for you to get hurt in those tunnels. They're very dark, you know."

He put the knife behind her and cut the bands around her wrists, then carefully pulled the tape from her mouth. It stung coming off, but the pain only lasted a moment.

"There, now, isn't that better?"

Esther's urge was to shove the man down and make a dash for the door, but she had no idea what awaited her on the other side. If he was telling the truth about their location, and they were truly underground and miles from civilization, she didn't stand a chance. She was at his mercy, at Harold's mercy. And after seeing what he'd done to William and Marny and hearing what he'd done to the Karstens, the thought made her shudder. She stretched her arms in front. Her shoulders ached, but she didn't care. She needed to move them.

Esther rubbed her wrists. "What do you want with me?"

The man smiled again, this time showing two rows of bone-white teeth. "Those are the secrets we keep." He patted her leg. "But no worries. None of it will hurt. Now, if you will, please lie down and get comfortable."

She didn't like where this was going. Lying down seemed too vulnerable, too passive.

His smile disappeared, and those empty eyes seemed to look right through her. "I can get some of my friends to help you, but we'd both rather avoid that. I simply abhor violence."

Hesitantly, Esther lay supine on the bed, arms at her sides.

"There now, that's a good girl. I'll be right back." He walked to the table and opened a drawer, retrieved something from it and put it in his pocket, then returned to Esther on the bed.

He knelt beside her and lifted a hand.

Esther tensed.

"No, no, no. Come now. Believe me, I have no intention of harming you. My desire is to give life."

He placed a hand on her chest, but the contact wasn't inappropriate. It reminded Esther of the gentle touch of a physician.

His smile grew big, and this time there was some true excitement in it. "Ah, there it is. Your heart beats strong. Did you know the average heart will beat more than two and half billion times in a person's lifetime? Nonstop, beating, beating, never quitting. It's a remarkable organ. The sustainer of life. And the substance it pumps, ah, there is where the magic lies. Life is in the blood, you know."

"You're a doctor."

His smile returned. "Yes, I am. A giver of life."

He reached into his pocket and withdrew a hypodermic butterfly needle and roll of medical tape.

Esther started to sit up, but he quickly and gently pushed her back down.

"Now, now, settle. It's only a needle for drawing blood. I won't be administering any drugs with this. We need your blood clean."

"What do you want with me?" she asked again.

"With you? Not a thing. It's your blood we desire." He tied a rubber band around the top of her arm. "Now make a fist."

She hesitated.

"Come now, dear, seriously. Fist, please."

There was no use resisting. If he wanted, he could call in his goons and have them hold her down while he did this.

"Did you know your heart pumps right around two thousand gallons of blood a day? Quite remarkable, isn't it?"

Esther didn't answer.

"It's okay to agree with me, you know? It *is* remarkable."

The man tapped on the vein in the crease of her elbow.

"And did you know the average adult body has approximately sixty thousand miles of blood vessels? End to end that would wrap around the earth two and half times. I bet you didn't know that, did you?"

Again Esther gave no response. If he was attempting to gain her confidence through his knowledge of mundane facts, he was failing.

"And I only need one small entry site," he said. His hands worked deftly, and she barely felt the needle go in. He had some experience doing this. He withdrew the needle, untied the rubber band, and placed tape over the butterfly portion. "There, now you can bend your elbow if you like. It's just a catheter in your vessel, just flexible tubing. Nothing will stick you. I told you it wouldn't hurt, didn't I?"

He then connected a vacuum vial to the tubing, and dark red blood filled it quickly. His eyes met hers, and in them was something vile and dark. "The life is in the blood."

"Are you going to kill me?"

He held up the vial of blood. "Now don't think about such things as death. Our goal here is life. And besides, if this is pure, we'll be keeping you around a bit longer." He sighed, glanced at the door. "They made mistakes, especially in the past. They were...vicious. Too vicious, I suppose, and got careless. They lost some to disease and such. Nasty little critters. But then they built this little clinic of sorts and found me, and since then we've progressed, evolved if you will. Our techniques have become more sophisticated, safer even. For you and us."

"And what if it's not pure?"

He smacked her hard on the cheek, and she let out an involuntary scream. His face changed, hardened, the lines deepened. "It *will* be pure. I was assured it was pure."

Chapter 60

THE SILENCE OF the room seemed to be another presence of its
own.

The man had left with the vial of blood and closed the door
behind him, leaving Esther alone with her thoughts and fears. She
heard nothing from the other side of the door.

Why did they need her blood? She supposed by *pure* he meant
free of disease, venereal, hepatitis, and such. And what were the
mistakes they made in the past, when they were too vicious? The
thought of that made her skin tighten and shudder. She looked at
the catheter in her arm and felt it. She had a notion to rip it out.
But what good would that do? There was no escaping this place. If
she tore it out, they'd only replace it and probably tie her down.

Despair climbed into her head and burrowed a hole. There was
no hope.

Esther closed her eyes and let the tears come. But there *was*
hope, wasn't there? There was always hope. Words, ancient yet
familiar, came back to her, words of comfort that she'd read and
stored in her heart.

Be strong and take heart, all you who hope in the Lord.

All those years of living with Gary, huddled in her room, flash-
light in hand, scanning the pages of the Bible, drinking in the
words, holy and true. They were an endless source of comfort for
her. And often, more times than not, she'd read aloud to William.

She loved to see his eyes widen when she read from those pages. His faith stemmed from them, from the promises they contained, the words of life.

Yes, there was hope. It was just a point of light in the darkness of her mind, but she reached for it and took hold of it. It grew, and as it did, its warmth infused her with peace. Her lips began to move in prayer, asking for strength, for courage, for faith like William's. And the more she prayed, the more she focused on the One who was the giver of hope, the brighter that light grew. William might be gone, but she wasn't. She still had a purpose.

The door of the room opened and startled Esther out of her prayer. Harold stood in the doorway, his hand on the knob, a pistol in his other hand.

"We need to move you." His voice was flat, even. "Let's go." He extended a hand toward her.

Esther didn't want to go with him, but what choice did she have? She climbed out of the bed and walked to her father. He pointed the gun at her, and in his eyes, those black, empty eyes, she found a shadow of uncertainty. Oddly, he feared her.

"Are you going to use that on me?" she said.

He ignored her question. "Come on. This way." He took her by the arm and led her down a different tunnel to yet another room. This one was similar to the other two in size and decor. It was furnished only by a wooden table and three chairs.

Harold nudged the gun in Esther's side. "Sit."

She did as she was told, and Harold closed the door behind them.

"Are you going to kill me?" She asked the question with all sincerity. The hope she had, the peace she now felt, brought no assurance of rescue or survival, only an assurance that no matter what happened, she would not be alone, and that was all she could ask for.

Harold lowered the gun but kept his eyes on her. "Eventually."

∽

Marny stood between the jambs and held his breath. He waited for something, but he wasn't sure what. Maybe for William to do some of his magic and conjure a light. He wasn't thrilled about walking down the long, dark tunnel with no weapon and no light. And if Esther was to be found at the other end, then chances were that Harold was too. Harold with his gun, big and black. The same Harold who had showed no hesitation in shooting William and him once already today.

Marny didn't like the feel of that, of walking into gunfire, a death trap. But if William was right, if *he* was right, and Esther was indeed there, then he couldn't just leave her. He had to move onward, regardless of the potential dangers involved.

Like the mouth of a beast with the corridor its endless throat, the doorway waited for them to enter so it could swallow them whole. Two thin copper pipes ran along the upper right corner of the tunnel, signifying that there had to be *something* at the other end of the blackness, something that needed a water supply.

"Can you glow?" Marny asked William.

It was a joke, but William didn't laugh. "Esther's down there, Marnin. We have to go to her."

Marny knew it. Esther *was* down there. Plus, it made sense, didn't it? Creepy tunnel under spooked-out house. Where else could she be? Marny doubted the tunnel led to Harold's man-cave where he got together with buddies and watched football and played cards. No, tunnels like this always led to something sinister, something evil, something that could only be done in a subterranean room at the end of a long passageway.

He had an odd sensation that on the other side of the darkness he would come face-to-face with his curse. He could sense *it* as well. Calling to him, luring him, bidding him come and witness the full power of its wrath and hunger.

He suddenly wanted to turn tail and bolt, but he was tired of running. It was time to face whatever was in store for him, whatever waited at the end of the tunnel.

"Okay," Marny said. "But we go slow. I don't want any surprises." He hesitated. "And if anything happens, feel free to do something miraculous, all right?"

Again, William didn't laugh.

Marny started ahead, but William stopped him. The boy stood still with his eyes shut.

"William, what are you doing?"

"This is probably a good time to pray, Marnin."

Marny smiled. "Yeah. Probably." He was glad the boy was doing what he did best. For some reason it made him feel safer.

William bowed his head but said nothing, at least nothing anyone this side of heaven could hear, then opened his eyes and nodded at Marny. "Are you ready, Marnin?"

"Ready as I'm going to be."

"Are you *ready*?"

"Yeah, buddy. I guess."

William paused and stared at Marny. His eyes made Marny uncomfortable, like they were peeling back the flesh and peering into his soul.

"Do you trust, Marnin?"

"Trust what?"

"God."

Chapter 61

WHEN GARY HIT the floor in the hallway, the first thing he noticed was the change in temperature. With the fire quickly engulfing the room, the parlor had been an oven, but here in the hallway the mercury had to have dipped near zero, if not below. The second thing he noticed was the frost that covered everything—floor, walls, ceiling, banister, doors, and knobs. It was as though when he'd busted through the door he'd passed through some space continuum and found himself stranded in the Arctic Circle.

He got on all fours, his hands and knees immediately stinging from the cold, then pushed up to his feet and folded his arms across his chest. The parlor door had shut again and was frosted over. The knob was caked with a thick layer of ice, like it hadn't been turned in months. Rubbing his arms and blowing out a puff of white air, Gary headed down the hallway to the bathroom. The water no longer ran and the light was off. He was curious to see what was in there.

It was an ordinary bathroom—sink, toilet, tub. Everything in there too was blanketed with a heavy frost, but the sink was filled to the lip of the basin with a solid chunk of ice.

Leaving the bathroom, Gary walked toward the staircase, ice crunching beneath his shoes. He navigated the steps carefully so as not to slip and tumble down them head over heels. At his size that would not end well. The foyer and entire first floor were no different from the second story. The house was a winter wonderland. The furniture was encrusted with frost; lamps were encased in crystal. Ice hung from the lampshades like glass fingers. Gary leaned against the banister at the bottom of the steps and tried to collect his thoughts. The encounter with Landon and his father in the parlor had left him shaken and nervous. The front door was closed and in fact was now covered with an inch layer of ice top to bottom. William and the punk were still in the house. He was certain they hadn't gone upstairs, which meant they had to be on the first floor or in the cellar.

Gary scolded himself again for leaving William. He'd had a miserable lapse in judgment and failed. But it wouldn't happen again. He'd never again let William out of his sight. Never.

An image of Landon in flames burst into Gary's mind, and he nearly screamed. He didn't try to drive it from his memory, though. No, he wanted it there. It served as a reminder of what could happen—what would eventually happen—if he neglected to protect William. Whatever in this house was causing these strange disturbances and visions, Gary was thankful for it. He needed it.

Marny rubbed his forehead. William's question banged around in there. *Do you trust God?* "Yeah, sure. Look, we had this conversation already."

Those eyes bore holes into Marny again. "But you didn't get it. You need to trust Him, Marnin. You need to let go of yourself. You're holding on too tight." He paused, swallowed, but his eyes never left Marny's. "He knows you better than you know yourself."

"Okay. Can we go now?"

Marny reached for William's good hand, but the boy pulled it away, hesitated, then gave him his crippled hand. "Trust, Marnin."

Marny took the hand.

They started off down the passageway. Marny expected the door to slam shut behind them, leaving them in utter blackness, but it never did. They walked by the light of the cellar as far as they could, but eventually the darkness overcame the light and left them blind. Marny stretched his left arm out in front, and they both slowed their pace. Neither said a word. It seemed the darkness demanded silence, and any sound other than that of the ground under their shoes would disturb whatever lurked in that underground lair.

Finally they came to a perpendicular wall. Marny felt the length of it and found that the tunnel turned right at a ninety-degree angle. He looked back at the small door to the cellar at the far end of the corridor. Funny how he could see it, but its light came nowhere near reaching them. It was like a distant star, there but out of reach, too far away for its light to have any impact.

Marny leaned down next to William's ear and spoke quietly. "This is it, William. Either we follow this tunnel or head back for the light. We make this turn, and there's no going back."

William was quiet for a moment as if he knew what awaited them and was debating with himself over whether or not to take the plunge. "Do you think Esther would come after me, Marnin?"

"She'd give her life for you."

"I know. Let's go get her."

His air of certainty encouraged Marny. He still didn't understand William's gift, what he could and couldn't do. At times it seemed the wonder boy could see into the future, at times it felt like he could see into Marny's soul, yet at other times he appeared to be no different than every other eleven-year-old out there. Just a kid.

"Okay, let's do it," Marny said. They turned the corner and headed down the tunnel. In a few feet they met another wall and another turn. But around this bend, a good thirty feet in the distance at a T in the tunnel, Marny saw the faint orange glow of a partially opened door. A room was beyond it, and in the room was light.

They inched closer, quiet, steady. William held Marny's hand with both of his now. Each step felt like one closer to the end of the world...like the ground in the tunnel would collapse at their feet and they would fall and keep falling until they reached the center of the earth.

When they were within twenty feet of the door, a scream emanated from the room.

Esther.

Chapter 62

ESTHER SWALLOWED HARD. "You don't have to do this."

"What do you know about what I have to do and don't have to do?"

"I know you don't have to do this."

Harold smirked. "You don't know anything about me."

"I know you're my father and at one time you were my daddy. I know I was your Squirt and we used to do everything together. Do you remember that?"

The look on his face, in his eyes, said he didn't. Either he chose not to remember or it had been wiped from his memory by whatever now indwelt him. This man standing before her was a stranger. Something resided in him, something dark and eternal.

If she could break through that wall and reach her father, she might have a chance. He was in there somewhere; she was sure of it. She'd seen it briefly on the mountaintop, right before he'd changed and killed William and Marny. She tried again. "Do you remember when we took hikes in the forest and chased squirrels around the trees? You almost caught that fat one. Do you remember that?"

Still his eyes showed nothing. He was gone, merely a shell of the man she once knew.

"Do you remember how I loved you?" It was her last effort to connect with him.

Harold's eyes shifted slightly, almost imperceptibly. Something had happened there, a breakthrough of some kind. Small, maybe, but it was something.

He opened his mouth to speak but was cut short by the door opening. Another man entered, carrying a rifle.

"They're coming."

They? Who? The police? How?

Harold glared at Esther as if she were responsible for whoever it was making their way through the tunnel. "You need to come with us. Now."

She hesitated, stayed put in the chair.

"Esther. *Now.* Let's go."

Still she didn't move. If someone was coming, her best chance was to stay here.

Harold cursed and closed the distance between them in two large steps. He grabbed a handful of Esther's hair and yanked her to her feet. She screamed.

Pushing away from the banister, Gary ventured into the living room but found it empty. No William. The dining room and closets proved no different. Only the kitchen was left. The linoleum was slick with frost, forcing him to take small, sliding steps. Other than the ice covering everything, the room appeared undisturbed. The back door was also covered in ice and hadn't been opened.

He then noticed the door on the far side of the kitchen. The cellar door. They had to have gone to the cellar, only it too was frozen shut. Thick ice sheathed the sliding bolt lock. The doorknob dripped icicles. Gary crossed the room and took hold of the knob. The icicles broke and clinked to the floor. He turned the knob—ice cracked and broke free—and rattled the door, but the ice covering the lock held. He banged it with his fist, but it was too thick to break. Using the butt of his pistol, Gary jabbed at the ice, but the steel did little more than scratch the surface.

Panic lashed at him. He had to get the door open, had to get to William. Who knew what lies the punk was filling William's head with? Protecting the anointed one was more than just a physical assignment; it was mental and spiritual as well. Gary had to keep William pure, untarnished by the filth of the world, filth the punk was no doubt piling on the boy's tender psyche.

He pounded more violently on the lock, putting his muscle behind it, and little by little it began to break away until the lock was exposed enough to slide and disengage. Once unlocked, the door opened with a creak. The air flowing up from the cellar was warm and dry and soothed Gary's numb, wet hands.

He stood at the top of the stairs for a few seconds, waiting, listening, but heard nothing. Gary descended the steps and again stopped at the bottom to listen. Still nothing. If William wasn't down here, then Gary had no idea where the boy was. He couldn't live with himself knowing he'd lost the anointed. But he would live if for no other reason than to devote his life to finding and retrieving William. This was his mission, and ending his life would be a sorry cop-out.

Gary turned and noticed the wall of boxes, some stacked neatly, some displaced and tossed to the side. He took a few steps closer and saw the open door. It led to a subterranean tunnel.

A tunnel that would lead him to William.

Chapter 63

A SHADOW MOVED IN the room.

Marny stopped, and William stepped closer to him. The tunnel was quiet, too quiet, and it put Marny's senses on high alert. The door seemed to grow and expand. Marny wasn't sure if it really was moving or if it was merely a trick of his eyes in the dim lighting. After what had happened already, he wouldn't be surprised to find it was either.

He took one step closer to the door and was stopped by a man's voice.

"You lost?"

Marny spun around and found a small group of men blocking the tunnel to their right. Darkness obscured their faces. In the tunnel they appeared to be larger than life.

One of the men stepped forward. He had something in his hand, but it too was hidden in the shadows. "You lost?" he said again.

This was no welcoming party bringing gifts to share. Marny and William were intruders and ones who should have been long dead.

Another man lifted something to shoulder height.

Marny stepped back and put his arm around William.

A light flicked on. The man held a lantern; its light was dull and moody but enough to illuminate the tunnel. There were four men.

Their faces were flat, even, as if they wore masks. These were not men with free will, they were puppets under the control of some evil master. The one in front carried a machete and held it waist level.

The men stepped forward in unison. By the light of the lantern their eye sockets appeared deep and hollow, the angles of the faces sharper and leaner.

Marny didn't like the look of this. There was obviously a maze of tunnels down here, and these men knew them. Running was an option, but not a very good one.

The pack of sinister puppets took another step closer.

Taking a step back, Marny turned to check the tunnel behind them and found two more men closing in, blocking the way. The only way out now was the way they had come. It was fight-or-flight time. Could he and William outrun these tunnel rats? Maybe, maybe not. There was only one way to find out. But Esther was behind that door. He'd recognized her scream.

The men on both sides inched closer, pressing Marny to make a move. His mind said run, get out of there, out of the creepy house, and go for help. But his heart said stay. Esther needed him to fight for her. He was her only hope. He and William.

Marny squeezed William's shoulder. "If there's anything you can do, now would be a good time."

To their left, the door to the room opened all the way, and there stood Harold, pistol in hand. Marny looked past him and saw Esther standing in the middle of the room. To her left was another man, shorter and older than Harold.

When the door opened and Esther saw William and Marny, she first thought she was seeing things, that under the stress her brain had misfired and fooled her. Only it was no trick. They were alive, and they'd managed to find her. Her hand went to her mouth and the tears came quickly. She'd watched as Marny went down from a shot to the head and William followed, shot mid-chest. How could a boy survive that?

William's gift, of course. Even death could not harness the power of faith.

Harold lifted the gun and pointed it at Marny. "I killed you once already."

Marny looked over Harold's shoulder and found Esther. She couldn't believe he was really there, that he'd come all this way and found her.

The other men came up behind Marny and shoved him from behind. He stumbled forward into the room, William with him.

Harold walked up to Marny and put the barrel of the pistol against his forehead. "I should blow your brains out right here, make sure you're good and dead before I leave you this time."

The men behind Marny stepped out of the way.

Esther held her breath and locked eyes with William. Amazingly, there was no fear on his face. He was as calm as he ever was, as if all this were just some game that everyone knew the outcome of and no one really got hurt.

Instead of pulling the trigger, Harold swung the gun around and caught William on the side of the head. The boy lurched sideways and crumpled on paper legs. Marny's hand slipped from William's, and Marny lunged at Harold. But Harold was too quick and sidestepped, shoving Marny in the back as he passed and throwing him into the table. The table slammed against the wall. Marny bounced off and dropped to his knees. Harold was right there, grabbed the back of Marny's neck, shoved him to the floor, and drove his knee into the space between the shoulder blades.

Esther screamed again and made a move for William, who lay motionless on the floor.

"No!" Harold yelled. "Stop her."

Two men stepped between Esther and William. She tried to fight, but they were much too strong for her.

Harold put the gun's barrel against the back of Marny's head and nodded toward William. "Hog-tie him and put a pillowcase over his head. I don't want him seeing or hearing anything."

Esther struggled against her captors. "No, leave him alone."

"Hurry up," Harold said. "And get her out of here."

Chapter 64

MARNY WAS ON the floor with nowhere to go and nothing to do.

Pinned there by Harold's knee and the barrel of the handgun, he couldn't move. The ground was hard and cold against his face, and Harold had his arms pulled so far behind his back his shoulders felt like they'd come loose from their sockets at any moment. On the other side of the room, William was lifted from the ground and carried out, and Esther, fighting and screaming and clawing, was dragged out by three men.

Marny was alone with Harold and was sure this was it, the culmination of his curse. The time had come to pay up. He'd known this day would come and had often wondered how he would react. Oddly, he felt little fear. Sure there was the fear of dying everyone experienced. For him, the fear of a bullet penetrating his skull and tearing through his brain. But more than fear he felt an overwhelming self-loathing. He'd failed. William and Esther were in the hands of madmen, evil, malicious monsters, and there was nothing he could do. He'd stuck with this ordeal because he'd wanted to do some good, do the right thing, and because he'd found himself more and more attracted to Esther and her little brother. But in the end he'd come to this, a helpless victim at the mercy of the one who'd started the whole thing.

Harold's voice came as a raspy whisper. "I killed you once;

I know I did." His mouth was inches from Marny's ear, close enough that Marny could feel the hot breath against the side of his face. "How did you get here?"

Marny said nothing.

"Did the boy, the *thing*, do this?"

William's words came back to Marny. *You need to trust Him, Marnin. You need to let go of yourself. You're holding on too tight. He knows you better than you know yourself.*

William believed in him, believed he could be more than he thought he could be.

You need to trust Him, Marnin. He was speaking of God, of course. Marny needed to trust God. He had at one time. During those nightly visits his mother made to his room when she'd read him the Bible. Those words often brought comfort and encouragement and planted the seeds of faith in young Marny. But as the curse grew and claimed more lives, and as his prayers to be freed from Karl went unanswered, Marny's faith and trust withered. And when the curse finally entangled his mother and dragged her down those steps, whatever inkling of trust he had left died altogether.

Let go of yourself. You're holding on too tight. Marny had learned a long time ago that life was an untamed beast and death even more wild and unruly. At first he'd tried to resist the curse, to control the uncontrollable. But time and time again he'd stood helpless as death bucked and charged and claimed another life. Eventually he'd given up and decided to ride the current of his fate and simply avoid tempting it. But when Esther appeared at the garage and that note followed, everything changed.

Harold took a handful of Marny's hair, lifted his head off the floor, and slammed it down again. The shock momentarily made everything go black.

"I'm going to kill you here, and I'm going to make sure of it this time."

He knows you better than you know yourself. The truth of William's words hit Marny full force. He *was* helpless, yes. All his efforts to control and hold tight were futile. And deep down he knew that, had known it all along. Years of hiding his fear and insecurities and self-loathing were suddenly exposed, the windows of his soul were thrown open, and light shone in, bright, cleansing light. Marny no longer felt the pain in his shoulders, no longer felt the barrel against his head or Harold's knee in his back. He felt something he'd never known before. Peace. He wasn't in control; he didn't have to hold tight to anything. God was in control, and that was all that mattered. Marny then understood that trust required selfless surrender; faith was about doing *God's* will, not his own.

God, I trust You. Four simple words, but to Marny they were nothing short of a manifesto.

Harold cursed and jammed the barrel harder against Marny's head.

A shot rang out but not from Harold's gun, not even from within the room. From somewhere else in the tunnels. Harold's pressure on Marny's arms lightened a little. Another shot, then a cluster of them. Muffled pops, rapid and successive. A man screamed.

Harold grabbed Marny's hair again and lifted his head off the floor. "You stay here or I'll kill the girl, you hear?" Then he jammed his face against the dirt again.

Marny felt warm liquid ooze from his cheekbone.

Harold released his hold, got up, and bolted through the doorway, closing the door behind him. The lock engaged.

More gunfire erupted outside the room.

Marny climbed to his feet and rubbed his head. He dabbed at his cheek, and his fingers came away red. The door was locked tight. He kicked at it, but the heavy wood didn't budge.

In the tunnel another man screamed, cursed, hollered something garbled.

Marny had an idea then. He thought of William back in Gary's house. The locks on the door, Gary rumbling down the steps. William had unlocked them. His faith had unlocked them.

Marny put his hands on the doorknob and closed his eyes,

focused his mind on the lock. Nothing happened. He prayed, asked God to unlock the door. Still nothing. The door was as dumb and still as ever. Marny backed away, confused. He knew God could unlock that door; of course He could. Marny believed it a thousand percent. So why wasn't it happening?

Frustrated, he charged the door, prepared to kick it again, when he heard the lock disengage. He reached for the knob and yanked open the door.

Esther stood on the other side.

Chapter 65

FOR GARY, THE tunnel was a pathway to freedom.

It led to William, and the boy would show him the way to loose his soul from the binds of this world. Gary was quickly realizing that William was not only the anointed one; he was a savior. *His* savior. And not only that, but more. Something much more, so unique and holy and special that Gary dared not even mention it, dared not even think on it for too long. But William had to know, the boy had to be told the truth. Gary had to get to him, bring him safely back into the fold and watch over him as a shepherd does his sheep.

When Gary crossed the threshold from cellar to tunnel, the door shut behind him, sealing off any light. He was in darkness now, but William would be his light. One hand holding his gun, the other running along the dirt wall, Gary moved forward, taking the turns cautiously, feeling his way through the lightless corridor.

The darkness was thick and oppressive, like a heavy fog he could feel in his lungs with each drawn breath. The air was stale and warm. Voices were there as well, surrounding Gary, whispering to him, taunting him. The innocent voice of Landon, his baby-like noises, that unmistakable speech impediment. The voice of his father, questioning, warning. He was so disappointed in his older son, so hurt, so angry. But above them both was the voice of William, calling to Gary, pleading, crying, beckoning him to come and provide rescue.

Gary picked up the pace and moved through the tunnel as though he'd navigated the maze a hundred times. William's presence was his eyes; William's voice was his light. It was as though the boy had some psychic tether with which he drew Gary forward, guiding him through the darkness.

Up ahead Gary heard voices, men's voices, talking in hushed tones. He crept forward, feeling the wall for the next corner, and stopped when he found it. He peeked around the corner and found a huddle of men illuminated by the light of a lantern. A door was just feet from them, and it was open. Soft light spilled out into the tunnel. From inside the room a voice spoke harshly, followed by a disturbance. Two men exited carrying a body, a small body, like that of a child.

It was William. *His* William.

The man in the room spoke again, and more people came through the doorway. Three men and a woman. Esther. One man had her by the hair and neck and forced her forward, in the opposite direction of William.

Anger jumped into Gary's chest, and he moved closer, keeping along the wall of the corridor.

The men with William disappeared down another tunnel, and Gary followed. He paused and poked his head around a corner. They were putting distance between him and William. He had to act now. Careful not to hit the boy, Gary took aim and squeezed the trigger. The discharge of the pistol sounded like cannon fire in the confines of the tunnel. The gun bucked, and one of the men dropped. The others scattered and hollered. Gary fired more shots, keeping his aim high so as not to errantly hit William. Shots came back at him, digging into the walls and spraying dirt, some dangerously close to finding their mark.

Gary's shots were dead on, dropping men one by one. The tunnel filled with thunder and the sound of men in panic.

The percussion of a weapon sounded behind Gary. Something

bit the back of his shoulder and pushed him forward, into the open tunnel. He squeezed off more rounds and found more flesh, but the pain in his shoulder quickly spread and rendered his arm useless. He leaned against the wall and sucked in a short breath. He had to stay on his feet, had to keep moving forward, keep firing shots.

William needed him.

He needed William.

Both of their lives depended on it.

Chapter 66

MARNY STOOD DUMBLY and stared at Esther, not sure if it was really her or an apparition.

She reached out her hand to him. "Come on, Marny. I know where William is."

He walked toward her and took her hand. She was real. She pulled him out of the room and down the tunnel opposite where the gunshots were heard. They rounded one corner, then another, following the curves of the tunnel with their free hands.

"Do you know where you're going?" Marny kept his voice to a whisper. In the distance, the gunshots continued but became more sporadic and muffled.

"We're doubling around. I think these tunnels form a big square."

It made sense, a square with rooms on the interior. They'd come up behind the men who had taken William.

They came to a third corner and Esther stopped, put her hand on Marny's chest. The gunshots were louder now, just around the bend.

She poked her head around the corner, then turned to Marny. "William's there, on the ground, about fifteen feet away. I'm going to get him."

"No, wait." Marny held her shoulder. "I'll do it."

"You sure?"

"You think I'm going to let you go out there in that gunfire?"

"I was hoping you wouldn't."

"You've been enough of a hero for one day. It's my turn."

Marny ducked around the corner, stayed low and to the wall, and moved quickly to where William lay, still unconscious. Two men had their backs to him, firing in the opposite direction. Whoever was shooting at them was just around the far corner.

Grabbing William by both wrists, Marny dragged the boy the fifteen feet, but just before he pulled William around the corner a deep voice bellowed through the tunnel.

"Noo! William."

Gary. The shooter was Gary. He'd found his way to the cellar and into the tunnels. He'd come for William. The gunfire picked up, and a man yelped.

Marny yanked William around the corner and locked eyes with Esther. "Gary's here. Help me get him up."

They got William onto Marny's back, across his shoulders.

"There's no other way out," Esther said.

"There has to be another way. Whoever dug these tunnels wouldn't have left themselves with only one way in and out. Too easy to get trapped. We only followed the interior wall of the tunnel, what about the outside wall? There has to be an auxiliary tunnel of some kind, another way out."

They backtracked, this time running their hands along the outside wall until Esther suddenly stopped. "Here's a corner. It must be another tunnel."

"Go, go." Marny pushed her gently in the back.

Quickly they moved down the darkened tunnel with no light to lead the way. Marny had no idea where it led or how long it was, but they didn't have time for other options.

Two more gunshots fired, distant, muffled. They were extending the gap between themselves and Gary.

Adrenaline surged through Marny's veins, saturated his muscles. He raced on blindly. Finally Esther stopped and Marny nearly ran her down.

"What? What is it?"

"A ladder."

Marny felt in the darkness, and there it was, a metal ladder.

"I'll go first," Esther said.

Marny didn't like the idea, but with William draped across his shoulders he would need both his hands and wouldn't be able to feel for any kind of opening above them.

"Okay, but be careful. Take it slow."

Esther's hand found Marny's face. Her touch was soft and once again reminded him of his mother's. "Slow isn't a luxury we have right now."

She started to climb, and a few seconds later said, "There's a metal door here."

There was a popping sound, then the creak and moan of dry hinges. The door swung up and open, and the waning light of evening filtered down into the tunnel.

Marny climbed the ladder, one hand working the rungs, the other holding onto William. When he reached the opening Esther helped him with William, and they both collapsed on the ground above.

"I just need to catch my breath quick, rest my legs." Marny's lungs were working overtime, and his legs felt like rubber from the climb.

Esther closed the door and sat on it. "Real quick. Time isn't our friend here."

They were in a hollow deep in the forest. The ground rose and sloped upward for several hundred yards all around them before ending in a circular ridge. The forest was dotted with mature pines, comfortably spaced, and little undergrowth.

Marny stood. "Do you know where we are?"

"Not a clue. Are you done resting?"

"I could rest the remainder of my life and it wouldn't be enough. But we need to keep moving. I say we head back toward the house." The Rose residence was on the other side of the rise, and beyond the house was Cranberry Road and the way out of this nightmare.

"How do we know which way is the house?"

Marny scanned the area. She was right. They were surrounded by rising ground and could see nothing but trees and dirt.

"The tunnel could have turned so gradually we didn't even notice," Esther said. "The house could be in any direction."

"Well, we have to pick one and go for it. I'm not waiting around here to see what crawls out of that hole. We need to get to high ground and see what's on the other side."

Once on the ridge they could survey the area beneath and find the house.

Esther helped him with William again, and they started to climb. The slope was not unbearably steep, not as steep as the trail Harold had taken them on in Massachusetts, but it didn't take long for Marny's legs to begin to burn again. Soon he was slowing down, fighting the urge to stop and rest.

Gary had finished off the rest of the men and found the tunnel leading out, the tunnel down which they had taken William. He would retrieve the boy, *his* boy. He had to. He ran full stride down the corridor. He had to make up time; they were well ahead of him. His shoulder burned and cramped, but he ignored the discomfort and pressed on.

Strangely, the voice in his head, the voice of his father, was silent. He'd finally rid himself of it. He had no need of it anyway; he knew what was at stake.

He met a ladder at nearly full speed and cursed loudly. It led to the outside world, the world that begged to corrupt his boy. Up he climbed until he reached the door above. He pushed it open and squinted into the dusty sunlight. This was it, the way they'd gone.

Gary emerged from the opening in the ground and stood erect. His shoulder throbbed and ached and oozed blood. In front of him was a shallow mountain with a gentle slope. More than halfway up he spotted two figures, and one was carrying a boy.

Farther down the hill was another figure, a man following them. Harold.

Chapter 67

MARNY PUSHED UP the hill, willing his legs to move forward, to step, to climb.

Esther was behind him, her hand on the small of his back as if she were supporting him and urging him onward. The incline didn't look this sharp from the base, where the tunnel emerged from the forest floor, but now that he was on it, the climb seemed almost vertical.

As they got nearer the summit, the trees thinned and grew shorter. Rocky outcroppings protruded here and there. The soil was thin and loose, and good footing was getting more difficult to come by.

Three quarters of the way up, Marny had to slow. He was beginning to hyperventilate and his legs were rubbery bands, barely keeping him upright.

"No," Esther nearly shouted. "Keep going, Marny; you have to."

Marny glanced behind them and saw Harold gaining quickly, his athletic form taking the hill easily. Shifting William on his shoulders, Marny dug in and pressed on. He began talking to his legs, begging them for just one more step. One more step. One more step.

"We're almost there, Marny. Keep going."

Marny looked ahead and saw the summit just yards away. But what then? So they reached the summit, so what? There was no magic door at the top of the mountain through which they could pass into another dimension, leaving Harold behind. It was over. Marny couldn't go any farther. All the trusting and faith in the world couldn't save them now. It was just them and Harold, and he wouldn't let them escape alive again.

As he reached the clearing on the top of the mountain, Marny stumbled forward and collapsed to the ground. William rolled off his shoulders and landed near a large boulder. Esther fell to her knees beside him. She too had to know it was the end.

Marny's head swam from lack of oxygen. He lay flat on his back, his legs throbbing, his diaphragm in spasms, sucking in short, shallow breaths.

It didn't take Harold long to reach them. He stopped a good thirty feet away and put his hands on his hips. His respirations were barely above normal.

Harold pointed his gun at Marny. "Seems we've been here before."

Marny climbed to his feet but did not raise his hands. It was a useless act of submission at this point.

William began to stir, to lift his head and move his arms, and Esther made a move for him.

"Leave him," Harold said. "Let him alone, Esther."

Esther stopped and eyed her father. For a second Marny thought she would defy him and go to William anyway, but she didn't.

William lay on his side now, his eyes glazed and distant.

"Look at him," Esther said, pointing to William. "Look what you did to your son."

Harold spat to the side, wiped his mouth with the back of his sleeve. "I told you, he's not my son. Your mother had an affair, and this freak was the result of it. She wanted me to raise him as my own, claim him as my son."

"It's not true." Tears spilled from Esther's eyes. "Mom wouldn't do that."

"She did. I couldn't stand the sight of him. How could I live with them—a woman who betrayed me and her illegitimate freak son?"

Esther said nothing. She glanced at William and put her hands to her face.

The gun trained on Marny again. Harold's face twisted into a scowl. "You've brought me enough trouble. It's time to end this."

"You're him, aren't you?" Marny said.

Harold's scowl froze on his face.

"You're the Maniac. It was you who killed all those people ten years ago."

"You shut your face." Harold's voice was a growl, barely human.

"You drained the blood from their bodies. They were all type O. The universal donor."

To his right, Esther shifted her weight. She dashed the tears from her cheeks. "Is that true?"

"Shut up!"

"I'm type O," Esther said. "You killed all those people for their blood? What were you doing, drinking it? Injecting yourself with it?"

Harold's mouth tightened into a thin line; his lips disappeared. "*We* did it. All of us. They gave us life."

"The life is in the blood." Esther's voice was low, weak. Disbelieving.

"Look at me." Harold hit his chest with an open palm. "I'm forty-seven and in the best shape of my life. I can do anything."

"Even take the life of your own daughter? Drain it from her?" Marny said. He wanted to push Harold. Maybe if they drove him further into a fit of rage, he'd snap and self-destruct, turn the gun on himself. It was their only chance of getting off this mountain alive.

Harold repositioned his feet, opened his stance. The gun moved in his hand.

"No, wait." Esther stepped in front of Marny. "It doesn't have to be like this. Haven't you killed enough? Please. I'll go with you. Just let them go."

"Let them go? You think I'm a fool? I let them go, and they run right to the police."

"But who would believe them? You're an ex-cop, a hero around here."

But Harold's eyes remained lifeless and dead. He had death in his blood now. He was fully given over to the darkness, a slave to its whims and lusts.

"Get out of the way, Esther."

Esther didn't move. "No. This isn't you; you aren't my father, my dad."

"Get out of the way."

Still she held her ground. "You'll have to shoot me first."

"Fine." Harold swung the gun around so it pointed at William, who was now sitting on the ground rubbing his eyes.

A shot cracked through the still mountain air, and Esther screamed. Marny's breath hitched in his throat.

But William didn't move. Didn't even flinch. His eyes remained trained on Harold.

Harold's face went blank, his jaw slack. He tried to speak, but nothing came out. He dropped his gun and lifted his hand to the back of his head, took two steps forward on stilt-like legs, teetered, and finally toppled forward like a felled tree.

Marny froze. Neither Esther nor William moved.

Seconds later Gary crested the mountain, gun in hand.

Chapter 68

THE BOY," GARY said. "I want him."

Esther shook her head. "You can't have him."

Gary pointed the handgun at Marny. "Give me William or the punk dies."

Esther hesitated. She looked at Marny, and in her eyes was the look of defeat. Everyone knew she had no leverage. Gary could shoot Marny and Esther both if he wanted to. In fact, he probably would. He was toying with them.

"No," Esther said.

"There's been enough death already. I just want William. I have a right to him."

"No one has a right to him. I won't leave him."

"I need to make sure he's okay. William, are you okay?"

William stood now. He swayed back and forth slowly and said nothing.

"No," Esther said again. She reached her hand out to William, but the boy didn't take it. "He's my brother. I won't leave him."

"Esther, you've always been in the way." Gary's voice rose, his face reddened. "I took you in, you and your mother and William. Let you live in my home. Provided for you. I cared for William, protected him, and obeyed my calling. And from the beginning you challenged me. Tested me. Made my duty difficult."

Marny was convinced Gary was raving mad. The more he talked this nonsense, the angrier he got. He had to be stopped.

"Listen," Marny said. "Maybe we can work something out here."

Gary stared fire at Marny. "You shut up! I should have killed you back in Massachusetts. But William wanted you with him. He *needed* you." His voice tapered a little.

Esther stepped forward. "Please, Gary. No more killing. Put the gun down."

The lines on Gary's face softened, the color faded, and the gun lowered a few inches. "I need him. He's my son." Gary looked at William, and Marny thought he saw tears in the big man's eyes. "You're my son. My boy. I need you with me."

Esther froze. To Marny, it seemed the rotation of the earth stopped while this news was processed. It was insane, of course, but insane enough that it made sense. It explained Gary's strange obsession with William and Harold's hatred of the man. It explained why Gary took the three Roses in after Harold left. He was no uncle to William and Esther at all; he had been their mother's lover, the man with whom she'd betrayed Harold.

Esther locked eyes with Marny for only a moment, then turned her head toward William. "No. It's not true."

William's eyes cleared and he nodded. "It's true, Esther. He's my father."

"He's my son." Gary's voice cracked. "Please, I have to keep him safe. It's my calling. My duty."

Esther extended her hand to William again, but still he didn't take it. "You knew? Since when?"

William's hands hung limp at his sides, his shoulders slumped. "When Harold told us about Mom. I figured it out."

Gary brought the gun up again and pointed it at Esther. "I'm not leaving this mountain without him."

Marny knew Gary was serious. He'd killed how many already in his quest to "protect" William? What were two more?

He had to do something. Marny's mind churned but kept getting stuck on Esther's words from the past couple days...

You're the right one, Marny...all part of God's plan...you don't have to understand it, just believe...it's called faith...we can all have faith.

Faith only works when it's filtered through love. Okay, so he loved her. He loved Esther...and William. But still the question was there: What could he do?

Gary's face reddened again. "I'm leaving with William, my son. And you're not stopping me."

The pines began to rustle and sway. A strong wind had suddenly kicked up.

"He's mine. I've been called to protect him, and I will not fail."

Wind whipped across the clearing and tore through the trees. Pine needles took to the air like rain.

And William swayed, still swayed. His head was bowed and palms turned up, as if asking for a handout or showing he had nothing to offer.

"You'll have to kill me first," Esther shouted. Her voice was mostly lost in the powerful gusts.

Gary leveled the gun on her, and a slight smile tugged at the corners of his mouth. Marny knew what came next, and he couldn't let that happen. He lunged toward Esther and in front of her as the gun popped and bucked in Gary's hand. The impact of the slug was like being punched in the chest. Oddly, no pain accompanied it. As Esther screamed, Marny hit the ground with tremendous force, knocking the air from his lungs, and rolled twice.

Things came in spits and bursts then. The wind still howled, more violently than ever. Esther was there, kneeling by his side, saying his name. Marny momentarily blacked out, then he opened his eyes and lifted his head. William still stood with his head bowed and hands up. Tears washed down his face. He cried steadily. The wind pushed the trees around like they were weeds in an open field. William's hair twisted about his head in sporadic patterns. But now the ground shook as well. All Marny could think was earthquake. Had there ever been an earthquake in Maine?

Gary was still in his spot, fighting to remain on his feet. The gun wavered. He fired a shot, then another, but they were wildly misplaced.

Esther lifted Marny's head and put it in her lap.

The ground trembled and quaked. It sounded like a freight train bearing down on them, storming up the mountainside. Gary's legs buckled, but he didn't fall.

To their right, a boulder the size of an SUV broke free and toppled out of view.

And still William stood and swayed, palms up, eyes closed so tight only the tips of their tear-wetted lashes were visible.

The soil beneath Gary's feet began to give way.

Gary looked up, his eyes wide and fearful. His mouth gaped...and the earth disintegrated. The ground opened. Gary lost his footing and sank to his knees, then his waist. He clawed at the dirt in desperation, grabbed at rocks. But he continued to slip, to fall, to be swallowed up by the mountain. He was down to his shoulders now; then only his head remained above ground, his face frozen in terror.

Then he was gone. The earth moved back into place, and the chasm sealed itself.

And just as quickly and suddenly as it had started, the ground stopped moving and the wind ceased blowing.

William's arms fell to his sides.

The boy dropped to his knees. The only noise was the sound of his crying.

Chapter 69

FIRE RADIATED FROM Marny's chest.

The slug had hit him just below the collarbone on the right side. His arm felt like someone had injected his veins with acid. A great numbness overtook his hand and forearm. Spasms tightened the muscles of his shoulder and chest. Hot blood oozed from the wound, life escaping him. He lay on his back, motionless. The ground below had stopped its shaking, but the darkening sky above seemed to swirl and rotate in a counter-clockwise direction, like water down a drain.

Esther leaned over and put her hand on his cheek. Her touch was warm and tender and did more than comfort him. "Hang on, Marny. I'll be right back."

She left and went to William. He was on his knees on the ground, covering his face with both hands, sobbing.

Esther took her little brother into her arms and held him. She rocked back and forth, stroked his hair, made calming noises.

"I didn't mean it, Esther." William sniffed and wiped at his eyes. "I only wanted to help you and Marnin. I just wanted him to leave."

"I know. I know." Esther stopped rocking and cupped William's face in her hands. "William, Marny needs you now. He's been hurt."

William looked over Esther's shoulder at Marny. Tears wet his cheeks; his lower lip trembled. He stood and walked to Marny, knelt beside him.

"You've been shot, Marnin." He sniffed. "You need to stop getting shot."

In spite of the pain, in spite of the life bleeding from him, in spite of the heavy fog that clouded his head, Marny smiled. "I'll have to remind myself to stay out of the path of speeding bullets."

William, the wonder boy, the giant of faith, placed his hand on Marny's chest over the entry wound. He shut his eyes and moved his lips slowly, speaking unheard words. Gradually, like the cooling of lava, the heat in Marny's shoulder dissipated and the pain subsided. The muscles relaxed and feeling returned to his hand.

William opened his eyes, and for the first time since Marny met him, smiled. It was a nice smile, warm and wide, genuine.

"Thank you, William."

"You're welcome, Marnin, but it wasn't me. It never is. God did it."

"Yes. I know that."

Marny sat up, and Esther put her arms around his shoulders. "And thank you. My hero."

"Hero?"

She pulled away and studied Marny's face. Those eyes of hers, deep pools of still blue water, washed over him and brought comfort and hope. "You saved me, you know. Only a hero would do that."

He had saved her, hadn't he? He'd taken the bullet. "It was—"

"Don't say it was nothing. It was anything but nothing. Marny, you have a heart big enough to fit the world in."

His mother's words.

"Are you okay?" he said.

She paused, smiled. "Yes. I'm still alive."

"We need to go, Marnin." William stared at Harold's lifeless body, facedown on the ground.

The sun was nearly gone, and they would need all the light

they could get to find their way off the mountain and back to civilization.

Marny took William's withered hand in his and patted it. With his other hand he took hold of Esther's. Together they made their way back down the mountain, back to roads and homes where people lived. People who did not want them dead.

Chapter 70

L IFE DOESN'T ALWAYS supply the answers to every question.
Milly's was the only diner in Comfort and was next door
to the White Pine Inn, the only motel. Marny sat at a booth and
sipped his coffee. Across from him, William worked on a chocolate milk. Four booths over, Esther was in deep conversation with
Mitch Wickham, a lieutenant with the Maine State Police.

William lowered the mug to the table, revealing a chocolate
milk mustache. He wiped at it with the back of his hand. "Do you
think they're going to put me in jail, Marnin?"

Marny smiled. "No way. You didn't do anything wrong."

"I killed Gary."

"You didn't. You saved us. You said so yourself. All you did was
pray for God to intervene. He chose how to do it."

Since the incident four days earlier, when they came down off
that mountain to be greeted by the flashing lights of a state patrol
car, William had worried he'd go to jail. There was no consoling
the boy. He grieved for Gary too. Deep in his heart Marny knew
William had hoped there was some chance for reconciliation, that
Gary's sins would be forgiven and wounds mended and he could
actually have a relationship with the man. William grieved not
only the loss of a life, but the loss of the opportunity to have a real
father, a real dad.

William stared at his hands. "Do you think he could have loved me, Marnin?"

Marnin reached over and covered William's twisted hand. "I think he did love you, in his own way."

"He had a strange way of showing it."

"Yes, he did. And a lot of people got hurt because of it. And Esther and I would have been next."

"I didn't want him to die."

"I know. All you did was have faith. God took care of the rest. All we can do is have faith and pray. We must agree with God's will, not the other way around. You taught me that."

William's mouth turned up in a subtle smile. "You were listening to me, Marnin?"

"Hanging on every word."

Esther stood, shook the lieutenant's hand, and made her way back to William and Marny. She slid in next to her brother and kissed him on the cheek. "Good news, little brother. You're not going to spend one minute in jail."

"Did you tell him what happened, Esther?" William said.

"Everything."

"Did you tell him I didn't want Gary to die?"

"Of course. They're saying a micro-earthquake hit the region and opened up a cave, and Gary just fell in. That's the story."

"Some story," Marny said.

"Stranger than fiction."

Marny pushed his coffee aside. "And what about the house? What about Harold?"

For three full days the Maine State Police had combed the home and tunnels on Cranberry Road. And after tracking Gary from Massachusetts to Maine, the FBI even showed up for a day, did their thing, and got out of there. They didn't appear to enjoy their stay in Vacationland.

Esther reached for a sugar packet and spun it on the table. "It's quite a story, the stuff of a weird novel."

"We have nothing else to do."

Esther took a sip of William's chocolate milk and swallowed hard. She took a deep breath. "For starters, no one survived the shootout down there. There were ten of them. Normal guys, I guess, working men. Construction types, a lawyer, a forest ranger, even a couple state troopers. And one was Dr. Martin Finkelstine, a hematologist in Bangor who lost his license to practice medicine for tampering with blood samples and performing experiments on unknowing patients, among other things. Unseemly things. But they were all family men. And they were all murderers."

"The guy next door. Why is it that the normal guy next door turns out to be the creep?"

"Their normalcy keeps them hidden, steers them away from suspicion."

"And they had some kind of ritual thing going on down there in the tunnels?"

"More than that. And much worse."

"*They* were the Maine Maniac?"

She nodded, spun the sugar packet again. "Together they formed a cult and did dark and disgusting things, things too gruesome even to talk about." She glanced at William. "The things they did are best left unsaid. To talk about it would be to memorialize what they did. And they don't deserve that."

"But the blood, type O, the victims. What was that all about?"

Esther paused, swallowed again. Marny could tell the more she talked, the harder it was for her to go on. The story, the nightmare, didn't get any better as it went, and though he was a monster and murderer, Harold, the man spearheading the disgusting acts, was still her father. She and he shared the same blood.

"It seems they got it in their heads that if they replaced their own aging blood with that of the young and healthy, the pure and strong, they would live longer. The life is in the blood. So they drained their victims and transfused the blood into their own veins."

William shifted in his seat but said nothing. He was all ears but clearly bothered by Esther's grisly tale.

Marny said, "A new breed of vampires."

"Drinking from a dark fountain of youth."

"Fiction doesn't touch this."

"I warned you."

"So what about the Maniac's murders?"

"Wickham said he thinks all the murders will be solved and then some."

"There were more?"

"Recent ones, unsolved, as recent as a month ago in Monroe Bridge."

Marny was about to take a sip of coffee but set the mug down again instead. "Harold."

"Seems he tried to run from his sins, tried to hide from his dark past and start a new life."

"Building ornate cupolas in Massachusetts."

"But eventually his demons found him."

"They almost always do."

"They *always* do. Sooner or later."

Marny ran his finger around the rim of his coffee mug. "What do you think drove him into such a dark place? I mean, from cop to killer is quite a fall."

"We'll never know now. My guess is that he was so hurt by what my mother did, and"—she paused and put her hand over William's withered one—"so repulsed by William that he just snapped."

"That's the understatement of the century." Marny downed the rest of his coffee. "And the house? Please tell me there's a perfectly rational explanation for what we experienced there."

Esther shrugged and shook her head. "Nope. They didn't find anything. No blood, no water, the temperature was a perfectly balmy seventy-eight degrees."

"So I imagined the whole thing?"

She tilted her head to one side. "And William and Gary imagined the same thing? Hardly. What would the chances of that be? There were some dark forces at work there. I saw it in the eyes of the men, the doctor, my father."

"I told you the house was alive, Marnin," William said.

"In a way, I guess it was."

Esther reached across the table and took Marny's hand. "But the light pushed back the darkness."

"It almost always does."

"No," she said. "It *always* does. Sooner or later."

Chapter 71

Saying good-bye is the hardest part.

One day after Marny, Esther, and William came down off that mountain, the bodies of George Condon and Pete Morsey were found buried in the pebbled beach behind Mr. Condon's shoreline home.

Petey's funeral was held a week later, Mr. Condon's a day after that. Marny attended both.

He hadn't realized the scope and breadth of Mr. Condon's influence on the people of Down East Maine. Hundreds came to pay their respects to the man some knew as Condy, some as George, some as Mr. Condon. They testified for hours of his dry humor and quick smile, of his toughness as a Maine native, of his kindness and generosity, and of his capable attention to the inner workings of any vehicle on wheels.

When it was Marny's turn, he stood before the crowd, tears in his eyes, and cleared his throat. "I've heard a lot of good things about Mr. Condon, sweet things and, I have no doubt, true things. Things I'm just now learning about him. He was more of a man than I ever imagined. And to me he was just that, more than a mere man—he was a father. I never had a father, not a real one at least, and Mr. Condon unknowingly filled those shoes. I'll miss him. I'll miss getting whipped at checkers by him. I'll miss drinking coffee with him every morning at the shop. I'll miss the tunes he used to hum while working on some engine or transmission. And I'll miss the way he used to say my name, *Mahny*. I still hear his voice in my head. He gave his life to save ours. What greater love is there than that?"

A month after the incident on the mountain behind the house on Cranberry Road, Marny, Esther, and William walked along the shoreline of Booker Island. William held a handful of shells he'd collected; Marny and Esther held hands. Water lapped at the pebbled beach and gulls circled overhead, always on the lookout for their next meal.

They walked mostly in silence, Marny thinking about the night they had spent there. It seemed like years had passed since he went through every match in that matchbook and William started the fire with nothing but faith. Years of memories and nightmares and unanswered questions. And for Marny, years of making up time and drawing closer to God. He was amazed at how much one could learn from an eleven-year-old boy wonder and his overly protective sister.

Eventually they came to the fire pit they'd sat around that night. The charred stones were still there in a neat circle, out of reach of the relentlessly surging and receding waters of the Penobscot Bay.

At the fire ring Marny stopped and faced Esther. He took both her hands in his. "My mother once told me that behind every rain cloud is the sun, just waiting to shine its light and dry the earth's tears. God knows I've been running from a rain cloud my whole life, trying to find the sun and never succeeding."

Esther's eyes never looked bluer, like they'd been chipped from the clearest sapphires. She smiled at him and squeezed his hands.

Marny turned his face toward the sky and took in the warmth of the sun, then looked at Esther again. "You're my sunshine, Esther. You're the one God sent to dry my tears and light my world."

Esther's smile grew wider. "Marny Toogood, that has to be one of the sappiest and sweetest things I've ever heard."

"Good. Sappy is just what I was going for. Never mind the sweet part."

She stood on the tips of her toes and kissed him lightly on the lips. "I love sappy. Now why did you bring us here?"

"To say thank you."

"Really?"

"Yes." He glanced at William and winked. "To thank both of you for believing in me and seeing me as a hero even though I still don't feel like one and think you're terribly wrong."

Esther and William both laughed.

"Thank you for teaching me the power of a little faith and how to truly trust." He gazed into Esther's eyes and blinked back the tears forming in his own. "And thank you for teaching me how to love, to *really* love. You remind me a lot of my mother in that way."

"Well," Esther said. "I'm glad you don't remind me of Gary. Or Harold."

"Or Karl Gunnison."

"Definitely not Karl Gunnison."

Marny paused and swallowed past the lump in his throat. Above them, gulls circled, riding wind currents and drawing wide, smooth arcs in the cerulean sky. "Esther, I have to ask you something."

"The answer is yes."

"Okay. Will you swim the English Channel with me?"

"Seriously, yes."

"I'm not a very good swimmer."

"Bummer. I'm not either. Maybe we could just take a boat."

"That's a sweet idea, but it's not really what I was going to ask."

She cocked her head to the side and smiled. "So get to it."

"Will you marry me?"

"I said yes."

She wrapped her arms around his neck and kissed him firmly. For Marny, those rain clouds had finally moved on, and the sun shone so brightly.

William tapped Marny on the arm. "So you're going to marry my sister, Marnin?"

"I sure am, little buddy. What do you think of that?"

William shifted his eyes to the gulls above, watched them thoughtfully for a moment, then said, "Good. Will I live with you?"

Marny ruffled his hair. "You bet. We wouldn't have it any other way."

William watched the birds again, that familiar disinterested look on his face. "I hope it's okay, Marnin, but I don't want you to teach me how to drive."

Coming in October 2012 from Mike Dellosso—
A Thousand Sleepless Nights

Dear Reader,

Cancer has a way of pushing you to reevaluate life. In 2008 I was diagnosed with colon cancer and took a break from writing while I endured chemotherapy. But it gave me plenty of time to think. And things started to come into focus.

You see, there's a side of me my readers rarely see. I'm a homebody. I'm sentimental to a fault. I'm a sucker for a good love story. And so, coming off my battle with cancer, I decided to focus on the characters in my stories: their relationships, their fears, their worries, and their struggles with faith. The result was *Darlington Woods*, *Darkness Follows*, and now *Frantic*.

My next book, *A Thousand Sleepless Nights*, will open a new chapter in my writing, a change of genres that will have me exploring matters of the heart, love, relationships, and life as it's really lived.

A Thousand Sleepless Nights deals with issues that are very close to my heart: family and cancer. Set in the beautiful horse country of northern Virginia, it is about a family torn apart by neglect and hurt and brought together again by a most unlikely force. If you or anyone you know has ever been touched by cancer, I know you'll enjoy this book. It is the kind of story you'll want to share with friends and family.

Thank you for taking this journey with me.

Mike Dellosso

Chapter One

NENA'S BLEEDING STARTED three weeks ago.

Now, sitting in the waiting room of the doctor's office, awaiting the verdict of his wife's recent colonoscopy, Jim Hutchins's stomach writhed and twisted like a rag in the hands of an accomplished dishwasher. Nena's father had died of...he couldn't even bring himself to think that cursed word. But there was a chance her tumor wasn't malignant, wasn't there? There was always a chance. It could be nothing more than just a clump of harmless cells. Something that could be easily removed and she would be spared the ongoing tests, the prodding, the radiation, chemo...the suffering.

He reached over and took Nena's hand in his, squeezed it gently. It felt no different than the first time he held it nearly forty years ago. She looked his way but did not smile. He could see the fear in her eyes, the uncertainty, so unlike her. She'd always been strong, defiant, full of fire and life. That's what first drew him to her. But now she looked small, scared, childlike even.

"It's going to be okay, babe," he said, even though he knew his words meant nothing, carried no weight at all.

"Don't say that," she said. "You don't know that."

She was right, of course. He didn't know it. This was one problem sheer will power couldn't fix, one problem hard work and late nights couldn't resolve. No matter how hard he fought for her this time, he was powerless. And that alone was enough to drive him mad.

Jim looked around the waiting room. There were only a handful of other people there, mostly older folk, reading magazines, talking quietly. None of them were even remotely aware of the storm raging inside him. How odd, he thought, that in a room of people they were each totally oblivious to the plights of one another. A wall separated them, cubicles around each individual, not allowing even the emotion within to show on their faces, in their eyes. Yes, he could see the strain on Nena's face, but could they? Probably not, partly because they didn't care enough to look.

The walls of the waiting room were decorated with framed paintings of horses. Some galloping in open fields, some grazing. There was one of a mare and her foal standing in a valley of lush grass by a pool of still water. The glasslike water reflected the rolling hilltops of the range beyond it. It was a peaceful picture, and for a moment Jim wished he was back on the ranch, in the saddle, the feel of polished leather beneath him, exploring the far corners of the open land. Anywhere but here in this blasted office.

The door beside the receptionist's desk opened, and a young nurse stepped out. "Nena?"

Jim squeezed Nena's hand again, and they both stood.

"Good morning," the nurse said. She stepped aside, allowed them to enter, and let the door close behind her. "Follow me. We'll go right to Dr. Van Zante's office. He's waiting for you."

They wound through a maze of hallways lined with exam rooms and more horse prints. This was Virginia's horse country, after all, and horses were the only thing most of the people around here knew. Finally they came to a door with a plaque that read *Richard Van Zante, MD*.

The nurse knocked and opened the door. "The Hutchinses, Doctor."

"Yes, let them in, Becky. Thank you."

She stepped aside as Jim and Nena entered the room. A wide mahogany desk sat in the center of the office, and behind it Dr.

Van Zante stood. He was an older man, had to be nearing seventy, with a lean build, narrow shoulders, and long face. His eyes were brilliant azure, magnified by thick glasses. He smiled and put out his hand to shake Nena's. "Good morning, folks." He gave Jim a firm shake too then motioned to two leather-upholstered chairs across the desk from him. "Please, won't you have a seat?"

Two of the walls in the office were lined with mahogany shelves stuffed with well-worn books and journals; the other two held more paintings of horses and one photograph of a man riding a muscular bay quarter horse.

"That's Buck." Dr. Van Zante admired the photo before sitting.

"He's beautiful," Jim said. "How long have you had him?"

"Six years." The doctor rested his hands on his desk and laced his long fingers. "But we're not here to talk horses. Let's get right to it, shall we?"

He shifted in his chair, rubbed his hands together, an odd show of uneasiness for someone so poised. He'd probably delivered this same news to hundreds, if not thousands, of patients throughout his career. And in an odd way, his apparent discomfort was, in fact, comforting. It showed the doctor cared, that Nena wasn't just another patient, a number on some chart; she was a person with real feelings and a family and a ranch that needed her.

Dr. Van Zante massaged his chin and studied a piece of paper he held in his hand. "I have the results of the biopsy here." He then met Nena's eyes and said, "I'm going to cut to the chase here, Nena. It's positive. I'm sorry." He pushed a color photo across the desk. It was of the inside of her colon, taken during the colonoscopy. There was a growth there, a terrible-looking thing, knotty and wartlike, a monster. The doctor hesitated…then said, "You have colon cancer."

The last two words Nena Hutchins heard before everything blurred were "colon cancer."

Dr. Van Zante kept talking, but Nena heard little of it, just bits and pieces, like scattered raindrops that occasionally land on your nose, catching your attention. She heard "MRI" and "ultrasound," "surgery" and "chemotherapy." But they were just isolated words, foreign almost. Her ears registered the sound of them, but to her brain they made no sense.

She looked at Jim, her husband, the man who had fought for her all those years ago and risked his life and won. The man who had never left her side because he'd promised he never would. His eyes were glassy and distant. He nodded in time to what Dr. Van Zante said, but he too appeared to be in some other place, a place where couples grew old together and enjoyed reasonably good health, where they traveled and spent lazy afternoons walking outside or sitting on the front porch, where they spoiled their grandchildren.

A place where people weren't blindsided by cancer.

He held her hand, but she didn't feel it. Her body was numb, paralyzed. She wanted to get up and run out of the room, but she couldn't. It was as if she was glued fast to the seat of the chair.

Memories came clanging into her head, just images really. Her father sitting atop Warlord, his prized Arabian. Her mother on the front porch of the house, rocking on the bench swing as a summer evening breeze played in her hair. Rocking her baby girl, her youngest daughter, and singing her a lullaby—"Baby, my sweet, don't you cry. Baby, my sweet, don't you fear. Mommy will take care of you, I'm here." Her children, grandchildren…how long had it been since she'd seen them? And the ranch? What would happen to it? She had managed to save what was left of it; what would happen now?

As these thoughts drifted in and out, that word, that awful word—*cancer*—clamored around like an old noisy cowbell, demanding her attention. She hated that word. It had taken her father from her and left her to run the ranch, a ranch that was dying a slow death of its own. It had taken her grandfather, the only man she genuinely identified with (except for Jim, of course). The word itself sounded like a death sentence, like Dr. Van Zante was not really telling her, "You have colon cancer," but instead, "You're going to die."

The room began to spin then, as if it had an axis running right through the middle of it. Slowly at first it revolved in a perfect circle, then faster and faster and off-center. Her head suddenly felt as light as helium, and she thought she would vomit.

"Nena, honey, you okay?"

It was Jim, holding her with both arms. Had she fainted?

"That's enough for now," Dr. Van Zante said. He too was near her, his hand on her shoulder. "Nena, we're going to fight this thing; we're going to throw everything at it." He handed her a paper cup of water.

She nodded and took a sip.

Jim helped her to her feet, but her legs were weak and the ground undulated beneath her.

"We'll set things up for the MRI and surgeon," Dr. Van Zante said. "Someone will call you with the appointment times." He bent forward and looked Nena right in the eyes. "Nena, do you need a wheelchair?"

She shook her head. "No. I'm fine. Jim will help me."

"Let me get Becky to get you a wheelchair."

"No. I'm fine. I just need to get outside and get some air."

"Are you sure?"

"I'm fine. Jim can help me."

But could he? Could he help her this time? It was cancer, after all, the same cancer that had taken her father and grandfather. A monster in its own right and one that had tasted blood—and not anyone's blood, but her family blood.

She nearly blacked out again, and the next thing she remembered was sitting in the truck with the seat belt pulled tight against her chest. She hooked a thumb under it and pulled it away, allowing her rib cage to expand and draw in a deep breath. The window beside her was open. She inhaled the cool air, filling her lungs.

"Nena, it'll be all right." Jim hadn't started the truck yet. His hand rested on hers, but she still couldn't feel it.

It would be all right. How did he know? He didn't, that was the plain truth. Those were the words everyone said, the words everyone *would* say to her. *It'll be all right.*

Jim turned the key and the truck's engine turned over and growled to life. "Did you hear what the doctor said?"

She shook her head again. "No." Her throat felt like it was the size of a straw and the word just made it out.

"He's going to set you up for an MRI to see if it has spread to any other organs. Then we'll see a surgeon and talk about getting it out of you."

It. He couldn't bring himself to say the word: *cancer.*

"The surgeon will set us up with the oncologist," Jim said.

"And then what?"

"Radiation, chemo."

"More tests, prodding, poking, cutting."

"Probably. But I'll be right next to you the whole time. We'll beat it, Nena. We will."

"Maybe it's not that bad," she said. The words sounded so hopeless, like someone lying there with a compound fracture, their bone jutting through the skin, leg cocked at a sickening angle, saying maybe it wasn't that bad, maybe it was just a sprain. "Maybe it'll just be a matter of cutting out the tumor and being done with it."

Jim looked straight ahead, out the windshield and across the parking lot. The doctor's office was a couple miles outside of town, and the lot faced the Winthrop ranch and its acres and acres of rolling green hills dotted with the occasional tree and sectioned off with white ranch rail fencing. "Maybe."

Sam Travis is a man on the brink of despair...

He awakens one morning to find an old journal by a Union soldier... written in his own handwriting. When new entries appear and begin to mimic Sam's own life, he is drawn into an evil plot that could cost many lives, including his own.

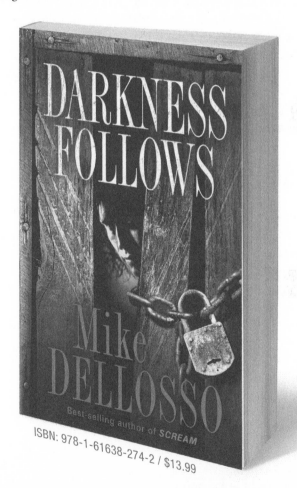

ISBN: 978-1-61638-274-2 / $13.99

FREE NEWSLETTERS
TO HELP EMPOWER YOUR LIFE

Why subscribe today?

- ☐ **DELIVERED DIRECTLY TO YOU.** All you have to do is open your inbox and read.

- ☐ **EXCLUSIVE CONTENT.** We cover the news overlooked by the mainstream press.

- ☐ **STAY CURRENT.** Find the latest court rulings, revivals, and cultural trends.

- ☐ **UPDATE OTHERS.** Easy to forward to friends and family with the click of your mouse.

CHOOSE THE E-NEWSLETTER THAT INTERESTS YOU MOST:

- • Christian news
- • Daily devotionals
- • Spiritual empowerment
- • And much, much more

SIGN UP AT: **http://freenewsletters.charismamag.com**

8178